". . . like a meteor flashing across the black sky of evangelical fiction . . . excitement of plot and characterization breathes from every page. I could not put it down."

> — Sherwood E. Wirt,
> Editor, retired

CODE NAME SEBASTIAN NOVELS

Code Name Sebastian

A Handful of Dominoes

The Nine Lives of Alphonse

A Piece of the Moon Is Missing

Code Name
Sebastian

ZONDERVAN HEARTH BOOKS

Available from your Christian Bookseller

A SEBASTIAN THRILLER

Code Name Sebastian

James L. Johnson

ZONDERVAN
PUBLISHING HOUSE

OF THE ZONDERVAN CORPORATION | GRAND RAPIDS. MICHIGAN 49506

Published by Zondervan Publishing House by special arrangement with the J. B. Lippincott Company.

Zondervan Hearth Books Edition   1978
Copyright © 1967 by James L. Johnson

Printed in the United States of America
Library of Congress Catalog Card No.: 67-14368

References to archaeological periods are from Nelson Glueck's
book *Rivers in the Desert* by permission of his publishers,
Farrar, Straus & Giroux, Inc., copyright © 1959 by Nelson
Glueck.

To my wife, ROSEMARY, *and son,* JAY,
And to all those
Who endured my restless spirit
And urged me to press on

"The hero in history is the individual to whom we can justifiably attribute preponderant influence in determining an issue or an event whose consequences would have been profoundly different if he had not acted as he did."

— Sydney Hook, *The Hero in History*
Humanities Press, Inc.

Prologue

Mr. Lester Bennington
Nashville Community Church
Nashville, Wisconsin

Dear Les:

I am writing from a delightful hotel on the crown point of the Mount of Olives outside Jerusalem on the eve of my departure from the Holy Land. It may come as a shock to you that I should be cutting my time short here. I've had a delightful seven days, but I don't think that another seven will accomplish much more.

So I do not leave now with any sense of total disappointment. But there is just so much heat in shrines, Les, and once you've had that first glow it begins to die, and you realize that there won't be any more. I actually feel a bit uneasy here now pulling out a few live coals from the museum of history to warm this chill of spiritual winter I've felt for some time. I am convinced that the experience I need is not in the past, and no amount of plowing up the old ground is going to really make a difference in my life. For some this may have sufficed, but I get the feeling that I have been digging in the ruins for some proof that Christ really existed or that He is not really contemporary at all but confined strictly to history. In other words, what I should be looking for has to be in the *now*, not in the *what-was*.

I know I place the burden on you to explain this to the church people who gave their money that I might get the "full treatment" of this tremendous Holy Land expedition. When you tell them of my plans ask them to continue to pray for me that I will find whatever God has in mind for me—perhaps in Kenya where I'm heading tomorrow. I expect to see David Mosley and his wife on their station outside Nairobi. Perhaps in that rugged country I will see and experience the workings of God in a new way. So then if this should be what God has in mind, the tour will not have been totally wasted.

This is not much balm I know to soothe expectant hearts back there who have been praying for some kind of miracle in my life brought about by this trip. But you know that I cannot be dishonest, and though it would be easy for me to stay here the full time and return to you with the stories people want to hear about "the stones crying out" and "Calvary still rumbling with the violence of the crucifixion" or "a new sense of commission has come upon my ministry as a result of standing on the Mount of Olives where Christ stood many times"—well, you know that I could not long live with that.

So—I'm booked on Zion Airlines for ten tomorrow morning. I couldn't get a seat on any of the main lines. Airline business is booming for the African runs. Don't worry—I made sure of this airline. It's a small outfit that handles charters mainly, but it has a good record. I'll be flying a four motor prop job with one stop at Khartoum and then on to Nairobi. Won't be quite like the 720 jets, but "I must learn to suffer hardship as a good soldier of Jesus Christ." I do not mean that to sound flippant, but I somehow really long to get out of the "smooth and comfortable" for a change. I hope the Mosleys give me the works.

I'm happy about the good report of the young man who

is filling the pulpit during my absence. You needn't apologize for talking so excitedly about him. After nine years of taking the dull and unimaginative from this poor excuse for a clergyman, an animated dummy would look and sound good. No offense to the young man, of course, and please give him my warmest regards and tell him I'll pray for him daily until I get the feeling he might take my job.

Please hang on to me before God in your prayers at this crucial point in my life. If I only have you, my friend Les, who have taken time to hear me out in my strange gropings for that which I do not even understand myself, then I have all I need. I will write you from Kenya in a few days. Blessings on you and all the people there.

Sincerely,
Ray Sebastian

* 1 *

It was because Sebastian knew himself to be a highly sensitive individual, sensitive that is to peculiar sounds or feelings that did not seem to fit his own concept of universal balance, that he did not immediately react to the bump that lightly tapped the bottom of the cushioned seat. It felt as though the plane had hit a solid pocket of "sky wall," a term he had heard airline pilots use when referring to a bundle of jet stream.

He glanced up once from his book, but apparently no one else had noticed it. Across the aisle, the two American schoolteacher ladies continued their comparison of their findings in the Holy Land, nodding to each other in mutual satisfaction while fondling their souvenirs—crucifixes from the Church of the Holy Sepulchre, a half-pint jar of what was sold as "water direct from the Pool of Bethesda," and nondescript ornamentary that would become the visual aids for their social studies classes. Behind him he heard the high-pitched chatter of a man talking about "excavations around Tyre and Sidon that produced history with every bucketful of sand." That would be the man named Brelsford, the retired archaeology professor who had been doing field work for Princeton. He had introduced himself earlier in the small, crowded waiting room of the airline as if everyone in the world were his friend or should be honored to have him consider them so. He was a medium-built man, not much over five-nine, and he kept bouncing up and down on his heels as if he were attempting to gain a few more inches. His round face was the color of beach sand, and his hair had been cut down to a short crew cut to hide the shafts of gray and white in it, which were not readily discernible except on close scrutiny. He smoked a long stemmed pipe and wore an open-necked, short-sleeved khaki shirt with tan trousers. Brelsford was definitely a man who wanted to create an image younger than his years. Even his high-pitched voice sounded a bit strained as if he were modulating to cover for what might be the heavy, shaky sound of a man in his early sixties.

Intermingled with that high-pitched voice, and sounding like the determined beats of a bass drum, was the conversation of another who kept insisting for anyone who was within earshot that "it was crazy anyway that the church should try to date man to 4000 B.C. when carbon 14 and every other geological device had already scientifically proved man to be a million years old. . . ." That would be Clark Dennison, a fiftyish bull of a man with a petulant sag to his wide mouth, who had just finished a three-year geological research project at the Hebrew University. It was Brelsford who had introduced him as "*Time* magazine's man of the year for sure." Dennison was scholarly in appearance with a good crop of straight black hair he was careful to keep combed back, a pair of small brown eyes that blinked nervously as if geological data were racing across his eyes daring him to catch it all. He kept the pose of a man who stood as the pivot between man's ignorance of the universe and the gateway to paradise which was, in essence, a geological kingdom of rocks and fossils that formed the missing link to man's purpose for life. He never asked anything, but stood waiting for the world to ask him. He had the appearance of a pompous king without a crown.

When the stewardess came down the aisle carrying a

tray on which sat two white paper cups as defiantly steady as twin Gibraltars, he went back to his book. But he could not shake the feeling of apprehension even though the plane's engines were throbbing on the same even pitch. Either he had flown too long or not enough, he told himself, so that unusual turbulence created exaggerated visions in his mind. He decided that the best thing would be to have a cup of coffee. If it did nothing else, it would at least give him an opportunity to watch the unruffled stewardess and let her reactions be the barometer for whatever the plane was intending to do.

He reached up to press the button when the plane suddenly lurched downward. It was a violent drop, the kind that shoved his stomach up hard against his breastbone and made him grunt. The full weight of his body lifted tight against his seat belt that he always kept fastened during flight for some reason. His book slipped out of his hand, and there came that weird and calamitous sound of falling things—that always sounded ten times worse in an airplane—and one or two excited yelps from passengers who apparently wanted to get their protests in first about this crazy business of flying. He instinctively glanced out the window to his right even as he shoved his feet up against the seat in front of him. He was shocked to see the jagged hills and sharp outcroppings of rock rushing up to meet him, the sandstone colors becoming as vivid as paint on canvas, while the white, sulphur-appearing sand that lay in lunarlike craters was suddenly changing to darker hues of red and brown. He had the feeling that a large hand had reached up from the desert to pluck this flimsy instrument of aluminum out of the air. Then he dropped his head and waited as the plane took on a high-pitched whine above the laboring sound of its motors, that deadly sound of tons of metal on a meteor course with earth. . . .

He had only seconds for his active mind to work before impact . . . and as he had read so often that a man can see his whole life before him in those last ticks of time before death, so did he; only all he could see was his church and the people floating across his mind's wide-screen vision, so sharp and clear now, so perfectly in focus, as if coming death had a way of enlarging the mental lens. They would never know now, he thought . . . those rows of people with faces that could not hide their boredom, who patiently endured his miserable stabs at eloquence, faces that reflected minds that had shut down operations and defied him to throw the switch again . . . and he felt an overwhelming sense of sadness . . . for they would never know now . . . all they would have was the one letter he had sent to Les, which was nothing more than a confession of missing connections with the "charisma," that spiritual Holy Land cure that had been the panacea for many like himself who suffered from theologically tired blood . . . they would never know now if he ever did find his Mount Horeb . . . and it seemed so unfair since they paid so much for him to pursue it . . . but then maybe this way was best . . . no fumbling explanations necessary, no attempts to gloss over the failures, no agonizing rehearsals about how to tell them that he had found nothing, and all they could hope for then was that he would resign and save them having to ask him to leave . . . but he felt sad that he couldn't have left them something more than he did with Les, anything positive that they could have used in their memorial service that would have vindicated their confidence in what this trip was supposed to do for him. . . .

Then he felt the first touch of the plane against the ground. . . . It skimmed the earth first, like a rock off water, a soft, kissing bump no more disturbing than when its wheels normally touched a landing strip. There was that pause of only seconds when the plane seemed to glide in the air weightlessly, and then came the next blow very harsh and demanding as the plane plowed deep, and all the thin threads of life were taut as people and metal had their encounter with the law of gravity. All he could smell and taste was burning metal. The air seemed filled with flying things, and over the sound of tearing fiber and aluminum he heard the high-pitched wail of terrified passengers, his own voice among them, in a long moan that seemed to be one big argument against what was happening.

Then . . . silence . . . and darkness.

His first feeling of consciousness was the stabbing flare of light that hit deep into his brain. It flashed on and off, sometimes turning to a bluish color, but never there long enough to guide him out of this deep underground mine he was in. He tried moving, forcing himself upright, and a wave of nausea swept over him—he vomited once, feeling the hard heat of the sand under his hands as he rolled over to get his mouth down.

He lay there for some time, fighting the spasms from his stomach and the pain in his head—and then he forced himself to sit upright again. Slowly he opened his eyes. Nothing stood still for him. But he saw the sand around his feet almost the color of salt, and the sun hitting it shot a sharp shaft of pain back through his eyes. He closed them tight and waited, feeling a rushing torrent of panic in this confusion of silence and pain until his mind slowly began to put out controlling fingers on his runaway nerves . . . slowly his lips began to move in response . . . you are the Reverend Raymond Sebastian . . . you are thirty-four years of age going on thirty-five . . . you are not dead or dying . . . you were on your way to Nairobi on a plane . . . flying over Egypt to Khartoum to Kenya . . . only something has happened to that plane. . . .

"Are you all right, sir?" The incongruous feminine voice sounded from way off. He tensed and groped for the direction from which it came. His fingers caught the feel of rough, coarse cloth, and he opened his eyes. It was a little better now. The glare was still there and the pain. But there was less double vision. Then he saw the uniform, the sprinkle of gold on blue and the symbol of wings stitched in gold on the breast pocket. The vision of the stewardess with two white cups on a tray weaved into his painful senses—and he was suddenly snapped back into the reality of his where and when.

"Yes," he said, his voice sounding hollow as if he were in a cave, "I guess I'm okay . . . but I feel like I got caught in a revolving door. . . ."

His vision was completely back to normal now. He realized that he was staring at the plane that lay not more than thirty yards away, trying to recall how he had experienced the peculiar mastery of gravity while committed to that so fragile-looking aluminum frame. It was cracked open in the center, the after section bent to the left a little. It reminded him of a hornet that had been snipped in the middle with a pair of scissors. Other than that, it appeared to have landed very neatly on the sandy pocket of a small crater in a world of rock that ran in crooked lines as if it had all been carelessly poured out of a giant cup and left to harden.

He looked up into the stewardess's face. She had an ugly bruise high on her left cheek that was caked with dry blood. But even so, she handled herself with the nonchalance and efficiency of one who had done this before.

"What about the others?" he asked, the blunt edge of the disaster slowly beginning to tap awareness into his foggy senses.

She didn't answer right away. She went on cutting strips of bandage from a roll she took from the first-aid box. "Only eight of us seem to be alive," she said finally, in a factual tone as though she'd been asked for nothing more than the time.

"Eight?" he said in some bewilderment, glancing back at the plane as if trying to visualize how sixteen persons could have died in what didn't appear to be a disastrous wreck.

"It happened too fast," she replied, almost in half apology as if she were assuming the blame. "Often over the desert we get freak air currents—we call them thermo-drafts. If one catches the plane right, it can smash it to earth in seconds. The passengers didn't have time to buckle in or get ready for it. . . ."

He could see the bodies scattered around him now in lumpy heaps. He hadn't seen them before. Luggage, half open, was strewn carelessly over the rocky surface, and personal belongings flapped and rolled in the hushed hot wind that whispered reverently across the spires of rock, ooing and aahing now and then over this rare calamity.

"Have you any idea where we are?" he asked, then, feeling the heavy sense of foreboding that so much death produced.

"Sparks would, I think," she said. "Probably not too far from rescue." And he couldn't help noticing how she forced the last line of cheer as a kind of afterthought. He knew human nature. The ministry had taught him that much at least.

He looked closely at her again. Her face was tan, almost the color of the Jews he'd seen in their kibbutzim in the hills around Jerusalem and Galilee. Her eyes though were deep blue, and her hair, cut short and straight, was very blond. There was a troubled frown between her eyes that could be the result of the glaring heat or the beginnings of genuine concern. She might be Jewish, but she had a definite English accent. He had been told that lots of English families stayed on in Israel after the British left in 1948. The children studied in the local universities and joined Jewish youth movements. Not many. But there were some. Maybe she was one of those.

"Can you walk over to where the others are?" she asked, and he turned his head slowly to look where she pointed, to the rocky wadi he had seen earlier.

"Of course," he said, and she put her arm out for him to grab for support as he stood to climb the mountain of dizziness that defied him to take one step. Half leaning on her, he moved off over the uneven rock that oozed the peculiar colors of red and blue, and then removed his arm from her shoulder as he felt the earth stop gyrating and his knees stiffen for the challenge. He stumbled into the half circle of survivors, plopped down on a smooth outcropping of rock with a grunt, and leaned his back against the natural backrest. Then he took time to look around through his aching eyes.

He recognized Brelsford next to him, a bulging bandage over the bridge of his nose taped down neatly to his cheeks and giving him the appearance of an Indian wearing war paint. He sat with his salt-and-pepper crew-cut head bowed toward the volcanic-looking pebbles under his feet, a man who knew history from rock like that, who could study the pain and sufferings and glories of the past there, but who now had to yield to the new pressures.

Beyond Brelsford was his seat companion, Dennison. He had a bandage wrapped around his head like a turban, and his left hand was bound up in gauze as well. He sat staring across the open ground toward the plane, one hand shaking the small pebbles as though they were dice and he were getting ready to prophesy their future on what they would show when he cast them across the ground. His eyes remained on the plane, a look on his square, scholarly, scowling face of a man who sought scientific explanations for the wreck as if his whole scientific way of life depended on finding the answers.

There were the two middle-aged schoolteachers who had sat across from him, entwined in each other's arms and trying to keep the blue and gold blankets around them. Why the blankets when it must be 160 in the shade? Only there wasn't any shade, except that which was made from your own shadow, he thought.

Next to the two ladies was the man in the uniform of the airline. He looked worse off with his left arm hanging uselessly at his side and a wide patch of black wetness spreading across his uniform near the left shoulder. Even at that it was comforting to have him. A uniform spelled out some kind of cohesion in a world suddenly pulled apart.

The last person in the rough semicircle was a wiry middle-aged man with a big bandage over his right ear, a lock of grayish hair hanging over his right eye, who still had on his blue bow tie neatly tied on a white shirt that looked as if it had just come out of the laundry. He appeared as casual and relaxed as a businessman waiting to catch a bus.

Sebastian began to shiver now as the shock waves hit him. Now he knew why the women had the blankets. But he would not ask for any. The women did. He turned his head to look for the stewardess and saw her working over the bodies lying around the plane, carefully covering each with a blue and gold blanket, hiding the protest on their faces, all the time trying to check them off on her clipboard so she would know the living from the dead.

"Somebody ought to help her," Brelsford offered, but without much sincerity. No one answered him, and no one moved.

After what seemed like a long time, the stewardess came to them and dropped some personal belongings on the rock, covering them quickly with a blanket before they all began to study each item for a clue to what those people were like who lay out there in neat mounds of blue and gold.

"Well, we've got something to write home about," she began, and though it wasn't necessary for her to try banter at this stage of the calamity, it was an admirable attempt to set them at ease. Brelsford grunted something which was either an acknowledgment of her attempt or else a dismal disdain for it. "I think we shall remain where we are for the night," she went on, her voice becoming more studious, but still like a guide conducting a tour and advising them about accommodations. "Rescue planes will undoubtedly be over us shortly. What we must do now is try to get as comfortable as possible. . . ."

Again Brelsford grunted and looked back at the chips of rock between his legs.

"Will they be long in coming for us?" one of the school-teachers asked with a quivering voice.

"I don't think so," the stewardess replied, avoiding the

look that the man in the airline uniform gave her. He sat smoking a cigarette impassively, not appearing to mind the spreading black wetness that showed up more clearly on his uniform.

"Is no one else of them alive?" Brelsford asked, lifting his head reluctantly and pointing his nose toward the makeshift morgue out by the plane.

"I'm sorry," she replied factually, and after a moment's pause added: "Come on, I think we should move off this rocky slope and down where we can get some protection from the wind and the cold that will come later tonight."

Sebastian knew that she wanted them to get out of sight of those bodies, and he kept thinking of what another day in this heat would do to decomposing flesh. That thought made him realize that he was getting his thinking processes back rapidly, and regretted it because the reality of their situation was becoming more and more apparent.

They half shuffled off the rocky plateau and down a gradual escarpment that descended fifty to one hundred yards to a larger crater of soft sand that was the texture of that which he had seen on many ocean beaches. The heat hit them hard here, bouncing off the sand to the metallike rock that hung over them and back again so that it defied them one long, easy breath.

He remembered then that there were things that should be carried from the plateau, so he went back up. The man in the airline uniform, who must be the radio operator since the stewardess had referred to him as "Sparks," met him on the top. He was dragging a small canvas bag that bulged with what little raw material he had been able to salvage. He went on by the man, accepting the crooked grin as a kind of foolish hello, to where the stewardess was trying to pick up two gallon flasks that flashed in the sun, a bundle of clothing, and a first-aid kit all at once.

He took the aluminum flasks from her, glad for the heaviness of them, which at least told him that there would be water for a while. He also relieved her of the bundle of clothing and slung it over his shoulder with his free left hand.

"We'll need petrol and some of the seats out of the plane," she said to him in a brisk voice. "It will help to have a fire when the cold hits us tonight. Would you help Sparks?"

"Certainly," he said. Then, as they began walking up the slight slope to the pinnacle overlooking the crater, he asked, "Did he get off a good radio signal before we crashed?"

He expected that she would give him that cheerio smile, but instead she looked straight ahead, her face set in an expression of intensive preoccupation. "He didn't have much time before the plane hit," she said simply, factually. "He got as much off as he could, let's put it that way."

He wanted to pursue that further, for he still didn't know how much "much" really was. Instead he approached it another way, "Will he try the radio again?"

"He has to fix it first . . . and he's not in very good shape physically as you've already seen. . . ."

They came to the crown of the slope now, and he paused to look across the endless expanse of wilderness, of broken rock erosions, thorny peaks of rocky protrusions here and there, and, in between, the flat stretches of red and brown rock mixed with that white desert sand.

"It's like a lost world," he said to her, awed by the pointed view of death and waste. She stopped now to look with him, her face set in unreadable lines.

Then she said, in a tone of quiet respect, "The Negev is a desert like no other . . . strange, mysterious, deadly. You walk ten miles here and it is equal to twenty-five or thirty in deserts like the Sahara or the Arabian. Every step costs you something." She paused a moment to reflect on what she had said, and then tossing her head to the hot wind so that the sun hit her hair with an explosion of silvery gold, a gesture that was half defiance, half optimism, added, "The Jews expect they'll tame it some

23

day as the prophets said. But the Bedouins say that when God created the world this was what was left over. And He could do nothing with it. It defied even His power to conceive life out of this void. The Bedouins call the Negev 'the bone that sticks in God's throat.'"

And before he could respond, she moved down the hill, and he was left standing there with well-used arguments on his tongue that seemed slow to come in this valley of dry bones. There had been no bitterness in her voice, only statements of fact, almost professorial in presentation. It was almost as if she were warning, as if she already knew that he was a clergyman, and that he must now reckon with something that even God had not been able to master. And as he stood there, watching her stride purposefully to the forlorn group of tattered humanity below, he felt a strange chill of apprehension mingling with and mocking the sweat that ran down his back. She had drawn a strange kind of challenge for him, a challenge no man had posed for him in peaceful Nashville, Wisconsin.

The hot wind brought the smell of burning rock to him again, and in that moment he realized that he was in a kind of crucible. And he felt the first tug of honest fear turn his throat dry and ripple the muscles around his heart. He coughed, seeking to drive away the pressures that were laying exploratory fingers on him. Then, shifting the load of clothing on his shoulder, he walked down the slope, his knees feeling weak again.

✳ 2 ✳

Sebastian calculated it to be about midafternoon when he and Sparks went back to the plane to see about draining off some gas for the night fire. As near as he could determine, it was near noon when they had crashed. His watch had stopped at 11:45, but he wasn't sure if it stopped on impact or later. He hadn't bothered to ask anyone else about the time because it seemed so ludicrous to be concerned about time in this world where time had lost its value and only mocked them in their feeble attempts to survive.

At any rate, since the crash the heat had become almost unbearable. The sun was a hot flame hanging still in the cloudless sky that was one big heat reflector matched only by the smooth, metallic, mirrorlike rock and volcanic ash that was supposed to be sand. Between the two moved the remnants of life, slowly being cooked alive, pieces of flesh turning on the spit of the hungry Negev. What added to the mounting sense of the inevitable was the fact that no rescue planes would come looking at least for another day. When they didn't get into Khartoum on schedule there would undoubtedly be a search. But they weren't due there until later this afternoon since the flight had gotten off the ground an hour later than expected because of a service problem. Their only other hope was that Sparks got off a radio signal. If he had, rescue planes should have been over them by now. The grim truth that hung heavy in Sebastian's mind now was that two gallons of water would not suffice for more than one day in this heat, even on short rations.

They came to the plane then, and he followed the radio operator through the forward half of the broken fuselage. They stepped over broken seats, more bodies covered with the official blankets, into the crew's quarters, which amazingly were still intact. He noticed the three officers in their relaxed poses of death, each one frozen in the pantomime he acted out before the crash. The pilot was half hanging out of the smashed front windshield as if at the last minute he had tried to reach out and hold back the impact. His copilot was jammed hard up against the controls and impaled on some kind of iron gear. The third officer was sprawled in the aisle staring at the ceiling, a dark reddish line running down from under his blue cap to his chin. Strange what details he should notice about them, as if the fact that they couldn't return his scrutiny gave him boldness to study them more closely. The third officer, for instance, with the heavy nicotine stains on his right index finger . . . probably a nervous man, smoked too much and had a nagging cough to go with it.

Sparks appeared again with a large adjustable wrench. He surveyed the cabin and shook his head. "Bloody thermodrafts," he growled, digging into his pocket with his right hand to come up with a big blue handkerchief which he used to mop the heavy, greasy blobs of sweat from his forehead. "One in a million times you get hit . . . you get caught in it and there isn't enough power in any airplane's engines to fight it . . . you don't know you're in it until your altimeter starts runnin' down like a bloody runaway clock . . . in seconds you're scrapin' the bloody deck. . . ."

There was some cockney in Sparks and some mixture of Irish and Scotch so that vehemence boiled out of him without too much provocation. His short, barrellike build

26

rode into his every word, and the cigarette butt that hung out of one side of his mouth flapped its own signals of alarm.

He sniffed loudly again, put the handkerchief back in his pocket, and said, "I think I got me a tool here to get the safety cocks off those petrol tanks . . . let's look for somethin' we can put the petrol in, shall we? You try the luggage compartment up forward, I'll check the galley aft. . . ."

Sebastian went forward and peered down into the shadowy hole that smelled of leather and clothes and cologne. He gingerly stepped down the small ladder into the luggage compartment. There was one big hole forward where the hull had cracked open. The sunlight streamed in on the tangle of suitcases, some sprung open with clothing scattered in heaps. He pawed around without too much purpose, feeling as if he were touching the live pulse of people who had intended to use these things. There seemed to be personality in white shirts, nightgowns, bow ties, underwear, and the bottle of French perfume that was cracked open and giving the grave a bizaare atmosphere of gaiety. Once he paused to look at another hole in the fuselage, a smaller one, not more than thirty inches in diameter. His mind kept telling him that that particular hole was peculiar, but before he could get his mind to concentrate on it, Sparks' voice came to him from the top of the ladder.

"I got me an ice-cream can, Yank, so it ought to do," he said.

Sebastian climbed back into the crews' compartment and found Sparks bending over the navigation plot board. "See here now?" he said, as Sebastian came up to peer over his shoulder at the flat graph paper with the long black lines drawn across it. "Young Mitchell had plotted our course right on the nose to the moment we went down. Note the time: 11:40 A.M. That was just before I could make my radio check with Eilat roughly sixty miles south of us. Notice our course running down from

27

Jerusalem, across Beersheba—we were just going to make a starboard turn for the leg to Khartoum when we hit that freak of an air current." Sparks paused a moment and sighed, a drop of sweat falling from his face to land on the plot paper, leaving a dark spot like ink on blotting paper. "That puts us, Yank, right in the middle of the wildest, loneliest, most godforsaken bit of desert in the world . . . north of us about seventy to eighty miles is the Negev with pasture land and water . . . east of us is Trans-Jordan across the Arabah range, a good hot walk of one hundred miles before you hit anything like an oasis . . . west of us is Egypt, Moses' Sinai, about as much hope there as an ant crawling into a furnace . . . south we can maybe hit Ain Ghadyan, about forty miles, I figure, or maybe some less . . . so that puts us right in the center of Wadi Iqfi, lots of rock and cliffs and sun, the place even the Bedouins avoid if they can . . . that doesn't help the morale, but we might just as well know the facts, hmm?"

Sebastian was subdued by the recital, almost mesmerized by the plot paper and the thin neatly drawn lines on it. He stood with Sparks a long minute just looking at it, and it was as if both of them were wishing that just by staring the whole grim picture it drew would change.

"Well, let's get at that petrol, shall we?" Sparks said then, and they moved out into the heat again. The wings of the plane were half-buried in the crater sand and so were the engines. The props were bent back, and one or two had broken off on impact sending parts of steel slamming into the fuselage.

They had to dig a hole under the portside wing tanks using their hands and the ice-cream can. The sand was soft enough, but heavy. After five minutes, Sebastian began to get dizzy from the exertion. Sparks tried to help, but his own physical condition was much worse. His one arm was totally useless, and though he made a game attempt, he finally sat back breathing heavily and gripping his left shoulder.

"Since you're built like a tree branch, Yank, have a go at crawling there, will you?"

Sebastian went at it again and finally got down far enough to crawl under the wing with the ice-cream can.

"Now you see," Sparks explained, "that's a sump drain right there sticking out like a nipple back of the engine housing and to the left . . . that's used, see, when a pilot has to dump his petrol in an emergency . . . they pop out automatically when the ship is running smooth, but twisting the bloody things off cold is a job. . . ."

Sebastian put the adjustable wrench on the metal flange jutting out and tried turning. It looked like just one piece of metal, a continuation of the wing not subject to twisting or unscrewing. He tried again and again, the sweat running down into his eyes, and the effort making his head ache. Finally, Sparks crawled in where he was, adding his weight to Sebastian's, so that the walls of the small sand hole caved in on them and jammed them tight against the wing.

"What a bloody show this is turning out to be," Sparks growled, his breath, smelling of nicotine, hot on Sebastian's arm. He finally gave one hard push and rammed his way back out again, letting the wind get back to where Sebastian lay. Sebastian felt the panic subside somewhat, and then Sparks called again, "All right, give it another try, Yank, and if she won't give we'll go back without our bloody fire for the night. . . ."

He put the wrench back on and dug his feet into the sand hoping for leverage, putting everything he had into it. He strained for some seconds until the sweat squirted out of his pores and stung his eyes and added salt to his mouth, already swollen from thirst. Then, suddenly, there was a snap and a yielding under his wrench. The gas whooshed out of the ruptured tank and poured over his arms, into his face, soaking his shirt. The fumes shut off his breath as if a giant hand had grabbed his throat, and the liquid poured over his mouth and eyes. He knew he would drown in a minute, and then Sparks tugged on his legs with strength that must have taken all of his reserves. Sebastian came out into the open air that, for all of its heat, smelled heavenly. He vomited the gas he had swallowed and sat gagging on the sand while Sparks rushed back into the hole with the five-gallon ice-cream can to get what gas there was before it all drained out into the sand.

They were sitting there, breathing heavily from the exertion, when Brelsford appeared. "I know I'm probably too late, but can I help with anything?"

Sparks said, "Right you are. We need to lug back some of the cushions from the plane. Would you start tearing them out?"

Brelsford went to the plane as ordered, and Sparks led Sebastian back into the plane's crews' quarters. He searched around the pilot's section and came up with a gun. "Maybe there won't be any need for this," he said, holding it out toward Sebastian. "But in any case, if there are no wild animals around to shoot, there'll be desert tribes sooner or later who'll pick us clean and leave us dead if we don't show some kind of weapon."

"I don't particularly like firearms," Sebastian said. "I don't think I even know how to use one. Why don't you keep it?"

Sparks looked at him for a long minute, not able to fully comprehend, and then shrugged. "Suit yourself, but I'm not a lefty. All I got is one good hand now, and I don't squeeze a trigger so good with a lefty's fingers. You might want to change your mind if the time comes. . . ."

After awhile they went back, each of them carrying one of the plane's cushion seats. The stewardess sent the other two men of the party back for a load, and they met the others coming in.

"Join the bloody party, mates," Sparks sang out. "We'll have a jolly good marshmallow roast tonight—nice big bonfire to bring our rescue planes in, what?"

No one bothered to answer. The heat had drained them

of their will to carry on any conversation. Even now, with a fresh wind blowing in, carrying traces of reviving coolness their preconditioned bodies could not break out of the ennui that the heat had created.

Back at the crater sand, the fierceness of the heat had diminished considerably. The sun had already turned to a tangerine color and was sinking rapidly. The far horizon took on deeper shades of orange as it did so, until finally it turned completely red. The cathedral architecture of the surrounding rocks turned into a misty purple with hues of orange. Each minute seemed to bring a change in the colors, as if the sun were a revolving stage light shining through a kaleidoscope.

"That's mineral rock," Dennison commented with some pride, glad for the opportunity to use his geology, even though it didn't make much difference to the rest now. "Some copper in there and iron, maybe some quartz. A lot of sandstone, mind you. That's where you get most of that color. But it's rich in mineral just the same. . . ." Finally, when no one responded to his recitation, Dennison lapsed into a silence, picking up small rocks and studying them closely.

"You better get that shirt off," the stewardess said to Sebastian. "You'll catch cold if you don't. In another hour your teeth will be chattering. And another thing, when that fire gets started, you're liable to go up with it with all those petrol fumes on you. . . ."

He did as he was advised, putting on a fresh khaki shirt she had found in the luggage and a heavy woolen brown sweater over it. The clothing felt good, and he was conscious now of the cold that was suddenly increasing as if someone had turned on a giant air conditioner.

He watched the stewardess as she broke out the rations of sardine tins and crackers. She passed out one half fish to each person and one half cracker, followed by two carefully measured swallows of water.

"If we are so sure of rescue in so short a time," Brelsford said after taking his ration of water and swirling it around in his mouth before swallowing, "why is it you have to be so abstemious with supplies, Miss?"

"Standard procedure, sir," the stewardess replied simply and went on to serve Dennison. "Anyway, we all look as if we could lose a few pounds without too much danger to our health."

Brelsford frowned at her, and then shrugged and concentrated on making the most of his half of cracker. The rest of them took their rations without question, although they looked longingly at the gallon aluminum flask as she poured the water from it carefully into the small measuring cup.

After they had finished, the stewardess stood in the small semicircle near the pile of maroon airplane cushions and said, "Now perhaps introductions are in order," and her voice became lighter to help them approach each other as intimates.

She introduced Brelsford and Dennison, then Sparks who nodded to the name of Roger Jordan. She introduced Sebastian as "the Reverend," and immediately he felt Brelsford and Dennison look at him in that way scientists often did as if clergymen were pieces of jetsam cast aside in the new order of superior technology. Even here, cut off from visible evidences of computers and graphs and the plethora of scientific wonder, reason and faith locked horns again. Sebastian glanced at Sparks next to him who also looked at Sebastian in a new way, a kind of surprised look on his face, but with a crooked kind of smile there, as if knowing he were a clergyman helped fill in some of the blanks in his mind.

". . . and then two Boston grammar schoolteachers, Ida Randolph and Mabel Stockton," and the two middle-aged women nodded together so that no one really knew who was Randolph and who was Stockton, but somehow it didn't matter. They were seldom out of each other's arms anyway.

"And lastly, Mr. James Eaton," and the man with the lock of gray hair hanging over the left side of his forehead simply stared back at all of them morosely.

"And what sins are you engaged in, Eaton?" Brelsford called across the circle.

"Engineering," Eaton muttered, "as if it makes any difference one way or the other." Sebastian caught just the faint accent of Eaton's, that pronounced "v" in place of the "w."

"And you, dear lady?" Brelsford went on, ignoring Eaton's tone of hostility, and turning to the stewardess.

"I'm Barbara Churchill, no relationship to *the* Churchill. . . ."

"Ah!" Brelsford exclaimed, lifting his heavy, muscular, tanned arms in a kind of mock appeal, looking so much like a hoary Indian chief with those white lines of adhesive running across his nose and cheeks. "With a name like that, a synonym for English courage, how can we lose?"

Sparks laughed hoarsely and coughed on his cigarette smoke so that he had to lean over hard to hold down the pain in his left side and shoulder.

No one else reacted to Brelsford's attempt at banter.

"Why don't we get down to the matter of rescue as to when and how?" Eaton cut in then.

"I'm afraid I can't be that specific," Miss Churchill responded with a smile.

"Did we get off a distress signal?" Eaton pursued.

"Not much of a one," Sparks answered.

"That's just fine," Eaton snorted. "And what about trying it again?"

"When I get it fixed . . . maybe. It took a bit of a beating . . . ."

"Well, in any case we are undoubtedly in a common traffic pattern, so it shouldn't be hard to find us," Brelsford offered confidently.

Miss Churchill glanced quickly at Sparks as if warning him to silence or inviting him to go on. Sparks rolled the cigarette butt farther to the side of his mouth and said, "That's something else again . . . we got a message when

33

we took off from Jerusalem that we had a peculiar weather build-up and that we should switch to the alternate course plot . . . we had no indication that we'd hit a thermo-draft," and Sparks went on to explain how the plane had crashed, his voice carrying that pummeling tone of outrage again, while the cigarette stub flapped its own emphatic beats in his mouth.

There was a long silence after Sparks finished. Then Brelsford said, "Well, this desert is not that big in any case, it shouldn't take them long . . . we can make do on what we have till then. . . ."

"Which is to my calculations," Eaton insisted, "less than two gallons of water and a couple of pounds of emergency food rations. All for eight people for who knows how long? We were due in Khartoum an hour ago as I reckon it. . . ."

"Two hours ago, Mr. Eaton," Sparks corrected.

"And that means it'll be dark before they figure we're down, and they won't get anything moving until tomorrow," Eaton went on, ignoring Sparks. "And they may take time running down the six to seven hundred miles from Khartoum northward, expecting that this flight followed the usual flight plan. . . ."

"Jerusalem will have notified them of the change," Sparks interjected.

"But even then it will take time to run it all down and pinpoint the place," Eaton argued.

"Where do you figure we are now, Mr. Jordan?" Brelsford interrupted.

Sparks squinted up at the purple shadows as if he could get a permanent fix from the curtain of approaching night.

"Somewhere around Wadi Iqfi," he said, "about in the center of the Negev."

Brelsford didn't answer right away, and he looked at Sparks steadily to make sure he'd heard right. Then he got up and started to make long lines in the sand with his foot. One by one the others got up to move in closer to see what

34

Brelsford had in mind, except for Sebastian and Sparks, who were only a few feet from Brelsford as it was.

"Now," Brelsford began, clearing his throat and sounding as if he were just about to begin a lecture in archaeological field methods, "this is a rough sketch of the Negev Desert." And the lines now formed an inverted triangle. "That is Beersheba," he said and dropped a flat rock high up near the top of the triangle's base line. Then he dropped another at the point near the apex of the design at his foot. "That is Eilat and Tell el-Kheleifeh, or Ezion-geber. Reverend, you undoubtedly know what Ezion-geber was in biblical history?"

Sebastian was caught off guard, and he hesitated as his mind sought to pick up his biblical geography. Brelsford didn't wait. "What about it, Dennison?"

Dennison didn't hesitate. "King Solomon's port on the Gulf of Aqabah where out went brass and in came the Queen of Sheba. . . ."

"Excellent, Dennison," Brelsford chirped, and Sparks looked up at Sebastian with that crooked grin on his face as if he were truly enjoying the undercurrent of combat that the two scientists were creating at Sebastian's expense.

"Now up the right side of the Negev is the Wadi Arabah," and Brelsford pointed his finger to the long line forming the border of the map. "How about that, Dennison?"

"The main stream of Israel, running straight up from the Gulf of Aqabah," Dennison obliged dryly, as if all this were the alphabet. "King Solomon's mines are there. . . ."

"The promised land, Reverend," Brelsford added, "that the Israelites told about in Deuteronomy, Chapter 8, verse 9, which says 'whose stones are iron and out of whose hills we dig brass.' Do you recall that verse, Sebastian?"

All eyes shifted from the map on the ground to Sebastian who was trying to find something with which he could retaliate to do justice to his holy office. "Of course," he said lightly, and Sparks coughed again as he smothered a laugh.

Brelsford went on in his geography lesson and finished with, "Well, we are not more than fifty miles from Ain Ghadyan over here," and he poked his finger in the sand just below Iqfi and to the right, "and less than that to Ain Gharandel across Arabah. It wouldn't take planes long to find us. . . ."

"In straight desert, maybe not," Eaton growled again, "but we happen to be in a country filled with rocks and ravines and mountainous terrain . . . not the easiest area for planes to see anything . . . . Our only chance is the radio, right now. . . ."

"There's only enough power for one good signal for rescue planes when they come over us," Sparks warned. "I suggest, Eaton, that you sit there quietly and relax like the rest of us. . . ."

No one had anything more to say. Then, after a long pause, Miss Churchill said, "I'm going to check the plane for more supplies . . . I wonder if you would mind accompanying me, Mr. Sebastian? The rest of you better wrap up in your blankets—it's going to get colder. We'll save the fire for dark."

Sebastian had no desire to go anywhere right then, least of all back to that empty cracked shell of an airplane. He was feeling cold, his stomach was still heaving from his bout with the gasoline, and he was beginning to feel a bit short-changed in all this, as if God might have forgotten that he was really on His side. Brelsford and Dennison hadn't bothered him as much as they thought they had. Still, it hadn't helped to be pushed off balance out here when the need for a deeper faith in God was all the more demanded. But maybe it wasn't that so much either. Maybe Brelsford and Dennison were but the embodiment of all the superior obstacles that had kept him bottled up in a small, safe place like Nashville, Wisconsin, all these years. He just hadn't expected to find them here, not in this land seemingly stripped of anything but a pressure to dare man to survive.

But he followed the girl up the slope, overtaking her halfway up. The sun hung on the rim of the far horizon for what only seemed a few minutes, taking one last look at its miserable journey of the day—by the time Sebastian and the girl got to the top of the slope, the sun was gone. The cold cut through Sebastian's sweater almost immediately, and he felt the large, sentinel rocks slip behind the lavender strokes of night. He felt almost suspended, out of sorts—and very cold.

He matched the girl's long strides and noticed how much athletic spring there was to her step and yet how feminine it was too. "Aren't you cold?" he asked, jamming his hands deeper into his far-too-light tropical gray trousers which he had put on a long, long time ago in a hotel in Jerusalem on the Mount of Olives.

"Some," she said simply, and he noticed that she had only a light gray sweater over her uniform. He thought that perhaps the thing to do was offer her his own, but then she could have put more on if she had a mind to. She was made of good, stout English stock undoubtedly—the great Nordic type who had built-in thermostatic control.

They came to the plane, and just as they were about to enter the yawning gap in the fuselage, she paused and turned to face him. There was a kind of half-light left over from what the sun had spilled over the far horizon after its far-too-hasty exit. Her blue-gray eyes were right in that light, and it was the first time he had looked directly into them. He had seen them in brief flashing glimpses during the day, studious in concentration, flicking over objects and people without emotion, measuring, computing, dismissing. But now they had just a shade of softness to them, perhaps from exhaustion, but the hard glint was gone, and there might have been a feeling there now like that of a child who must succumb after all to mounting pressures of life and acquiesce a little.

"Mr. Sebastian," she said, her voice just the same steady tone of half inquiry, half demand but with a slight ingredient of appeal, "I think you can sense yourself that someone has to start thinking about holding this group together. Rations are short, tempers can get shorter, and everything depends on how well we organize and keep to the rules. . . ."

She trailed off, waiting for him to volunteer before she had to start recruiting him. He felt a little sadness because he had hoped she wouldn't put him in this position. He liked her, but not really knowing why—there was that something about her that made him want to rise above himself.

He pulled his hands out of his pockets and cupped them around his mouth to blow on them. "Well," he said lightly, "if you ask me, I think you are doing a bang-up job. For what time we have left here before rescue comes, I don't foresee any real problems with the way things are."

"I am a woman," she said tartly, and her eyes were a little harder again, studious, as if he had suddenly become another obstacle to be coped with. "There are three men with powerful personalities and their own concept of personal genius. They could pull this survival group to shreds."

"But not in the few hours remaining before we can expect help to come," he insisted. She didn't answer him, and he knew why. He sighed and said, "So you don't think they will come that quickly then?"

"I can hope like everyone else," she said. "But I'd rather plan it the other way. I'd rather plan that we would be here a few days, maybe a week. I don't think I can control the party for that long."

"So I just walk into that camp and tell Brelsford and Dennison and fireball Eaton that I'm their new commander-in-chief?" he asked, keeping his voice light and on the bantering side because he didn't want her to think he was backing out deliberately.

"Maybe not just like that," she replied, her voice harder now too, a bit indignant that he should take that approach. "But you ought to prepare for the time when you will have to step in. . . ."

"Because I'm a minister. Is that why you chose me?"

"No, it has nothing really to do with it. You happen to be the only one who has come out of the crash more physically capable than the others."

"Ouch," he said and smiled, although he felt a little sharp twinge deep within himself in the knowledge that his clerical cloth pulled no real weight.

"Well, it's not exactly in line with my parish duties," he tried again, keeping his voice steady on pleasant conversational tone, giving no hint of his own rushing tendency toward noninvolvement. "And you know how Brelsford and Dennison feel about clergymen. . . ."

He looked up to find that the light was gone suddenly, and there was only shadow hanging over where she had stood a few feet from him. He felt her move into the murky desolation of the broken fuselage. It alarmed him that she would dismiss his excuse so completely.

He followed her into what must have been the plane's galley where she was digging through drawers and knocking over things, the sound of clanging objects so incongruous in this world of heavy, mysterious, deathlike silence.

"I'm sorry I'm not being of much help to you," he tried, only sensing her there somewhere in the darkness.

"Forget it," she said, and her voice was back to that crisp, detached tone as if she had decided she had been asking too much of him, and it was best to drop the whole matter.

He didn't want to forget—or at least he didn't want her to relegate him like that to the least common denominator of humanity. He paused, hunting for something on which he could get her back on more disarming conversation, when she said suddenly, "I hear something. Listen."

He listened. He heard it. "For the love of heaven," she exclaimed and rushed by him and out into the desert night. He followed, falling over rock and sand until he would have stumbled over her except for the small flashlight she had flicked on. She was bending over one of the small bundles of blue and gold blanket, and as he stood there he heard a baby's cry come from that misshapen lump, a punctuating, almost terrifying sound of life in so vast a cavern of death.

"A baby?" he said, bending over her as she picked up the little body.

"I was sure the little thing was dead," she exclaimed, "when I checked it over earlier. I swear there was not a pulse flickering. Come on, little one, let's get you to some food and water. . . ."

"Can't be more than eighteen months old," he offered.

"More like a year," she corrected, standing erect and cradling the bundle close to her. He took the flashlight from her, casting the light over the small face buried deep inside the blanket folds.

"That could complicate matters," he said.

"Saving life is always a complicated matter," she snapped at him, "or don't they teach that in your religion?"

She walked off quickly, and he followed, keeping the light in front of her path. "I didn't mean it quite like that," he added. "What I meant was that keeping a baby alive on short rations is going to take a bit of doing."

"Which makes it complicated for everyone, I know," she answered shortly.

"Yes, I guess what I said was not very good at all," and he followed her back into the plane's fuselage and to the galley. "But that child will need milk to survive, and I hope I'm not being an alarmist in suggesting it."

"Then we'll find a way," she said. "Didn't you ever have any complications in the ministry for which you had to find a way through?"

"To tell you the truth, not many."

"I presume you're joking, and I don't think it's a subject for jest," and he played the light over her activities as she took the child out of the blanket. It was a girl—dressed in a yellow party dress with little black shoes and yellow anklets. There was a yellow ribbon in her long curly blond hair. She cried harder now as the touch of human hands awakened the will to live.

"I'm not joking," he said, wondering why he should feel it so important to share his air-tight compartmentalized life with her in this impossible moment, to a woman he hardly knew and who already had formed her own opinions about him. "Sometimes even in the ministry you can be cushioned from complications."

"Religion is a complication in itself," she countered, and she began running her hands over the child, probing for hidden injuries.

"True. But when you've been raised in the atmosphere of religion all your life it becomes uncomplicated . . . like a sword swallower, it looks tough to people outside the community of sword swallowers, but to them it's just a matter of a conditioned esophagus and tonsils. For religion it's a matter of knowing the points of stress and conditioning yourself against them. . . ." He had meant to say "avoiding them" but he was not prepared to admit that—yet.

"I'm not sure I get the analogy," she replied, her voice reaching him, but her thoughts obviously more on the child she folded the blanket back over the frail little body exposed to the sharp night cold. The baby began to cry, so she picked her up and held her close in the blanket, rocking her lightly in her arms. Soon the hard gasping cries were muffled down to short hiccups, and then soft cooing.

"You're quite efficient in all departments," he said.

"You never had children?"

"No. My wife died five years ago in an automobile crash. . . ."

"I'm sorry."

"It's all right—five years is a long time, they say. Whoever said that never lost anyone close."

"I suppose it's hard being a minister without being a

family man?" she said, humming softly now to put the child to sleep.

"Of course. The church understood though. Anyway, I had the Sebastian name. Sebastian is to theology what Argentina is to beef, if you know what I mean. My father was and is the most famous Bible expositor in America on any side of the theological spectrum. As long as I had my father's image, it didn't make too much difference to my church if I were married or single, I suppose. From the day I entered seminary, I had churches writing to me to ask me if I were interested in their church. I felt like a bonus baby—but I suppose you don't know what that means. . . ."

"It's what they use in American baseball when they sign up a man for a big sum of money," she said factually, and he could see her body swinging lightly as she rocked the child.

"You are quite an expert on most everything," he said in admiration. "When I graduated I had about a hundred pulpit committee delegates in the audience waiting for me—no one heard me preach or teach, they didn't even know yet if my doctrine was right. But that magic name of Sebastian was all they needed. It wasn't their fault really—it's just the way we do things and sometimes the world's ways rub off on the church. . . ."

"You don't have to tell me all this," she said, then, and her voice wasn't any more warm for all his attempts. "It really isn't that important."

"It is important to me," he replied, and he knew he was going to say it all, even though he didn't know why. "It's important that you know all this so you can understand that some of us haven't had the opportunity to jump into complications of this degree and swing away at it like Prince Valiant. Some of us never did get our noses bloodied, fight with the gang on the block, or solve anything more complicated than an algebra problem. Some of us have lived antiseptic lives, not by choice, but by dictate." He paused and realized that he had switched

42

out the flashlight. "They say a hothouse rose is never as good as the ones that learn to fight the wind and rain to survive. I say all this because when the time comes that you expect me to act like Field Marshal Montgomery, you'll understand if I am diffident or fumble like an actor who's missed his lines." He paused again, and she stood there in the shadows not moving, just waiting. Then he gave a snort of disbelief at what he was doing and saying, and added lightly, "So I say all this because it's the first time in my life I've ever had a chance to say it to someone who had no place else to go . . . and maybe too because I didn't have to look into anyone's eyes when I said it. There are times when the darkness and desert help. But I guess I said to you what I never really said to my father or even my closest friend in that church of mine in Wisconsin . . . I said it to you because you live with turbulent Jewish history, in a land that can't afford anyone who hasn't prepared to die in complications . . . and for some reason, since you act the part of an Israeli soldier in a kibbutz, and since everything is hung out here on very thin margins, I thought you ought to know . . . just for the record. . . ." There was another long pause, and he added with a little laugh, "And Miss Churchill, that is the best sermon I have ever preached, would you believe it?"

Her voice had the same steady, unruffled, and detached tone when she spoke, but her words were more precise as if she were picking them carefully out of her brain. "I'm not very good at theology, nor do I have much of the world view," she said. "But if there is a God, and I'm inclined to believe there is, then there's got to be some reason that He has for permitting you to live for this particular moment and some other more capable man to die. There has to be some reason why He permits the helpless infant to live through a crash to have to depend on someone like you for survival. Or me. I'm not much for analyzing human nature, so I'm not going to try. You have to live with yourself and God . . . I'll let that be your judge. Meanwhile, you have a pair of hands. Using them won't involve any great stress. See if you can find anything I might have missed that a baby can use. . . ."

He let the conversation die there on that note, feeling better for what he had said, even though she gave no indication that what he had said did anything to alter her opinion of him either way. So what did it matter? He went on rummaging around in the galley and came up with four tins of powdered milk and held them up to her in the light of the flashlight.

"This could be a sign from God," he said lightly.

"It's the first step in meeting a complication maybe," she countered dryly, and walked on out into the night that was filled with the brilliance of a full moon coming up over the horizon as fat as a pumpkin. They walked back toward the others in silence. He felt a flood of shame when he thought of his impulsive admission of a secret problem that he had never felt ready to share with anyone else. Why to her? Why was she so important to him? But it was past now . . . and he felt that perhaps he would never walk with her quite the same again whatever lay ahead.

* 3 *

The flames from the gasoline-soaked airplane cushions had settled down to a comfortable snapping of orange, giving off the same welcome heat in the increasingly bitter cold desert night air. The baby let out a cry of half excitement and half need, and for a moment the atmosphere in the sand crater took on a new kind of family closeness. Miss Churchill worked over the child with her usual easy proficiency, humming softly in a rather good alto while putting on paper diapers she had found in the emergency kit in the plane.

But the presence of the child did little to soften the undertow of forboding that hung over them. The fire had taken out the immediate chill of the night, and for a few precious moments it took away the loneliness and the isolation they felt in this wilderness. But the quiet, inner calculations of survival showed on each face, the mind computing the percentages, the heart pumping the will to live at any cost.

They all watched sullenly as the stewardess poured six precious ounces of water into a tin cup and then added three teaspoons of powdered milk. After stirring it awhile, she poured it into a small baby bottle she had improvised from a medical flask and some rubber tubing. Soon the child was happily sucking away in her arms.

They waited, watching the child drink greedily, licking their own parched throats, and then they dropped back into their blankets, staring at the fire or the stars that hung so big and bright overhead, like the over-ripe fruit of heaven bulging in promise, trying to find refuge in their individual islands of hope.

Sebastian fell asleep after the fire had died to sporadic flames that flashed on and off, bouncing strange semaphore signals off the rocks. The sleep was not more than fitful dozes, and finally he jerked awake, feeling very cold. He lay there trying to control his shivering. He tried tightening the two woolen blankets around him, attempting to shut off the shafts of cold that seemed to be creeping in from everywhere. Finally he resigned himself to a night of sleepless discomfort and turned to controlling the muscle spasms and the chattering of his teeth.

It was then that the vision he had seen earlier in the day flashed across his mind. Strange that it should come to him now. Again, what significance did it have anyway to this time and place?

He lay there most of a half hour thinking about it, trying to dismiss it and trying, too, to get back to the sleep that would dissolve it. But the cold kept on jabbing him—so he sat up, realizing it was useless to lie there a helpless victim of the elements and decided, instead, to walk back to the airplane in hopes of finding extra clothing.

He got up slowly, biting down hard on his teeth against the fresh attack of cold that hit him with a double wallop once outside the blankets. None of the shapeless lumps scattered around the winking embers of the fire indicated their discomfort, and he thought he could detect light snores coming from the direction of Brelsford's blankets. He did a light jog up the slope to get the circulation back, and it felt good to get the blood running warm again. The plane lay there, gleaming in its false coat of silvery promise. He entered the fuselage and moved forward, feeling the eeriness among the dead, but forcing himself to ignore it now.

He dropped through the small hatch leading to the luggage compartment, using the small three-step ladder. It was the same atmosphere of twisted clothing, smelling mustier now, the moon casting weird shadows over it through the large hole on the left and also through that peculiar one on the right. It was an odd hole all right. He peered at it closely. About thirty inches in diameter, as he had figured earlier that day when Sparks had sent him down here to hunt for the jerrican. The peculiar thing about it was that it appeared to have been punched outward from inside the fuselage. Little spears of aluminum jutted outward, as if some fist had smashed through leaving tatters of the paneling hanging there.

"Found something?" the voice came from the dark and upward from the hatch leading back to the cockpit. He jerked around quickly, surprised at hearing Miss Churchill's measured tone of inquiry here.

"Not what I'm looking for," he replied casually enough, wondering how she could have known he had come here. "Thought I could find my suitcase in this mess . . . got some extra heavies in it that I thought would keep off the cold. . . ."

He watched the long, slim shape of her tanned legs come down the ladder, and he had that feeling about her again, of neatness, efficiency, sureness.

"How'd you know I was down here?" he asked, the moon splashing her face with light, bringing her blond silvery hair to a splendor of light contrasting the deep tan of her face and the blue-gray sharpness of her eyes.

"Saw you leave camp," she said lightly, factually, and he saw her eyes dart past the hold behind him like she knew it was there all the time. "So I thought you might need some help in whatever you were after . . . it's a mess here, isn't it?"

"Quite," he said simply, and they stood there a long moment in the awkward silence like two assailants not really sure of one another and each waiting for the other to make a move.

"Sparks is getting weak from loss of blood," she continued, picking up a piece of clothing and throwing it aside. "I thought I might find more tourniquet material."

It sounded like a good excuse, much like his own, so he waited, hunting for more conversation to play with. Then, as they stood there, the new sound came to them in the heavy velvety night, and it froze them for a moment in wonder.

"That's the radio," she exclaimed, and shot up the ladder before he could make the first move. He was right behind her as they got to the radio compartment, and the high-pitched sound of dots and dashes was strong and clear. "It's Morse code," she said in disbelief, staring down at the gleaming eyes of the gauges.

"Thought Sparks said it didn't work?" he demanded.

"Receiving is okay . . . it's the sending that's weak."

"Can you read it?"

"Not the slightest," and he looked at her steadily to see if there might be just a trace of hesitation to indicate that she might be lying, although the accusation forming in his mind rather startled him.

"Why should a signal be so strong out here if we are so far out from radio contact?"

"Doesn't make sense," she admitted, bending down to touch the dial, the signal continuing in nervous patterns. "If we got any signal at all it would be faint on these batteries; and then it would be from some high flying aircraft or from some military outpost a good fifty to sixty miles off. This sounds like it's right on top of us. . . ."

"Maybe it's a rescue party?" he offered hopefully.

She shook her head almost too emphatically, as if she knew. "It wouldn't be an overland rescue since that would take another day at least to get within that powerful a signal . . . and if it was coming in that strong by air we'd hear the engines over us by now I'm sure. . . ."

He thought it odd that she wasn't asking him to go to Sparks. "Shouldn't I be going for Sparks?" he asked bluntly then, and she looked up quickly as if she'd been caught in a glaring oversight.

"Of course, but you better hurry," she returned, making a good recovery. He hesitated just a moment, really not sure if he should leave her there alone and yet not knowing why he felt that way. Finally he moved out of the compartment and into the moon-splashed night, starting out in a dogtrot up the sandy slope.

He got to the top of the slope when he stopped, paused for just a moment to look back at the plane. And then he cut sharply to the left running in a low crouch on a course parallel with the stern of the airplane. He had a feeling he'd be sorry for this, and a kind of explosive laughter boiled up inside him as he thought how stupid this really was anyway, a minister running wild in a desert after something totally illusive and undefinable. But he was propelled by a hunch that seemed to demand vindication, and, though he didn't want his suspicions verified necessarily, it was as if proving her now was absolutely essential to himself and to survival.

He came up to the plane from the rear, off to the right side, opposite the radio compartment. He inched himself past the break in the fuselage and up to the small circular window that opened on the navigator's compartment, facing straight across the radio cubicle. The light from the moon opened up the scene.

She was sitting at the radio with the earphones on, listening carefully and scribbling on a pad of paper in front of her. He stood there feeling the mixed emotions of triumph and shock. She had lied to him then. He was vindicated in one sense, but disappointed at the same time. He felt a sinking feeling that turned to a rising jelly-like panic in his throat, and he wanted to run and keep running before he became too involved and experienced too much disappointment over what she was turning out to be. He stood there in a half crouch, leaning against the still warm fuselage, his eyes staring out into the night, his mind groping for the next move, while his heart kept putting wings to his feet.

The logical thing to do was to run for it. A whole lifetime spent in disentangling himself from irrelevant situations, a reflex triggered on the sensitive feelers of a narrowly defined ministerial role, militated against anything that might demand action outside of those confines. And he knew that if he did face her now, he would have to be pulled into the tightening web of mystery that was building up as the night progressed.

But there was that other feeling too—the sudden need to prove her innocence. He wanted to hear her explain this one way or the other so that he would not have to wonder about her anymore . . . whether innocent or guilty or whatever was going on here, he wanted to be sure.

So he moved back, stepped into the plane and walked casually into the radio compartment. She looked up quickly as his shadow fell across her writing pad, but she went on writing for a full minute, stopped, waited, and then took off the earphones slowly and carefully. The radio was silent now. He leaned against the compartment wall and waited. She didn't say anything, nor was she giving any indication that she was about to.

"Well, at least some things have become more clear," he began trying to keep nonchalance in his voice as if all this was but a game anyway. "For one thing, I don't think you believe we crashed from a thermodraft any more than I do. In fact, I think you are positive we didn't."

She looked up at him quickly, her eyes large and bright in the pale fire of the moon. She looked very lovely like that, with enough shadow to blot out the ugly bruise on her cheek and the light just hitting right so that her dry, pinkish lips were soft looking and her blond hair seemed to take on that brilliant appearance of a halo. He saw the innocent question in her eyes too, so he knew that she'd play this now as defensively as she could.

"I don't know what you're talking about," she replied,

trying to dismiss him with that sound of incongruity in her voice.

"I think you do," he insisted. "I had a foolish dream maybe . . . I woke up and saw that thirty-inch hole down there in the luggage compartment . . . that neat hole that you saw and that I think you know all about . . . I don't think it was made on impact at all. Something else punched out that hole, and I have a hunch it was made while we were a few thousand feet up."

"The next thing you'll be saying is that we had a bomb go off up there," she cut back, her voice sounding dry with intended sardonic humor.

"Now that you mention it, that's exactly what I think."

"And wouldn't we have heard the explosion?"

"Maybe. But I have a demolitions expert in my church back in Nashville who gave me a lesson once—I know that there are ways to knock out a wall with these new explosive substances without a sound. In fact, I understand that you simply paint it on a surface to do its dirty work very neatly without a noise louder than a grunt. . . ."

"Mr. Sebastian," she retaliated with a toss of her head, "I don't know what has wound you up, but when Sparks says it's a thermodraft, that's what it has to be. He would know the difference between an explosion aboard and a down draft, don't you think?"

He stared at her a long minute, not liking this tension building up between them, hating even more her insistence on playing it dumb.

"Okay," he said with a sigh, "I would have gone along with that before I caught you just now at that radio and handling that message like a real pro. For a gal who claims she doesn't know Morse code, you do pretty well at the motions. So one bit of double cross here has to reflect on everything else, don't you agree?"

"I don't think it's any of your business what I'm doing right now," she said abruptly, "and it certainly doesn't concern you."

"That's exactly the way I prefer to play it," he replied,

"because I don't really care one way or the other about whatever subterfuge you desire to carry on here, except that what you are doing now touches on our survival."

"So this whole business is suddenly really beginning to touch some nerves, Mr. Sebastian?" she taunted.

He coughed against the ripple of palpitation around his heart and was glad for the semi-darkness that hid the flush of his cheeks. "Don't get me wrong, Miss Churchill," he slugged back, trying to restore his tone of calm detachment that was gradually yielding to his own mounting indignations, "whatever you're up to doesn't concern me at all—but I don't particularly like to experience suffering that is brought on by someone else's manipulation of events. And there are now six others in this party who become victims of the same plot, whatever it is . . . and if rescue is out there somewhere in the night, and you know it, then it behooves you to share it with all of us. . . ."

"I'm sorry, you'll have to let me handle this," she said with finality.

He shrugged. "Then I think it only fair to let the others know of your noctural activities with the radio. It's their skins too you know. . . ."

"That's blackmail. . . ."

"Call it what you will, Miss Churchill . . . I'm playing this by your rule book so far."

She sighed wearily, hesitating, playing for time, perhaps debating. She leaned her head against the wall so that her face was hidden in the shadows.

"You are becoming quite a paradoxical character, Mr. Sebastian," she said coolly. "A few hours ago you were defending your lack of ability to get involved and to assume responsibility that should be commensurate with your sex at least. Now you are elbowing your way into involvement with seemingly no observance of caution."

"Dimensional I may be, but not paradoxical," he replied. "Every man has his other side, it has been said, held in reserve for specific circumstances. Some men wait a whole lifetime before they are forced to use it. Anyway, I'm not sure what I'm asking is motivated by anything more than curiosity."

"Curiosity has been the beginning of the end for many people. . . ."

"Then so be it. But I'd rather know what form that end is going to take than to walk into it blind."

There was a pause again, heavy with silence, except for the cracking of the plane's metal as its taut muscles relaxed in the cold night air, sounding like someone's knuckles were popping in rhythmic tempo.

"I must warn you then," she said finally, her voice suddenly sounding very weary, "that you are sworn to secrecy of the highest degree. If you share this with anyone else in the party, then you will be asking for serious trouble for all of us."

"I'm not exactly a novice in keeping confidences," he reminded her lightly.

He waited for her to speak, a bit amused now that he could put her on the defensive for a change. It stimulated him to have the mastery for just a few brief moments. It helped him forget the cold and the fact that she deliberately deceived him, a fact that marred his image of her perfection. On top of this was an inner skepticism of the peculiar dramatic projection she was giving all this, like some wild tale of a child she was dreaming up for effect.

But as he listened to her, he realized almost immediately why she had hesitated. And though each word only added to the farcical image he had of her mysterious intimations, yet he felt increasingly the desire to stop her before he found himself too far in to withdraw.

She was a professor of history at the University of Tel Aviv. While teaching there, she also served as agent for the Israeli Secret Police to keep an eye on the head of the geology department who was suspected of being middleman feeder of Israeli top secrets to Russia. It became known a few months ago that this man was getting high priority secrets smuggled out and putting them on microfilm for shipment outside.

"The documents were of the highest priority," she explained, "but we felt we ought to wait to see who the geology man was going to use to get the documents out of the country. We were sure that he would pass them to an agent we called Christopher, who was the key man to the whole espionage system in the Middle East. We want that man more than anyone in the last ten years."

The ISP learned from a defector that the geology man would pass the secrets to the "Big Man" who would take a Zion Airlines flight to Nairobi where the film would be passed on to a Russian agent.

"The only trouble was we didn't know who Christopher was or what he looked like," she went on. "What we did find out was that this flight was it—so I was assigned as stewardess to make sure no one got off at Khartoum. Once our man got to Nairobi, we had another defector who had just come over who could identify him. It was just a matter of keeping him aboard."

"Well, Khartoum is only a refueling stop," Sebastian cut in, "no one gets off there anyway."

"True, but if the agent suddenly decided to jump, he could use the forward crew's hatch or even the rear loading hatch during the time we were loading the afternoon tea boxes."

"So we didn't get to Khartoum," Sebastian said, still feeling as though this was pure fiction because he couldn't picture her as any kind of spy at all, or that anything so fantastic could actually have come into his own uneventful life. "We were sent off course and bombed in the air— which brings us to the glorious present. How do you figure this?"

"It's obvious," she continued, "that the Russian and Arab underground got wind of our plan to intercept them in Nairobi. It was probably too late for them to change flight plans without throwing suspicion on their man, because they undoubtedly knew we were looking for any sign of just such a move. So they took the only way out. They planted the bomb, the silent type as you mentioned earlier. . . ."

"To kill off twenty people, and their big key man besides and all that microfilm?" Sebastian asked in astonishment.

"Twenty people mean nothing in this kind of game," she retaliated with some impatience. "And if you knew what was on that microfilm you'd know that Russia couldn't afford the embarrassment of having one of their men caught with it. There is no unexpendable agent, even in Russian intelligence."

"Yes, well, you haven't yet told me what's on that microfilm," he reminded her.

"And you don't need to know," she returned bluntly.

"Very well," he said with a sigh. "One thing bothers me among others—when that bomb went off up there, how come the plane didn't go up with it? Pressurized cabins normally run on an atmosphere as volatile as a house full of gas fumes."

"We were flying below 10,000 feet over the Negev to keep out of the headwinds higher up so as to save fuel. That saved the day. The bomb put the plane out of control, and even at that the pilot did a masterful job in trying to keep it from going in nose down."

"So as far as we can conclude then the Russian big wheel is dead, the microfilm is probably destroyed with him—so everything ends happily for Israel. That leaves us with what you got on that radio. . . ."

She hesitated only a second and then said, "The fact is simply that our Russian agent is not dead . . . he apparently survived the crash with the rest of us."

Up to then Sebastian hadn't followed it with any feeling of alarm, but now he suddenly came alert. He tried to see her face hidden in the shadows, just to be sure there wasn't some kind of smile on her mouth or in her eyes that would indicate the joke. Instead, she turned the white pad of paper on which she had been writing towards him.

The bright light of the moon showed up her neat penciled block letters:

RECVD YR MESSAGE 1900 HRS
WILL STAND BY FOR WORD

"Which means what?" he asked.

"Which means that the people who sent that just now are a special team sent in to make sure our man Christopher is dead—or if alive, to make contact and get him out of here into Egypt."

"Which means the agent sent that—what time is 1900 hours anyway?"

"Last night at seven o'clock."

"Well . . . he couldn't have sent it on this radio. We were here at that time."

"Correct," she replied, her voice carrying that note of indulgence as though he were a child groping through a stiff math problem. "He probably sent it on a small transistor sending device, no bigger than a fountain pen."

There was a long silence during which Sebastian let the astonishment filter down into his brain. He shook his head slightly to clear it of the heavy fog that always came when he had to make deductions in areas out of his normal line of thinking. "Would you mind, Miss Churchill, getting your face out of the shadows, please? I want to look at you when you talk just to be sure you're not either half mad or having a good time with me. . . ."

She stood up and leaned forward so that the moonlight hit her face squarely only a foot from his, so close that he could smell the warmth of her, feel the light touch of her breath on his chin, and look into those pentrating blue-gray eyes that were dead serious. He cleared his throat and dropped his eyes instead to her tan, long legs, but everything about her was disturbing. So he discreetly backed a foot out of the compartment, eased his gangling frame half out into the aisle, and found a spot over her head to look at.

"What I don't get is how our Russian agent knew that he had friends out there in the desert? It almost looks as if he knew he was going down right from the start—and how could they be sure he would die anyway and that microfilm would be destroyed?"

"Your question begs the obvious answer. He was probably tipped off at the last minute that the intercept was on, so he knew he would have to give his life. All agents are prepared to swallow cyanide when caught, so going down in an aircrash is just another way to make it appear more legitimate. But those agents out there in the desert were sent in here to make sure—one, that he was dead and, two, to make sure that microfilm was found and destroyed. Or—if he just happened to live through it, get him out and over into Egypt fast."

She was beginning to talk more rapidly now, and he knew she was feeling nervous about sitting out here with the dead bodies of the crew still in the cabin and Agent Christopher somewhere plotting his own moves.

"So he sent the message to his friends," Sebastian went at it with his insistent lint picking, giving her unreadable face a hasty glance, "but did he get what you just got?" that radio?"

"Probably not," she said quietly, in preoccupation as if thinking this one out to herself, standing half crouched in the radio cubicle, studying him now with careful scrutiny. "These little transistors can send Morse code but can't receive—it's an emergency device only, a one-way transmission. I'm pretty sure that's all he's carrying, anything with receiving would demand a larger piece of equipment. . . ."

"They took a chance sending it on this radio then."

"Of course. They gave him time to get here. He probably told them to send a reply exactly at this time and keep sending until answered."

Now Sebastian began to feel the sweat trickle down the long valley of his backbone. "This agent of ours then knew there was enough power on this radio to send and receive a short distance," Sebastian said.

"And you will remember that Sparks told everyone in the group that fact last night, especially addressing Mr. Eaton," she answered quickly, anticipating his thoughts.

He kept looking at that spot over her head and went on as if not hearing her. "And one thing more—this radio transmitter was on, or must have been when I got here. Which means that Agent Christopher, or whoever he is, was out here before I was, waiting to get in on that frequency."

He looked down into her face then, looking hard for that one sign that would confirm his suspicions. But her eyes remained steady on his, her face unreadable, her mouth set in that soft, firm, unyielding line.

"Which means," she continued factually, "that you scared him off when you got here. He didn't expect anyone to come looking for heavy clothing at this time of night. And I know that you think I could very well be that person, and you have every right to conclude that. All I say is that I was not here before you. I followed you out. It's as simple as that. In fact, I figured you were my man up until an hour ago when you started grilling me about desert wigs and bombs. . . ."

He laughed, half in relief in knowing that she was being very insistent on declaring her innocence and half in the sheer amusement of her remark. "Me? Seven days in Palestine? All the way from Nashville, Wisconsin, where nothing more exciting happens to a minister than dropping the collection plate?"

"You're the type the Russians use," she remonstrated. "The tourist type, no interesting background, very little to excite Israeli intelligence. You could be Agent Christopher as well as any of the others."

He laughed again, but it sounded feeble this time.

"You think this is funny," she said with some irritation.

He nodded. "Yes, it is very funny. Me suspected of being a Russian agent—but more so I guess that I, a

58

minister with a very carefully laid-out life, should land right in the middle of a most macabre situation. Heaven surely has its signals mixed."

But he didn't laugh long. He just stood there after a minute or so savoring it all, his mind chasing through all the possible alternatives, debating his own responsibility in it.

Then, suddenly aware of another matching piece for the puzzle, he said, "You said the transmission would stop when they got an answer. The code has stopped coming over now—what does that mean exactly?"

"I sent them an answer," she said simply. He glanced down to the small table in front of the radio and saw the sending key half hidden by her right hand.

"You know the more I ask and the more you have to answer, the more I get the idea that you are closer to Agent Christopher than any of us."

"I can't help that."

"What did you tell them?"

"That I'd transmit later on as to when I'd rendezvous and where."

"And what if our man—assuming it isn't you—gets to this radio in the meantime and tells them to come on in?"

"They'll come. . . ."

"And?"

She sighed again and sat down in the cubicle. "They'll probably kill us all."

Sebastian clucked in the back of his throat, but he felt the dampness of the sweat on the backs of his hands even in the cold night air. "My, my," he said trying to make it sound less final, "must it be so serious?"

"They couldn't chance us getting out to tell what we saw, obviously."

Silence again. "You know what I think?" he ventured.

"I have an idea," she replied dryly, "but don't keep me in suspense."

He smiled wanly at her, but her face remained impassive.

"Well, I think our man Christopher wants to make contact so he can get out there to his buddies. I don't think he wants to sit around here with that hot film on him . . . so I think we ought to let him make contact and get out. That way it will save us all from getting shot up over what is none of our business."

"Yes, I thought you were thinking that way," she said, and the cutting edge of sarcasm was there again.

"What's wrong with that?"

"Two things, if you can't see for yourself. One, he's probably not sure if one of us is an Israeli agent or not . . . he may have been tipped off that one was aboard . . . if he has suspicions, then he's not going to chance making a quick move out. He knows he can't afford to get caught—he'll play it close and cozy until he can get to this radio and call in his friends to get him."

"What's the other criticism?"

"Namely the matter of the film . . . I can't let him get away with it. That's why I was assigned this job, to make sure he didn't get away with that film."

"I still don't know what's on that film," he prodded her.

"You don't need to know . . . anyway, it's top secret."

"Anything top secret at this point is rather ridiculous, don't you think? You led me this far, and the way you sound I get the feeling you're asking for help. So it's obvious you're going to need another pair of eyes. Which comes down to one obvious fact—I'm all you've got from here on in. I'm no door prize to be proud of, but nevertheless I'm it. I don't like it. You don't like it. But if we're going to be one for all and all for one, then I think in all fairness I should know what's up for grabs."

She sighed again and leaned forward into the light, propping her elbows on the bent wooden radio table. "Very well," and her voice reflected some notes of defeat as she gave in reluctantly to his demands, and even now she hesitated a long minute before proceeding. "The microfilm carries the full picture of Israel's National Water Carrier—its system of water routes from Lake

Galilee to Tel Aviv, Jerusalem, and down to the Northern Negev. Power stations, pumping areas, diversion areas, and especially the underground channels and conduits."

Sebastian thought about that, realizing something of the long stretches of dry, desertlike sandy plains he had seen in Palestine. "I see the need for water," he admitted, "but it sounds a little too simple. After all the attempts to crush Israel with military might, it just doesn't seem possible that water could have that much of a hold."

"Water is our life blood," she argued, "and the Arabs know it. So far we've kept that underground conduit pattern out of their reach. The main thing is it has taken us nine years and millions of dollars to put in that system—if they blow it, we probably won't get to build it again. Besides that, we have close to a million Jews planning to come in this next year—we need those million to man the frontiers of the Northern Negev. To put them there, we must have water."

"So they wreck those channels," he went on doggedly, "you can still build new ones or tap emergency supplies."

"The Arabs will attack not long after," she countered. "We won't have the time to do anything but defend ourselves. And you can't move an army without water."

"But there's the U.N. or even the United States . . . surely, they'd step in to prevent any Arab push?"

"Russia will tie up the U.N. the moment anything is brought forward concerning Israeli water and Russian tampering. They've timed everything with that film. As to your country, well, they won't detour the U.N. on this one, what with other commitments demanding too much of their resources. It will take too long for your country to make any major policy move—and by that time we will be swallowed up."

Sebastian sighed, his breath sounding a little shaky in the quiet compartment. "Well, you know the sons of Ishmael have been trying to gobble up little Israel since 1948. They've struck out every time so far."

"Militarily, yes, but never had they so natural a weapon as water before," she declared in half appeal to him.

"Again here's where you and I differ," he said, swinging on a new tack now. "You are not a student of Scripture, but I know that the timetable in prophecy doesn't call for Israel to go under like that. Whatever God has in mind for that nation must be a plan that goes beyond us, and it must be for the good. . . ."

"You mean like Hitler's plan that put six million Jews in the ovens?" she remonstrated, and he blinked in surprise at the vehemence that came into her voice then.

"God let it happen for a purpose," he replied lamely, not sure he could handle this kind of argument.

"And the church let it happen, I suppose, because the Jews were the apple of God's eye?"

"Well . . . I don't see where the church had anything to say about it."

"The Roman Catholic Church could have stood against it by open statement if nothing else. The Lutheran Church could have demanded cessation of any such practice."

"Well—maybe. But you can't judge the church in total for one mistake in history. Some of us weren't in Germany then."

"But you are with them by the very answer you just gave me—if God wants Israel dead tonight, then far be it from me to dabble with His sovereign plan. Do you let the suffering in the world go on charged to God's account? Or do you as a man of God seek to relieve human suffering when and where you can?"

She seemed to have argued this before and lost. "There are certain things I'm not ordained to meddle in," he tried again, but he knew he was not reasoning with any sense of confidence. He was beginning to feel genuinely disturbed.

"On what basis do you make distinctions?" she jabbed at him. "You see a child run into the street and a car comes roaring down on her—do you stand there and ask yourself if it is God's plan that that child should die with you standing within rescue distance?"

"You are drawing a poor analogy for the Israeli problem," he reminded her, but feeling a twinge of guilt deep within himself.

She didn't answer him, and she heaved a sigh again as if she had become aware that this argument was foolish and her intensity a waste. She sat back in the cubicle again and looked out the broken window into the night.

"Well, now you know," she said to him with finality.

"Yes," he said, and then after a pause added, "What's the next move then?"

"We'll have to move at dawn or before. . . ."

"Where?"

"South I suppose . . . try to make it to the nearest outpost . . . anyway away from this place. We have no choice. We've got to stay ahead of that crowd out there."

"There's still a possibility of rescue."

"We can't take the chance. Time is not with us anymore. Death could come on us at any minute."

"Death could come even more surely if we try that desert," he reminded her, a little angry at himself for making it more difficult for her. "Even I know that. And how can we stay ahead of them with this man Christopher keeping in touch with them with that transmitter of his? And how do you expect Christopher to let us move away from the wreck without a fuss? He wants to get to this radio and return a signal to his friends."

"It's a chance we'll have to take," she replied flatly.

"And he's got a gun undoubtedly."

"Then we'll have to try to find one as persuasive."

"I detect that first person plural again," he defended. "You are assuming that I intend to become so directly involved in this cloak-and-dagger?"

She was a bit taken aback by this sudden turn of conversation and turned to face him again. "I would think your interests in Israel would bring some identification, yes," she said, her voice heavy with sarcasm now.

63

"Political identification with political Israel is not my responsibility," he argued, irritated at his own headlong bent to disentangle himself. "I don't intend to be an unwilling pawn in this. . . ."

"You've made your point quite clear," she retaliated. "But if you can't get identified with Israel as the cradle of your theology, then try to view it as any red-blooded American does in sympathy for the underdog . . . even you a clergyman must have at least that much iron in your system!"

He felt her voice grow cold as the night desert air, and it was as if a light had been snuffed out, a light that had given him warmth. He did not want to argue further. He wanted that light back, so he said, "I would say that my interests are purely in the matter of survival . . . and in that connection I think I can supply you with a weapon. . . ."

She didn't get the significance of what he said at first, because he had swung back on her side too quickly. Then she arose slowly and leaned toward him again in expectancy, in urgency, and he moved away quickly to avoid that rising pulsation within him. "Sparks picked up a gun earlier today," he said, standing outside the cubicle and peering around him aimlessly, conscious of her a few feet from him. "He offered it to me . . . just in case . . . I refused it and told him he ought to use it when the time came for whatever it happened to be for. . . ."

"Good," she said, and he felt a strange exhilaration at knowing he had done something that apparently pleased her. "Then we must get it from Sparks as soon as possible."

He wanted to say more, to reestablish new ground upon which he could approach her. The slashing dialogue between them had left him feeling cold, alone, and uncomfortably detached from her.

But she was already moving by him and down toward the break in the fuselage. He followed. She paused once before going out into the bright night, looking across the desert. "I'll go into camp alone, you follow in ten minutes," she said crisply, and then she was gone before he could say anything more.

He watched her until she disappeared over the hill. She didn't look back once. That's the way he wanted it, he thought. She wasn't asking him to become really involved at all—she intended to face the problem thrust upon her with the ingenuity that her training gave and the loyalties to Israel that had become the most important thing in her life. She was a civil servant schooled in espionage—and though she faced a situation never intended by her superiors, she rose to it with a kind of magnificence that thrilled him.

But though she had diplomatically taken him off the hook, he felt no sense of relief in it. For the first time in his ministerial life, the antiseptic-safe world of his Christian isolationism was caught in the balance, and it carried very little weight at all. She had been precise in her summation of what could be expected of him, of the church—and the indictment moved beyond him to God Himself.

And he couldn't help but feel the pressure of uncertainty—and not a little shame.

He followed her into camp fifteen minutes later. He felt naked in the exposure of the moon, knowing that Agent Christopher was at that moment watching from his blankets. He moved quietly across the sand crater to his own tangled blankets, and as he settled down in them he felt a movement to his left and turned to see her coming across to him, crawling slowly, using her elbows and wriggling her curved, athletic body like a reptile against the sand. She stopped when her head was not more than inches from his, and exertion of the crawl forced her to breathe heavily so that the warmth of her breath touched his cheek.

"He hasn't got it," she said in a whisper.

"Sparks?" he queried. She nodded.

"Are you sure he had it?"

"Of course. I saw him put it in his belt."

"Well, it's not on him now," she replied.

"Maybe our man Christopher took it off him?"

"Perhaps," and he noticed the frown that came between her eyes, always a sign that a new pressure point had arisen within her.

"We could wake him and find out," he offered.

"No—he needs to rest, and we'll only disturb the camp and get our man a little jittery about what we're up to . . . if he doesn't already know." She paused, thinking to herself, looking slowly around the camp from her prone position. He studied the soft curve of her chin, the tilt of her nose, the clean sculptured lines of a face that had aristocracy and scholarship in it. He wondered what it would be like to sit with her in candlelight and soft music, if the beauty of the face hidden by the intensity of the business at hand would come to the fore, if she could laugh and what it would sound like and what her eyes would look like in that laugh and the glow of candles.

"I think we better sleep," she said, then, "we'll need it in a few hours."

"You sleep," he said softly. "I'll keep my eyes open to make sure our man doesn't try for the radio out there again."

He thought he detected a look of gratefulness for his offer, but he knew he was reading that into her eyes. "We'll check Sparks later," she added, and turned slowly and started her crawl back to her blankets. Her legs touched his arm as she moved off, and it was the first time he sensed the actual humanness of her, the smooth firmness which was at the same time intensely exciting.

He watched her until she was in her blankets, lying on her side, her shapely form defying the bulky woolen covering over her. He knew he wouldn't sleep. Already he thought he could see a faint finger of light reaching across the sky, the first probing vanguard of dawn, two hours away maybe. He lay there in the blankets, feeling the warmth relax his muscles. His mind kept whirling with the incredible design of which he was involuntarily but inexorably a part. Even now his mind, exposed only to the normally uneventful, refused to absorb the facts of the situation—he had the feeling that he wanted to smile all the time, as if this was after all some wild joke conjured up by some person of exceptional imagination, who at any moment would take off the disguise and reveal that the gun he held was nothing more than a piece of licorice.

But behind his constant tendency to smile was the slowly developing awareness of the actual genuineness of the elements so suddenly projected here. All of the nagging questions that had nipped at his mind since the crash had now been answered, ridiculous as these answers may have appeared. The blank spots were filled, the circle complete, the parts fitted in. Though he did not have a mind disciplined to following the patterns of intrigue, he did have his father's relentless spirit of exposition. And he knew now that the outline was there, the analysis in one sense complete, and the shape of the whole coming more and more out of the fog.

"The heavens declare the glory of God and the firmament showeth His handwork," he said in a whisper, staring up at the brilliance of the stars. His spiritual quest was taking on strange and bizarre overtones. He had no reason to question the sovereignty of God as to the purpose of all this or the outcome, yet he could not see how this would meet the need of his own ministerial life, which demanded more of Bethel than Jericho. "What is man that thou art mindful of him," he went on, "or the son of man that thou considerest him. . . ."

His mind went back to the girl again—how warm, how fiercely spirited she was. Not like Carol really. Carol was a leader in her own right, and while she lived the church knew it, even more than they knew it in him. But she could never rise to the heights under real pressure any more than he could. She, too, had been a product of an environment that kept the pressure at safety valve level. But Barbara Churchill had will, a flashing glow of intense desire actually, developed in a world of life-or-death conflict. And the hotter the flame of adversity, the more that will glowed to match it. And the more beautiful she became. . . .

Thinking of her moved him to explore his face, rubbing his fingers against the day-and-a-half-old stubble that covered the angular lines surrounding high cheekbones and prominent jaw line. He glanced down the blankets over his six-foot-two gangly frame to his size eleven feet that jutted up from the blankets like the grotesque web-like protusions of a penguin. He wished many times for a more compact, well-coordinated frame that seemed to go with successful people. And anything but an Abraham Lincoln face. "Four score and seven years ago," he whispered. How many times had he given that address at the Lincoln Monument in Nashville . . . well, nine Lincoln birthdays now . . . the high school always asked him because he did resemble Abe, the young Abe of Spring-field, Illinois . . . and once the Nashville *Courier* ran a picture of him alongside the statue of the famous presi-dent, the wood chopper and champion wrestler . . . and the resemblance was striking even to himself. Like his father, the almost eagle-beak shape of his nose, the greenish-blue eyes set back into receded sockets, the wide mouth with full lower lip and shock of wiry, bushy black hair that always stayed short and close to his head . . . well, it helped on Lincoln's birthday anyway, and all he had to do was stand near that statue, grip his suit lapels with both hands, put one foot forward to match that famous pose, and the kids cheered.

For one hour of the year anyway he was the personifica-tion of history, sentimental as it was . . . the rest of the year he had to live with the Lincoln image of gentility and humility and homeliness . . . but Carol had described his appearance as "rustic handsomeness" whatever that meant, "with a dash of the rugged woodsman and the sophisticated bearing of a senator." Carol was a beautiful woman, too. What she saw in him then was not all that drastic.

But what did Barbara Churchill see in him? Nothing probably. Such physical proportions had to grow on a person from long association. So he hadn't much going for him there, and he was no match for her aggressiveness and spirit either. Anyway, what did it matter now . . . they were worlds apart. . . . She had her world of espionage, the turbulence of Jewish history as her propelling purpose . . . he could not entertain any thought of future association, except for what lay ahead in the desert . . . she would use him now as she had to, and when and if by the goodness of God they got out, she would go back to her duty, and he would go back to his. . . .

And then his mind drifted slowly and casually to Nashville, Wisconsin, where things like this only showed up in the newspapers, and people read about it with a detached provincial viewpoint—and he smiled as the warmth of the blankets lulled him to a doze. . . .

And he did not see the form rise out of the blankets across the camp, blended skillfully against the dark outcropping of rock that defied the brilliance of the moon . . . he did not see that figure dart up the slope, moving quickly and masterfully using the landscape for cover . . . he did not see the figure pause at the top of the escarpment and look down with a grin, the figure of one hand caressing a fountain pen.

The early morning desert stood still, but forces were at work—while Sebastian slept.

* 4 *

He awoke with a jerk, opening his eyes to a peculiar liquid
red haze, and he had the impression of blood running
down a wall, and it was Carol's blood, her life oozing down
the fuselage of that sports car, her light, petite body
smashed in the entrails of aluminum and plastic—forever
gone, forever out of his life, taking with her the big
meaning of his own life and the drive that had kept him
alive in the ministry. . . .

But it wasn't blood at all. As he continued to stare at it,
almost paralyzed by the wonder and terror of it, he
realized it was a fine mist, or fog, and that behind it was
the sun pouring in the promise of the inferno to come . . .
and then someone coughed, and the sound rose flatly in
the damp air like a sharp thud. It snapped him hard in his
mental solar plexis, and he sat upright in his blankets,
looking around for the others, realizing suddenly that he
had slept and experiencing the sharp shaft of shame that
came with it.

He picked out Brelsford first who was sitting in the
middle of his blankets pulling on a pair of hard shoes with
high tops that came over his shins. His gray crew-cut hair
looked like a wild crop of bramble tinged with frost, and
standing out even more in contrast to the bizarre morning
of red. Dennison, a few feet away, was on his knees

70

staring at a few rocks in his right hand through a small magnifying glass looking as scraggly as an old prospector checking his nuggets. Eaton was propped up on one elbow, refusing to come out of his blankets totally, peering around at the world of rocks and sand and strange hues with a woeful look on his face. Farther to the left, the two schoolteachers were doing brisk pacing in the sand to the rhythmic cadence counts of Miss Churchill who, while prodding her charges, worked carefully over the morning rations.

Sebastian stood up quickly, feeling embarrassed that this camp would wake up and feel no need of him—they faced up to the day and the task of survival with their own individual approach to it, and he had the smiting stab of guilt that even here the church slept while humanity mustered up its own courage to weather the elements.

He went over to Sparks first, anxious now to fit himself into the discordant scene, to form some spiritual vortex around which they could rally. Sparks did not look well. His face was very white against the blue blankets that were tucked up around his chin. "Would you light my butt, Reverend?" he croaked, his voice sounding raspy like his throat was raw or closing up on him. Sebastian looked down at the familiar stub of a cigarette hanging out of that wide mouth that turned up in that half smile, then at the brass lighter that lay by the limp right hand. He had never lit a cigarette for any man in his life, and he felt no particular desire now to violate a custom of his holy office. But the eyes that stared back at him were not taunting, critical, or judging. They were the eyes of a man in pain, trying to draw what comforts he had accustomed himself to in the trying hours. This was no time for sermons on the evils of tobacco nor inner debates with his conscience. He swallowed, picked up the lighter, flicked the wheel clumsily. He tried four times, and then Sparks reached out and touched his hand gently.

"I think the fluid's gone, Reverend," he said quietly. "Thanks anyway . . . ." Sebastian indignantly flicked the wheel three more times before snapping the cover back, as if it was suddenly very important that Sparks know he wasn't diffident about lighting his cigarette for him.

"I'm sorry, Sparks," he said, putting the lighter back on the ground. "Can I help you up now?"

"Sure thing," and the radio operator was breathing more rapidly as he made the first move out of the blankets that set off a short coughing and retching spell. Sebastian lifted him from the waist and eased him back against the smooth wall of rock. "Fancy me turning out to be an old woman at my age," Sparks bantered after he got his breath back. There was the smell of dried blood on him and that peculiar pungency that came from an open wound that was taking on an infection.

"It takes nerve just to wake up with what you've got," Sebastian said, wishing he would not sound so negative in his attempts to be light. He tucked the blankets around him again, searching for ways to make his ministry more effective.

"I'm glad you took the gun off me," Sparks said then, sighing a long shaky breath. "Like I said, governor, you might be needing it. . . ."

Sebastian smiled, wondering if he ought to tell Sparks that he didn't have the gun . . . but then there was no point in alarming him further. "I'll get your ration," he said.

"Don't forget me hat, Reverend," Sparks said, and Sebastian looked back in the sand where the blue and gold of the airline lay. He picked it up, and placed it on the small round head with its familiar shock of black hair that looked very thin now up close.

"Have to cover me bald spot," Sparks added, "and we don't want anybody forgettin' do we?" He tipped the cap to a jaunty slant over his left eye. He grinned so that his face took on a clown's features.

Sebastian smiled, trying to think of something humorous to say to match the admirable spirit of this man who was dying and yet defied the world of death to take him kicking his outrage. "You are about as easy to forget as Captain Bligh," he managed, and though it wasn't a very good attempt, Sparks grunted a short laugh of appreciation, his dull white teeth looking even yellower against the paleness of his face.

Sebastian moved on over to where Miss Churchill was standing by the ration bag. She had already dished up the rations and was busy taking inventory when he approached.

"You slept well, Mr. Sebastian?" she said casually, and he felt the limpness within him at the direct confrontation with his failure. He was glad she didn't look at him when she said it.

"I'm really sorry," he said, but she went right on working without even giving notice that she had heard. Then, "I know I'm at fault for not watching for the dawn, but shouldn't we be moving now?"

"The fog is good cover for us now," she replied quietly. "No one will try to move vehicles with so little visibility. It gives us time and won't appear that we are too eager. Anyway, I'm not sure yet how to tell them we have to move on. . . ."

She handed him a half cracker and sardine. He took it and said, "I'll take Sparks' to him. By the way, I think he's about had it, and I doubt he can walk very far. And he doesn't have the gun . . . he just thanked me for taking it off him last night."

She paused for just a few seconds to think on that, her eyes focused on the ground. She glanced once toward Sparks and said, "We will have to help him, carry him if necessary . . . as for the gun, it's not our concern right now. The main thing is to get moving and soon. I think the fog is beginning to lift. Let's be ready in five minutes."

"Fine," he said and plopped the cracker into his mouth, sensing his body ripple with the feel of nourishment and taking on that peculiar ache too of a system that wasn't getting enough. She turned back to the baby, who was cooing softly in her blue blanket, delighting in the color of the mist that had the promise and innocency of a nursery.

Sebastian coaxed Sparks into eating after exchanges of bantering remarks that Sparks accepted readily but he now peered up at Sebastian studiously as if he weren't sure the attempt at humor was genuine or only superficial, available for only certain conditions.

Sure that Sparks was all right, he walked over to the two schoolteachers who sat with an airline blanket around them, as if it was some kind of fetish designed to ward off further evil.

"Anything I can do?" he offered pleasantly, and he thought how much he sounded as though he were standing outside a clean hospital room, as he had done a hundred times, offering his dutiful assistance to people who didn't know what he could do except pray anyway.

They both put on their smiles, nibbling at their ration with dexterity and proper Bostonian protocol.

"Thank you, but we seem to be managing," the one on the left said, and he noted that she had intelligent brown eyes and a high forehead and seemed to be very calm and more sure of herself than the day before.

"Excuse me, but which one of you is Miss Stockton?"

"I am," the same lady said with a good smile that flashed nice teeth, and Sebastian thought that she didn't appear to be old-maidish at all up close. Mildred Randolph, though, fit the bill. She huddled close to Miss Stockton, her eyes carrying the melancholy and open fears of a totally insecure individual who appeared to be ready to cry at any moment.

"You're not hurt, either of you?" he went on.

"Some scratches," Miss Stockton admitted for both of them, "and a few bumps. We're thankful—really we are. . . ."

"Thank God is what I do," Miss Randolph cut in, leaning toward Sebastian now as if her confession would declare her allegiance with him and thus offer leverage for Sebastian's role with God in the future. "I'm an Episcopalian, you know, have been all my life . . . my mother was a

74

Presbyterian, my grandmother a Quaker . . . our whole family tree from the precolonial days were believers in God . . . that's why I'm glad you're here, Mr. Sebastian, because I believe God is going to get us out of here . . . and with you a man of God among us, how can He refuse?"

"Well, God is mindful of His own," Sebastian said, and he wished he could be more original, less lyrical, less pontifical on a cliche like that that he had said so many times as a kind of ritual to people in crisis. And then Miss Randolph began to cry, and pieces of the dry cracker clung to her twisted lips so that she looked like a child who had been scolded in the middle of her meal. Miss Stockton took a quick, dainty swallow from the aluminum cup and handed it to Sebastian.

"We've had ours," she said, and he felt a peculiar kind of sureness in her that not only well balanced Miss Randolph's rivetless structure but seemed to carry beyond that.

"Let me know if I can be of assistance," he said, and she gave a quick smile that was only an upturning of her mouth as if to say she would handle whatever came up from here on in.

He went back to Sparks, gave him his swallow of water and was walking back to Miss Churchill when her voice, rather muffled in the pink mist, reached him.

"All right, people, let's gather around. . . ."

They collected in a loose, uncertain group almost as if they were afraid of getting too close to each other lest they reveal their own feelings or betray their own sense of interdependence. Sebastian crouched down a few feet from the standing Miss Churchill, drawing his finger idly in the sand, looking at her brown loafers and the tan of her legs and then back to the sand again. He cleared his throat and waited, and when he looked up at them he realized that they were different to him now. Each of them constituted a threat, for one of them had other interests here, driven by an uncertain desperation, biding the time, but using those interests for whatever they were worth to further his own ambitions. Though it was difficult for him to accept the fact that any of them would use violence here to achieve personal ends—for his view of the world was still optimistic and man was still endowed with that main stream of mercy—yet he could not deny his attitude toward them had changed. And this was creating a confusing crosscurrent of responsibility toward them.

"We have to move on," Miss Churchill said, her voice as clear and as sure as always. No one said anything. It was if they hadn't heard. She let it sink in and then added, "If we had gotten our signal through before the crash, there'd be rescue planes over us by now. Our only hope is to start out walking for the nearest outpost . . . I make it Ain Ghadyan forty miles east. . . ."

Still no one said anything. Finally Brelsford said, "Aren't you pushing this a little fast?" and his voice was deliberately condemnatory of the suggestion. "If we are ever to be found, I would think it would be around the wreck . . . anyway, to go out into that desert, dear lady, is an act of suicide, and I trust you'll take it from a man who has worked deserts before in his day. . . ."

She apparently had anticipated the argument, although Brelsford's gift for dialectics seemed to dare further exchange on the subject. "There is the question of water, Mr. Brelsford . . . we cannot go another two days on what we have here, and it may take longer than that to find us. . . ."

"You'll need twice as much water out there," Eaton chimed in dourly, "since we lose much more body liquid walking. If we sit quietly and conserve we'll stand a better chance."

"You couldn't conserve even if you were as quiet as a corpse, Mr. Eaton," she retaliated keeping her voice polite but firm, and there was the sound of Sparks' chuckle in the background. "The heat in this desert will suck every drop out of you and leave you a useless chunk of dehydration within twenty-four hours. . . ."

"May I ask, then, where you expect to get water out

there in the desert?" Dennison interjected then, and it was unusual to hear Dennison asking anything of anyone. "You're asking us to cover forty miles—we can at best expect to cover three to four miles a day. That means ten days walking . . . have you calculated all that?"

"There are supposed to be Bedouin springs between here and Ain Ghadyan," she insisted, rising to the grating hostility that seemed to build up in them now. "There are water collections in these wadis and perhaps wild pome-granates. . . ."

"Do you happen to know the average rainfall for this area of the Negev, Miss Churchill?" Brelsford challenged again, seeming to rise taller in his boots now, his adhesive scarred face lifting into the pink mist.

"Four to six inches," she said.

"Wrong," Brelsford replied flatly, with a triumphant smile on his face. "All of two inches, Miss Churchill . . . and that's an optimistic best at that. Two inches over a winter period here . . . and we are at the height of the summer, so where does that put your Bedouin springs or water collections in your wadis?"

"Oh, dear," Miss Randolph moaned, and Mabel Stockton put her arm around her, holding her up.

Miss Churchill hesitated a moment, and Sebastian knew her problem now. The fact was that no one knew where they were. The false radio message that sent them on this wild run into the Negev was not recorded back in Jerusalem or Khartoum. The Russian agent who had cut into the radio traffic had done that deliberately to make sure they crashed in this wildest stretch of terrain—and any search party was probably hunting them in Egypt. But she could not make this known to them without explaining all of it, and this would tip off Agent Christopher.

It was time for Sebastian to say something to support her, anything, just as long as he could provide her some leverage.

"Well, Mr. Brelsford, there's still the Old Testament

history which you are apparently well versed in . . . the old patriarchs had water here, so it is within the realm of possibility that nature hasn't altered that much. . . ."

Dennison laughed, and it sounded like a high whinny of ridicule. Brelsford merely smiled indulgently, but it was that of a debater who knew he had the upper hand. "Mr. Sebastian, ten millenniums ago they may have had wells here . . . but since then a lot of things have happened to the Negev. Of course, if you are thinking of using Moses' rod to smite the rock, I have no argument for you that would pass the empirical test. But I think a practical course dictates for the moment. I would prefer not to wait around while you attempt a miracle in the name of your Deity. . . ."

"And I have lived in Israel most of my life, Mr. Brelsford," Miss Churchill cut in then, "and the rule is always to move when caught in a desert, especially this one. And my airline orders are to move . . . the longer we stand here arguing the later it gets and the hotter. . . ."

"I say we stay," Dennison snapped, his body leaning into his works with intensity. "I think we ought to vote. . . ."

"There'll be none of that," Sparks' voice suddenly rose above the argument, and they turned to look where he lay, propped up on one elbow, his ruddy face turned almost yellow by his pain and infection. Despite the pallor, he still kept his grin curling around the cigarette butt. "You don't vote as long as there is an officer of the airline alive. I happen to be in charge, and after me comes Miss Churchill. What she says makes sense. I order all of you to move out."

"You are ordering us against our will?" Brelsford snapped.

"And what law governs us here anyway," Dennison wanted to know, "except that of the majority?"

"Water is the law, Dennison," Sparks cut back, and he grinned at that as if he had waited a long time to say it. "The airline happens to have that water, so the airline

78

decides what to do—and you don't have much choice but to obey."

"But, man, you're asking us to head out into uncharted wilderness, yourself badly wounded, most of us banged up, and a helpless child on top of it," Brelsford kept pummeling with heavy insistence. "Can't common sense show you the folly of that?"

"Water is common sense," Sparks replied. "An order is an order, Brelsford."

There seemed to be nothing more to say. Eaton stared at Sparks as if he wanted to say a lot more. So did Dennison. After awhile they all looked from Sparks to the reddish mist that was lifting rapidly now allowing the red beach-ball sun to come through, jabbing them with the reality of what had to come later.

"Well," Brelsford said finally, giving off with a heavy sigh of resignation, "you two women can't walk anywhere in those shoes—not in this country," and he pointed to the cuban heels that both Mabel Stockton and Ida Randolph had on. "While you people slept I did some prowling in that airplane . . . that's where I got my boots, and I saw a lot of good walking shoes up there that'll save a lot of bruised feet later. . . ."

Sebastian wanted to look at Miss Churchill, but he kept his eyes on Brelsford instead. Brelsford had been out of camp last night, perhaps while he slept—and now Brelsford wanted go back to the wreck again. There was too much eagerness in Brelsford right then, and it seemed to incriminate him.

"Then take the women to the plane with you," Miss Churchill said lightly, almost casually.

Brelsford hesitated, frowning a little, wanting to argue with her again. "Well, I can bring those shoes back without any trouble. . . ."

"It would be quicker for them to try them on rather than making several trips . . . take them with you, Mr. Brelsford."

Brelsford shrugged and marched on up the slope, the

two women following. Sebastian watched them disappear over the escarpment, and the mist seemed to dissolve right then as if a curtain had suddenly been pulled up by invisible drawstrings in the sky. The raw, naked world of the Negev lay before them, its terrible dimensions even more awesome now in the contemplation of their having to battle it hand to hand from now on.

Sebastian turned to look westward and toward the north, where the ragged rocks did not close in the view—and he caught it, just a wisp of it, but it was real enough. A light puff of dust far out, probably never really discernible except at the particular moment when the sun wiped the air clean and clear so that visibility was good for miles in any direction. He studied it for a few seconds, making sure of what he was seeing. Then he glanced at Miss Churchill. She had seen it too, and she gave him just a passing glance in return to let him know she had, and then went on to tend the baby. As she came by him, she said softly, "If Brelsford isn't back in ten minutes, go after him."

She went on to the baby lying in the blue blanket, who had begun to fuss some now, and he bent down to the ration bag picking up one of the gallon jugs, shaking it carefully and hefting it. He did the same with the other. A half gallon of water at the most . . . it meant then that their ration would be less later in the day. At the same time he felt the sweat come out of his face and hands and soak into his shirt—the Negev was turning up the thermostat, and the furnace responded. The insatiable desert began its sucking, and no one knew how long it would be before the body could no longer sweat and then the slow broil begin.

Sebastian licked his already dry lips and said, "This is the day the Lord hath made; let us rejoice and be glad in it." And Sparks, only a few feet away, looked up and grinned and gave him a quick wink.

∗ 5 ∗

Brelsford came back with the two women in their new footwear well within ten minutes, as if he had known exactly where to go for those heavier walking shoes all the time. He came down the escarpment carrying a long, thin aluminum shaft he apparently had found in the wreck, brandishing it like a scepter of authority one minute and a walking stick the next. He had wrapped a yellow scarf around his head like a turban, using it as a protection against the sun. It only added to his comical facial features already slashed by the adhesive strips which were showing out as strongly like weird latticework over his broken nose. He came down the slope shouting about "this is the closest thing to Moses' rod we'll ever get" for the benefit of Sebastian, lifting it over his head like a spear and mockingly aiming it at the rocky cliffs.

No one said anything in response to Brelsford's playful satire. They stood around waiting uncertainly, reluctantly, none of them wanting to be the first to lead out into the desert. "Now look at those shoes," Brelsford said, pointing to the low-cut walking shoes that both the schoolteachers had on. "We hit it right on the nose the first try, not exactly a perfect fit, but they'll do, and mind you, they didn't come out of their suitcases either. How's that for dead reckoning, Mr. Sebastian?"

"If you can find water that easily, Mr. Brelsford," Sebastian said with a smile, "I'll be the first to congratulate you."

"Well," Brelsford chirped back, "it could be a good omen all the way around. Nothing like starting the day positively I always say. . . ."

It was obvious who was assuming leadership now. Brelsford stood in the midst of them with his crown of yellow nylon, the official boots of his archaeological prowess which seemed to give him a peculiar sense of height and the aluminum shaft that stood out as symbolic of command as a shepherd's staff. The contrasting colors of his person were enough to set him apart from anyone else anyway, and if anyone had cause to question his role, he began immediately to dogmatically declare the rules for the wilderness road:

"I put Ain Ghadyan along this line," and he lifted his rod to point southeastwards over a range of purple-black rock and distant hills that hung behind a haze of blue smoke that rose from already sizzling rock. "I figure it not forty miles as Miss Churchill but more like twenty—I got the navigator's charts out of the plane," and now Sparks looked up quickly as Brelsford took out the map case with the initials of Zion Airlines on it. "Now I don't think, Mr. Jordan, that you would object to using your airline's navigational equipment at this point?"

Sparks leaned back on the pillow of blankets Miss Churchill had made for him. "It's your show now, governor," he said and dropped back without further argument.

"Very good, then," Brelsford went on, putting the map case inside his shirt. "Now if we walk steady for thirty minutes, rest ten, we can cover a good four miles today, maybe more. The thing to remember is not to think about water or the heat. Think of anything but that. We don't have a compass. I presume, Mr. Jordan, you don't have any such device?"

Sparks shook his head from his lying position on the

sand where Miss Churchill was now examining his shoulder.

"So that means dead reckoning," Brelsford added, smiling at Sebastian again, and there was a peculiar kind of exhilaration in Brelsford as if he were anxious to prove something in the coming ordeal. "And if we keep our eyes fixed on those hills yonder, we won't keep going in circles . . . that means we can't go drifting off the course . . . keep your eyes on me . . . all right, I presume we are ready to go, Miss Churchill?"

Sebastian knelt down to look at Sparks' wound along with Barbara Churchill. There was a jagged kind of cut high on his right shoulder that oozed a yellowish liquid. The whole shoulder had turned a light greenish kind of purple and the swelling ran down his right arm and back up under his right ear.

"There's a piece of the propeller in there, Sparks," Miss Churchill said. "I should get it out, but I wouldn't trust my probing in there without anesthetic of some kind— not in your condition right now. . . ."

"I don't want anybody slowing up for me," Sparks reminded her, his breathing coming more rapidly now as she tried to swab the wound with cotton gauze.

"The bleeding's stopped," she said, trying to give him some encouragement.

Sparks coughed on his laugh. "Good show, Barby, but this old man ain't about to depart yet. Now if you can fix up some kind of a sling, I think that'll do me fine. . . ."

"If Brelsford is right about Ain Ghadyan being only twenty miles off, you have a good chance, Sparks," Sebastian said and picked up one of the khaki shirts lying next to Sparks and started tearing it into strips to make the sling.

"Twenty miles, is it?" Sparks croaked under his breath, not wanting Brelsford to hear. "Well, like somebody said, twenty miles here in this furnace is like fifty anywhere else. He'll know the fight he's in before the day is done."

Sebastian managed to improvise a sling from the khaki strips, and Sparks almost passed out when they bent the

83

arm to fit into it. But he gamely hung on, his face running with sweat, until they had completed the job. The rest of them stood waiting and watching, their faces blank, showing neither sympathy or the lack of it. They were gazing on a man who was slowly dying, and it brought the reminder of death closer to them. They would rather not touch him or even get close to him, lest the smell of approaching night linger on them.

"All right, let's be going," Brelsford's ludicrous sopranolike voice rang in the crater, and Sebastian helped Sparks to his feet. The radio operator coughed hard with the exertion, and a fleck of blood appeared on his lower lip. Then he removed himself from Sebastian's support and stood a moment, getting his weak legs under him, lifting his head in a kind of proud defiance of his condition.

"Well, Yank," he managed with a wry grin, "they say the last miles are the best. And as they put it in golf, never up, never in . . . so let's get this jolly game on the road, what say?"

Sebastian smiled, shaking his head in admiration for the spunk of the man, and slung the canvas bag with water and food over his shoulder, while Miss Churchill picked up the baby and wrapped the blue and gold blanket carefully around its face and hands. Then they began to move out, Brelsford's broad back ahead of them, the black sweat patches showing up already on his khaki shirt. His yellow turban and aluminum walking stick flashed in the sun that had now lost its blush of dawn and had become a hard brass pan, bouncing its murderous rays off the sky and defying this presumptuous bit of life here to take one step without heavy cost.

Behind Brelsford a few yards moved Dennison, his own bandaged head bobbing in contrast to Brelsford's yellow, and it appeared that Dennison was having trouble holding his head erect as though it had become a weight too heavy for his neck muscles to hold. He was still wearing a light blue sweater over his white shirt even in the mounting heat, since Brelsford had said that white only attracted sun where dark repelled it. He kept looking down at the rocky surfaces over which he was traveling, now and then favoring his bandaged right hand, but unable even now to keep from bowing to his geological instincts as if new secrets would pop out of the ground at any moment.

The two schoolteachers came next, walking close to each other so that their hands touched now and then as if they were lovers seeking assurance of each other's mutual concern. Mabel Stockton's body moved with a kind of easy swing, her carriage also ramrod straight, as if she were daring the Negev to make the best of its attack on her. Ida Randolph, though, was bent in the shoulders as if every step were an anticipation of crisis or that she was bracing herself for her inevitable surrender to the death.

Sebastian, Sparks, and Miss Churchill moved out together, passing Eaton who still stood in the sand crater with a look of disenchantment on his sullen looking face—disenchantment with the world around him, the people in it, and the general direction they were taking now. He stood there in his white shirt and neat blue bow tie, his bandaged ear standing out from his head like a careless piece of sculpture that had been left by mistake. He kept turning his head back toward the wreck out of sight over the escarpment as if drawn by some peculiar affinity.

"Come on, Eaton," Sparks sang out, trying to reach the man with some levity, "there's a bucket a' beer in Ain Ghadyan waiting for you. You'll get nothing standing there but a mirage. . . ."

Eaton still didn't move. It seemed that he, too, kept looking back at the far horizon as if he had seen something, that wisp of dust that Sebastian had seen earlier perhaps.

"Close it up back there!" came Brelsford's high-pitched command from up ahead. "Miss Churchill, you'll have to push these people along!"

Whether it was the sound of Brelsford's piercing command or the sudden realization of the fruitlessness of standing there forever, Eaton finally shrugged and moved forward, carrying the bundle of blankets under his right arm. But his steps were heavy and deliberate showing his contempt for this move which was seemingly directly contrary to his will.

Brelsford led them for the first forty minutes without a break, keeping close to cut-out caverns in the Wade, trying to keep them out of the sun as much as possible. They followed behind in a loose group with no particular discipline, forced only to single file when the ledges of rock closed in. They felt no particular sense of Brelsford's leadership apparently, but were content to let him lead the way assuming that he had as much sense of direction as any of them.

When Sparks began to weave and stumble, Sebastian called up to Brelsford to halt. They gathered in the shade of a giant overhang of rock facing out toward the desert that was a mixture of bright sand and dull, black rock. Their faces showed the flush of the exertion in the heat that was now getting to their lungs, burning down their bronchial tracts, and turning their mouths and throats to raw tissue. They coughed on it, sucking at already dried up saliva glands for some wetness to soothe, while breathing became heavy and rapid. They said nothing to each other, but their eyes showed both fear and respect for this desert, like people who had had their opening exchange in a duel and were suddenly aware that their opponent was cleverer, harder, and capable of dealing real hurt.

Sebastian leaned over Sparks who had dropped flat on the ground, his hat rolling off to one side. His face was not wet with sweat now. It was hot to the touch. He lay with his eyes closed, his breathing rapid and rattling a little in his throat. A slight trickle of blood oozed out the corner of his mouth.

"I think he's got a lung punctured in there," Sebastian said to Miss Churchill, who had come over to check.

"Could be," she said quietly. "Temperature is very high. We've got to get that down somehow. . . ."

"How?" Sebastian asked, noticing the luminous sweat pockets on her upper lip.

"A damp cloth might help," she said, and Sebastian looked quickly at her. Water was too precious to use for anything but drinking, and he knew that was exactly what the others were thinking right then. She didn't exchange his glance, because she knew what she was asking too—and she was leaving it up to him to make the move. It was her first declared statement of his responsibility, that it was going to be up to him to control that water.

Sebastian looked from her to the others. They sat looking at him very intently now, their mouths half-open in that fishlike sucking of air that went with people who were dying for a drop of water to help cut the burning in their own bodies. Even Ida Randolph stared at him with a peculiar intensity, her eyes and pointed nose framed by the wild cascade of her hair, daring him to make the move. There was nothing in any of their faces that would suggest he perform this act of mercy, and he could not for the moment fathom how their normal human capacity to tend to the weakest among them could be so distorted by their own sense of personal survival.

He looked back at Miss Churchill whose eyes were on him now, and in them was the direct challenge to make his decision. Now he realized what she had meant, when she said his guarding the water would be no easy job. And now, though his ministerial sense of compassion for Sparks urged him to disregard the selfishness of the others, he was caught in the dilemma of equal priorities. Was he right in pouring out water to ease a man who had to die anyway? Or should he save what he had to maintain whose who had a better chance for survival?

But then he could not ignore what he knew to be the action relevent to his station in life without appearing to be less than what they would expect him to be. So he reached quickly for the water bag and was about to pull out one of the aluminum flasks, when Sparks' voice suddenly rasped out in a grating jab to all of them: "Who threw the switch, Yank?" and suddenly his hands dug into Sebastian's khaki shirt, and he was pulling himself to his feet before Barbara Churchill could restrain him. He stood erect, looking around at them with disdain as if they were the weaker ones. They, in turn, stared back at him, confused and surprised that he, so apparently debilitated in body, could still stand and demonstrate a will to go on that was not half as strong in themselves. "What about it, Brelsford?" he went on, weaving a little now, "do we make those four miles or don't we?"

Brelsford got to his feet with the use of his aluminum stick and peered at Sparks to be sure he was hearing and seeing right. "All right," his high-pitched voice echoed against the canyon rocks, "you heard the man—let's move it now, pick up the pace a little, and let's make some progress. . . ."

They responded slowly to the challenge, coughing in the heat and moving uncertainly down the small slope to the canyon floor, using Brelsford as a fix for their wavering and confused steps.

Sebastian took hold of Sparks who looked as if he might fall again, put the airline cap back on his head, and put the good left arm around his own neck and shoulders. Barbara Churchill picked up the baby, and as she did so it began to cry. The sound echoed down to where the others were, and they all stopped, looking back. But it was not a gesture of concern for the child, Sebastian felt, but an intent curiosity to see if he would tap the water bottle to give the infant a drink.

"She's just wakened, that's all," Miss Churchill assured, as if she, too, knew that he might do just that. "She'll be all right."

"Look, if she needs a drink, I'll give her one," Sebastian retaliated, feeling now as though she were deliberately trying to make it easier for him, to ease the weight of decision which she knew he was finding hard to make.

"Save it, Reverend," Sparks said hoarsely, his voice close to Sebastian's right ear. Sebastian looked at him quickly and noted there was seriousness in the radio operator's eyes now, a kind of urgent intent to communicate as if he knew he didn't have much time in which to do it. "Don't give a drop you can keep . . . stretch it out as long as you can even when it looks like you'll all drop dead without it. The others have to know how much you guard it before they'll respect your decisions on what you give them later . . . you understand?"

Sebastian didn't fully. "I've always lived my life with the heart controlling the mind, Sparks, not the other way around. Miss Churchill, though, seems to operate purely on head and no heart as if all this were some kind of exercise in the fine art of chess, as if people weren't involved at all. . . ."

"I don't know her that well," Sparks replied, and he was smiling. "She had only this one flight with me . . . but be sure of one thing, she's got desert sense . . . most of these lasses that grow up with the Jews know all about water shortages . . . she's made of good stuff, Yank, and could outlead a lot of men . . . so don't grind your valves over how she handles you, she knows what she's doing. . . ."

"Then she ought to be out there leading this show rather than Brelsford," Sebastian said in a half grumble, and started walking, trying to get into a kind of cadence that would match Sparks' slower, dragging pace.

Sparks coughed a short laugh again. "Well, she could do it too . . . but it's a job for a man . . . and anyway it's important to that man Brelsford that he do the leading here . . . such a man of science has to always prove things, one a' them being the superiority of mind over matter . . . he'll run everything on his slide rule percentages like he's learned all his life . . . and he may score that way . . . but chances are he'll miss because this kind of world doesn't follow the normal pattern of things. . . ."

He began to cough again, and this time he vomited blood. Miss Churchill came back to see what she could do, but Sparks only smiled weakly and said, "I got a few gallons more to go yet, Barby. . . ."

They walked most of the morning, winding through the wadis and into connecting caverns, sometimes down in the valley between walls of multicolored rock, other times walking on the higher ridges and across longer stretches of flat prairielike land sprinkled with sand and shale rock. The heat had become more and more of a torment. The sun was now everywhere in the hard sky, as if it had been cut open to spread its hot magnesium from horizon to horizon. This created a world of blazing heat waves that offered no respite in the world of mirror rock, and it boiled off their sweat before it came out of their pores, leaving them with no temperature control in their bodies. They had to walk, then, in a perpetual fever, their body mechanisms running hot like an engine without lubricating oil. For Sebastian, it was one long walk on a hot bed of coals. Sparks began to shift his weight more and more towards him, and after awhile it was a matter of half-carrying him rather than helping him to walk. In all this, he tried to ignore the pounding, feverish pulse in his own head, the agonizing burning in his throat and lungs, and the tortuous, swirling world of perpetual sun.

They stopped twice, each time their reluctance to keep moving even more apparent. The ten-minute break of Brelsford's dragged out to twenty minutes and then the second time it was thirty minutes before Brelsford had the heart to drive them to their feet again. During these intervals they merely sat, the effort to make any kind of conversation too much on them. They watched Sebastian sullenly, waiting for him to break out the bottle of water, licking their dried, blistered lips in anticipation. Each time Sparks seemed to be worse, until finally he went into delirium, babbling in a strange tongue at times. Each time Sebastian fought the temptation to break out the water and help assuage the fire that was raging through the likable radio operator's body. He fought what Sparks had told him about conserving what water he had and the rising pressure of compassion. Miss Churchill, meanwhile, offered no assistance in his decision-making.

Though he wanted to ask her, he felt he could not demonstrate before the others that he wasn't sure himself. So he sat with the water bag over his shoulder, trying to ignore the agonizing groans of Sparks and the dry flecks of blood that came from his cracked open lips, swelling from the fever and lack of water.

On the third stop, however, the issue had to be faced. This time the child began to whimper pitifully in her blankets, and then her cries became louder, rubbing hard against the already frayed nerves of the group and reminding them of their own desperate need. Sebastian walked over to the child who was lying on the ground next to Miss Churchill. He pulled back the blanket and saw the fiery red lips and the little tongue darting out for some touch of wetness.

Sebastian didn't bother looking at Miss Churchill, because he didn't want to see anything in those eyes that might condemn his action. He pulled the water bag around in front of him, withdrew the lighter of the two aluminum bottles, and unscrewed the cap. The sound of water in the aluminum cup was almost too much for him to bear, and he sensed a strange quietness come over the rest of them, and he could feel their bodies leaning forward, straining to taste vicariously that precious fluid for their tortured bodies.

Miss Churchill held the baby up out of the blankets while he gently placed the cup to the small mouth. The whispering cries subsided as the wetness reached the swollen tissues of the lips, and there came instead the sounds of soft murmuring as she felt the first relief. Sebastian gave it to her sparingly, making sure he wasted not a drop, using just a bit on his fingertips to rub on her face and forehead to ease the burning there. When he finished, he got up and went over to Sparks and did the same thing. The radio operator choked on the first of the water, but it brought him out of his delirium, and the eyes that looked up at him showed gratitude, while at the same time some questioning as to why he was bothering.

Sebastian finished with Sparks and sat back, putting the water bottle into the canvas bag.

"I'd say it was time to move on, wouldn't you, Mr. Brelsford?" Sebastian said, but none of them moved. Even Brelsford sat looking stupefied and unwilling to lift himself to the march again. They had the looks now of desperate people. They had heard and smelled water. They had seen the revival of an infant and a dying man. Suddenly they were conscious of the fact that they were being denied, and the thought of another mile without some relief had taken hold of them now so that to a man they were ready to make their demands.

Brelsford didn't say anything, but he did get to his feet slowly, using the aluminum stick for support.

"I presume you are not giving us our water ration now, Mr. Sebastian?" he asked.

"I think we can go another stretch and hold out until we finish for the day," Sebastian said calmly.

Brelsford nodded and looked at the ground. "Mr. Sebastian, we all admire your calling in life that makes you sensitive to the less fortunate," he continued, carrying that tone of exaggerated indulgence again. "A cup of cold water to a child and a dying man is a great gesture, a fine demonstration of Christian charity, but you cannot, in this practical world of very small percentages, use your own code of morality indiscriminately. I remind you that that child and dying man figure in the same average as the rest of us—I hope you won't let your sense of values work against the common good of us all. . . ."

"Mr. Brelsford," Sebastian replied, standing to his feet, feeling the first flush of indignation sting his ears, "when and if you should find yourself in as helpless a condition as these two, I will remind you of that statement. I trust it will sound as categorical to you then as it does now. . . ."

"Mr. Brelsford is right," Mr. Dennison cut in then. "Anyway, by what authority do you control that water ration? Because you are a clergyman does that give you the right to play God with us, withholding and giving as you see fit?"

"The airline gave him the authority," Sparks' rasping voice jabbed, and though his eyes were closed, there was that familiar smile on his lips. "Remember that, Dennison, the airline still controls. . . ."

"The airline, indeed," Dennison snorted, and there was a wild look in Dennison's eyes now, peculiar lights flashing off the brown, hard glaze of his eyes. His face, covered with a two-day shadow of a dark beard, was a balancing contrast to those eyes, intensifying what they said. "We left the airline a few miles back, and it would seem to me that new authority is called for here vested in those who know deserts particularly. . . ."

"Let's put it to the other more lucid member of the airline," Brelsford pursued, turning to look at Barbara Churchill. "For one of such sagacity, I should think you would know how to advise Mr. Sebastian about water control in situations like this, Miss Churchill!"

Miss Churchill looked from Brelsford to Sebastian. There was just a moment of hesitation, as if she didn't want to be forced into the issue. But then she said, "As Sparks put it, the airline gave Mr. Sebastian the water ration detail. I'll leave it to Mr. Sebastian to decide who gets it and when, Mr. Brelsford, and I suggest we all follow that policy from now on. . . ."

Brelsford only smiled, as if he knew that would be her answer all along, and it appeared as though he were taking some kind of satisfaction in his own confirmation of her attitude.

"Well, if we're not going to get a drink," Eaton suddenly broke in, rising to his feet, "we are not getting any further along by arguing about it." He strode through them then and headed out into the desert quite disinterested in whether they followed or not.

The rest of them waited just a few seconds, looking to Brelsford for further argument. Brelsford, however, turned and walked on, moving with some alacrity, seeking to overcome Eaton and take the lead again. The rest of them followed suit, except for Ida Randolph who paused to say, "You can do no wrong, Mr. Sebastian, a man of God can do no wrong . . . I believe this. . . ." She coughed harshly, and he could see the desperate look in her own large, strangely luminous gray eyes that stared at him out of that scraggly frame of disarrayed hair. Then she stumbled back to where Mabel Stockton waited, and leaning heavily on the stronger woman, she staggered on out into the shimmering heat waves.

Sebastian faced Miss Churchill who was gathering up the baby in her arms again. "That wasn't much support for what I had to do," he said, trying not to sound petulant.

"Actually Brelsford is right," she replied bluntly. "You can't give water to one or two and not all of them . . . next time they may tear you apart like animals to get their share."

"You know I'm going to use this water as the need is there," he defended, "and not on percentages Brelsford dictates."

"In any case you make the decisions . . . the sooner they see that you are doing that, they'll respect you for it."

"I get the feeling I'm being manipulated into a far too influential role in this business, more than I'm willing to assume," he argued.

"Events will manipulate you, Mr. Sebastian," she shot back and walked off, that same athletic stride and swing of her body taunting him.

There was no point of return then for him now. Events were speedily forcing a new mantle on his simple garb of a man of God.

He went back and helped Sparks get to his feet, but the radio operator was unconscious again. He looked up to where the others were standing on the ridge—there was no offer of help from there. He picked up Sparks bodily then, hefted him across his shoulders and started the long, torturous walk up the ridge.

"But God has not given you the spirit of fear, but of

power and love and a sound mind," he repeated the words of Paul's counsel to Timothy. He would soon know if any of those spiritual attributes would stand the test of what was to come. And for the first time in his life as a minister, he experienced a solid jab of doubt.

✳ 6 ✳

Sebastian carried Sparks on his back for most of a mile until Sparks suddenly came to and demanded to be put down. Then they walked awhile until Sparks fainted again—it was this way for the rest of the morning, carrying Sparks, then walking him. Once Eaton came back and helped Sebastian by taking one of Sparks' arms and helping support him so that Sebastian didn't have all the weight. But when Sparks passed out, Sebastian told Eaton he might just as well move up front and join the others, that it would be easier carrying the radio operator from then on.

"We ought to stop and let him die in peace," Eaton said dourly.

"Don't for a minute think that this Scotch-Irishman is going to go that easy," Sebastian said lightly. "He may make it to Ain Ghadyan yet. . . ."

"Your optimism is unrealistic," Eaton grumbled and moved forward with the others, content to let Sebastian carry the burden of a man so close to death that the smell of it was already very strong on him.

Sebastian knew that he could not continue the torturous journey much longer carrying Sparks. Once he fell flat into a bed of sharp rock with the full weight of Sparks on top of him. He lay there with the knifelike stabs of rock digging into his flesh, waiting for the others to help Sparks off him, all the time the pounding of sharp spikes of heat slashing into his brain from the back of his head straight into his eyeballs. His heart beat heavy against the ground, his lungs seemed to swell for one breath of clear cool air and his tongue, already swollen so that it felt like a chunk of inner tube, threatened to choke him to death.

When Brelsford and Eaton got back to him and got Sparks rolled off, Sebastian could not rise from the ground. It was only after the two men had lifted him that he was able to stand. He vomited twice, hanging on to the two men, all the time sucking for air.

"Give him some water," Eaton was saying from way off.

"No," Sebastian said, although it took all his will power to refuse it.

"Don't be such an ass," Eaton snarled. "You've been carrying the radio operator for the last hour . . . you must have a drink if you expect to go on. . . ."

"I'll wait with the rest," Sebastian managed to gasp out.

"Very noble, but very impractical at this stage, Mr. Sebastian," Brelsford said in his usual sardonic tone.

"It's got nothing to do with nobility, Mr. Brelsford," Sebastian replied, leaning over to rest his hands on his knees in order to get leverage for his dragging lungs. "The way I figure it, a sip of water now would about drive me crazy, and I'd end up making a fool of myself—and that I cannot afford to do after what I've already demanded of everyone else. . . ."

"Suit yourself," Brelsford said shortly, and after awhile both he and Eaton left to walk back up front. Miss Churchill came back to stand with him for a moment. She checked Sparks who lay sprawled on the blazing rock totally oblivious of anything.

"His pulse is still steady for all of that," she said.

"Probably stronger than mine right now," Sebastian answered and finally straightened up to look at her. "Do you intend to walk all day, Miss Churchill? If you ask me, this sun is going to kill us faster than thirst. . . ."

"I intend to get Brelsford to stop in a minute," she replied, "when I see a suitable place that offers some protection. Are you all right now?"

"Sure . . . perfectly. Now I know what a bug feels like getting squashed under a boot . . . but other than that, what's holding up the show?"

"You don't have to prove yourself by this kind of heroics," she reminded him tartly.

He gave a half laugh. "Heroics? Well, I happen to like Sparks for one thing, and I'm a poor loser for another. If that's heroics, then let it go into the book. What would you have me do, Miss Churchill, let him die out here somewhere?"

"No, but we could ask the others to help," she suggested.

"The fact that their assistance to this point has been rather sparse says enough of their feelings about the matter . . . so why don't we push on so you can find a place to rest . . . okay?"

She moved off again, and once more he got Sparks up on his shoulders, feeling the stabbing pains run down into his groin, gripping deep into his lower back and making him cry out in pain. But once he got walking, it eased up some, and since the going was gradually downhill into another small cavern it wasn't as bad.

He hadn't gone more than a hundred yards, however, before he noticed the rest of them gathering together in a loose circle around Brelsford and Dennison. When he got up close Eaton reached out to help him with Sparks. Dennison was the center of attention now, and he was holding a small rock the size of a golf ball in his left hand.

"Mr. Dennison has made a significant discovery," Brelsford said to them, sounding even now with all the heat and weariness of the trek, as though he were introducing the guest speaker at an archaeological lecture series. "He has a piece of rock with some interesting precipitation on it. Tell us about it, Dennison?"

Dennison kept frowning at it as if he weren't sure, but

then after scratching the black surface with his thumb, then smelling it, and, of course, tasting it, he said, "There's water erosion on this rock. . . ."

"Water erosion," Brelsford repeated for them, as if they hadn't heard or as if his own voice would lend weight to the statement.

"And it's recent," Dennison went on.

"It's recent, you hear that?" Brelsford followed.

"Which means what?" Eaton said skeptically.

"Which means a freshet of water went through here, or fell in here, not too long ago," Brelsford said with triumph as if all of science had been vindicated already by this rather peripheral discovery. "And that means there could very well be a substantial water collection in these rocks—and who knows, the real possibility of wild fruit. . . ."

They looked around them at the same black rock that had marked their journey thus far, some of it towering over them, pointing bony fingers toward the sky, others cutting down into jagged outcroppings to form weird shapes. There was a real sense of feeling of the agony of nature here, as if the sun had twisted even this unmovable, impenetrable canyon rock into grotesque shapes of pain. There was nothing to justify any of Brelsford's or Dennison's hopes, in fact, there seemed to be less justification here than anywhere else they had been this morning.

"Well, if there's water, it will wait until tonight," Miss Churchill said.

"Tonight?" Brelsford echoed, a look of shock coming over his face which had now turned deep red-brown, indication enough that even he as accustomed as he was to the sun, was suffering from the slow, torturous broil of the Negev.

"Mr. Brelsford, we're all dead tired and in need of refreshment," she insisted. "There's a good overhang of rock up there that will serve our purpose—we'll sleep it off for the balance of the day and start out tonight when the moon is up. It may save us from killing ourselves in this sun."

"The wisdom of night travel is fine," Brelsford acquiesced, "but to try to find water collections even with the brightest moon is far less than right now. . . . Miss Churchill, this is one time I have to insist that we go on, spread out in these caverns and look for water. Look, it's only a mile through this cavern, one mile to cover both sides won't take long . . . and if we find it, it could change our whole outlook on this journey."

She hesitated, and Dennison added, "I'm for trying it with Brelsford."

"Another hour won't make much difference," Eaton added.

"I'm not sure we can do it," Mabel Stockton spoke up, and they turned to where Ida Randolph had fallen into a misshapen heap on a large table-sized rock. Miss Churchill went over quickly to examine her. "She's fainted," Miss Stockton said simply.

They stood there waiting, not sure what was the best course of action, but mostly waiting for Miss Churchill to respond to what Brelsford urged. She didn't respond immediately. She looked up at Sebastian, and he knew that it was his turn again, that she was shifting the weight of decision his way, seeking that "leverage" for her own decisions she had asked him for back at the wreck. If that wasn't manipulation, then, he didn't know it at all, he thought.

"I'll compromise with you, Brelsford," he said, and he caught Miss Churchill's quick glance. "I say we camp up there by that big rock overhang, refresh ourselves for a few hours and when that nice breeze comes up later in the afternoon, we'll try it—at least those of us who are healthier. . . ."

Brelsford frowned. He didn't like to compromise. He was about to make a major discovery in his book, something that would put tremendous credence to science and his concept of "dead reckoning."

"That makes sense," Eaton threw in, in his own inimitable unplanned but beautifully timed way, as if he had been rehearsed.

Finally Brelsford shrugged and, with an air of dubiousness, to let them know he wasn't happy with the arrangement, added, "An hour or two makes a lot of difference here—I hope we don't miss it by dilly-dallying. . . ."

They gathered on a small slope of rock under a rooflike tower of red cliffs. It offered them a perfect view forward of the canyon spread out a mile or two, but shut them off from any view behind unless one climbed a little. This was what Barbara Churchill had in mind, Sebastian knew, when she picked this spot—she didn't want any of them looking back and seeing any sign of the pursuing enemy.

Sebastian broke out the water as soon as they had settled. He explained to them exactly where they stood with regard to it. "There's a half inch to be poured out in this cup for each of you now, another half inch tomorrow morning. That means three-and-a-half inches we will drink now. That takes care of one bottle. Tomorrow we will have but seven inches left in the other, enough for one more day of careful rationing, maybe a day and a half if we watch it closely. . . ."

Then he poured the first half inch and took it to Ida Randolph, who had been carried up the slope by Brelsford and placed with her back to the wall of rock. She had come to now, and her narrow face, half-hidden by her moppish hair, was very red from the sun while her eyes were big and feverishly lustrous. She stared at the water a long time, her mouth trembling as though she might cry before she got a drop of it into her. She hiked her hair back with a snap to her head and took the first sip, her long, tapered fingers wrapped around the cup as if it might collapse at any minute and the water splash on the ground.

"Let it stay in your mouth awhile," Brelsford yelped in the background.

"God bless you, Mr. Sebastian," Ida Randolph said as she finished the drink. "I pray all the time . . . what have we now but prayer?"

"It'll go a long way," Sebastian said and moved on to the others, watching them drink, noting their eyes that seemed to widen with the first touch of the wetness on their tongues, their throats moving jerkily then as their dehydrated bodies reached up to pluck at the promise of life. When he got to Miss Churchill, she said, "I'll take a sip, the rest goes to the baby. . . ."

"Who's playing the heroics now?" he said lightly, hoping he could draw some kind of a smile from her, anything to make her let him know that she viewed him as more than necessary equipment.

"It's got nothing to do with heroics," she replied, framing a parody on his own statement earlier, her face just as impassive and studiously intent as always—and he marveled how beautiful she could continue to look even after the day of ravaging heat. Except for a few light patches of dirt that perspiration had made on her forehead, she looked as she had the first time he opened his eyes after the wreck and saw her bending over him. "I'm actually half camel, you know, like all us Jews who live in Palestine. . . ."

He was delighted that she would try banter now, but his short laugh got none in return. She took her sip, then gave the rest to the baby who took it with relish.

Then, giving the cup back to him, she said, "You're missing Mr. Eaton, did you know that?"

Sebastian turned to survey the camp, trying to fix on the familiar wiry form with the bright blue bow tie.

"Didn't he come up with us?"

"He did . . . but a few moments ago he started climbing, up there. . . ."

Sebastian looked up the natural trail leading over the rocky aperture to a flat ridge above.

"Why didn't you stop him?"

"How? If Mr. Eaton wishes to relieve himself at a

higher altitude, I doubt that it's a woman's place to question him. I hope you begin to understand why you become more important to me all the time. . . ."

Sebastian was a bit taken aback by her frankness with him, but he picked up the prod in a hurry. "Will you see that Sparks gets his ration?" She nodded, and he left her, cutting out of the camp circle, darting up the rocky ledge, feeling the first heady pulsation of tension with the realization that he could be confronting a very dangerous man at this moment. He didn't know what he would do when he found Eaton—if it were an innocent move on the man's part as Miss Churchill so bluntly referred to it or if Eaton were actually trying to make an escape or establish some kind of communication to the pursuing element behind, he still had to explain his own reason for following him.

He came up over a shelf of rock and saw Eaton almost immediately. He was standing on a flat table of rock, his hand over his eyes, studying the far horizon very intently. Sebastian waited just a few seconds to see if Eaton was doing anything other than admiring the view and also to form his own stock question for his own presence here.

"Mr. Eaton. . . ?"

Eaton turned quickly, dropping his hand from his eyes, glowering sullenly at this interruption. "I missed you when I came around with the water . . . thought I'd better check just in case. . . ."

Sebastian climbed up next to the shorter man who went back to his hand-over-eyes study.

"Quite a view all right," Sebastian offered, his own eyes staring intently to see if there might be any evidence of the pursuing agents.

"It's not the view I'm concerned about," Eaton said shortly. "I know I've been seeing something back of us most of the morning . . . every now and then I'd turn and see just a puff of dust . . . and there's no wind at all, so that can't be the reason. . . ."

"Well, the Negev has its strange phenomena, I understand," Sebastian offered innocently.

"And now something flashed out there, like the sun hit something metallic," Eaton went on, as if he hadn't heard Sebastian at all, as if he were talking to himself.

Sebastian waited, watching, searching, and hoping nothing more would show, and yet wondering, too, if Eaton didn't know all along what was there and had merely come up here to check out the distance of his own friends. And how was he going to get Eaton off this rock, because sooner or later there would come some sign out there again. . . .

"An old Indian friend back in the States once told me that all deserts move," he tried again. "I guess he meant that you can see things that really aren't there. . . ."

Eaton turned his head quickly and his eyes were glowing, snapping gray black. "What do you know about deserts? What does a simple clergyman whose life is cut along so plain a line know anything about complex things like deserts? You with your spiritual common denominator for everything in life—you who try to divide God into everything and expect it to come out all wrapped up in gay ribbon? You with your blind concept of the universe that says everything runs like a big watch and all you have to do is let it run by itself and life will be one big garden of roses, ha?"

"Well, Mr. Eaton," Sebastian tried, feeling the heat of the man's vituperation singe something deep inside that he had always thought incombustible. "I really didn't mean that I knew. . . ."

"Well, I know!" Eaton retaliated, so that his voice bounced off the rocky caverns and reverberated in mocking echoes. Sebastian noted that Eaton, though a bit shorter than himself, was not really a small man. There were muscles bulging in his arms under the transparent nylon shirt, and the cords in his neck stuck out like small tree branches. There was in Eaton a mainspring of unusual strength, disciplined into a kind of power one would expect in a top athlete or military man. "I know deserts,

Mr. Sebastian." He hit his chest with his fist. "I lived in deserts, fought in deserts, spilled out my guts in deserts! If there is something out there, I know! It is not a mirage or a trick of the eye—not with me!"

Sebastian let the ringing denunciation die in the cavern, waiting for Eaton to turn his glowing eyes off him, almost glad to have him go back to his hand-over-eye study of the horizon. When the head finally turned off and it appeared that the thunderous rebuke was finished, Sebastian said, keeping his voice steady,

"Mr. Eaton, I need you back at camp."

Sebastian didn't know what he would say if Eaton asked why. He went on looking at the horizon by the shade of his hand, sniffed once or twice in a kind of disdain either for Sebastian or the empty horizon, and then backed off the rock and moved on down toward the camp.

When Sebastian got back to the camp, the rest of them were lying about without any apparent desire to move. The heat was now rolling over them from the white glare of the cavern in peculiar undulating motions taking a little bit more of their precious body chemistry with every wave and leaving them with less will to fight off the insistent hand of defeat. This was the worst time for them, because the elements had time to do their work while they gave themselves passively to the almost inevitable draining process. As long as they were moving something kept them believing they could make it out all right. But in this state of immobility every nerve slipped into limbo. What will they had was short-circuited by the pressure of the deathlike world around them, so that the mind never got the signal. They were slipping into that dangerous attitude that welcomed death rather than trying to rise to the inferno around them.

Sparks was no better off, but he managed to stay conscious now, the little bit of water apparently having revived him some. There were times when his eyes became vacant as if he were staring into another world somewhere. His breathing was quieter, but it was as though he was straining to control it, as if he didn't want them to hear the rattle. Now and then he coughed, and the same little flecks of dark blood appeared on his lips. The familiar cigarette, which had become a kind of bold pennant to announce his defiance of death, was no longer hanging in the corner of his mouth. His lips had swollen so badly that they just hung loosely over his teeth. There couldn't be much time left for him, and Sebastian realized then, with a start, that he had allowed the shadows to creep in without attempting to help Sparks know the way to eternal peace.

The sudden realization that he had not as yet, since the crash, even uttered a word to any of them concerning their own spiritual destinies caused him to feel a fresh flood of shame. This was so unlike him in Nashville. Every occasion in society, calamity or festivity, had offered him direct opportunity for a timely word on the significance of the spiritual. Calamity had always been his natural seed bed for sainthood—fear, sorrow, confusion, these easily argued most men to silence and inevitable surrender to God.

But here the normal patterns had changed. He had found himself preoccupied with personal survival and adjustment to alien forces. Or was it that here in this desert filled with its own malignancies the faith to believe that God was even there demanded much of his own belief that had always functioned in an atmosphere of tangible symbols of Divinity. The thought stirred him, for he had never thought his belief to be contingent on altars and organ music or the friendly spirit of community life. But up to now he had faltered, allowing himself to slip into the physical properties that governed all of them, and though he hadn't rejected the presence of God here, he had indeed permitted other factors to command first place.

Anxious again to communicate the values he felt were uppermost to all of them, and concerned too that Sparks somehow get hold of the bridge to eternal life, he pulled out the worn pocket-sized Bible from his back pocket, the one thing of his he was able to salvage from the wreck of personal value. His mind shifted to those passages that might be applicable here, and as he flipped through the pages, Ida Randolph's voice rose through the heavy, stultifying heat, almost whimsical, childlike:

"Would you read something to us, Mr. Sebastian?"

He looked up at her sitting a few feet away, Miss Stockton lying prone beside her, her eyes closed. She had the wonder and hope of a child on her face at that moment, erasing the intense, pointed features of a woman desperate to stay alive. Sebastian smiled, then glanced at the others, looking for some sign of invitation. Dennison merely rolled over on his stomach to rest his chin on his hands and stare out across the cavern, indicating clearly enough that he was not interested. Brelsford sat on a rock digging his aluminum walking stick into the hard slab, his facial expression neutralized by the confusing pattern of the adhesive strips, his eyes concentrating on the ground. Barbara Churchill had her back to him, her knees drawn up under her chin, her arms resting on them, her pose one of casual study of the cavern below. Eaton was sprawled out on his back, his face turned upward toward the sky, half shaded by the big overhang of rock.

Their reaction didn't seem much different from his own congregation in Nashville—the same combination of casual interest mixed with total indifference.

He was anxious now to begin reading before anything interrupted, so he paused at Isaiah 35, clearing his throat, gearing up to a lyrical reading, for he was not good at projecting his voice.

"The wilderness and the solitary place shall be glad for them," he began, lifting his voice deliberately so they would all be sure to hear, making it sound too forced. "And the desert shall rejoice, and blossom as the rose."

He went on reading, conscious of nothing but the page in front of him and the sweat marks on the paper from his thumbs.

". . . Say to them that are of a fearful heart, Be strong, fear not: behold, your God will come with vengeance, even God with a recompence; he will come and save you.

"Then the eyes of the blind shall be opened, and the ears of the deaf shall be unstopped. Then shall the lame man leap as an hart, and the tongue of the dumb sing: for in the wilderness shall waters break out, and streams in the desert.

"And the parched ground shall become a pool, and the thirsty land springs of water: in the habitation of dragons where each lay, shall be grass with reeds and rushes.

"And an highway shall be there, and a way, and it shall be called The way of holiness; the unclean shall not pass over it; but it shall be for those: the wayfaring men, though fools, shall not err therein.

"No lion shall be there, nor any ravenous beast shall go up thereon, it shall not be found there; but the redeemed shall walk there:

"And the ransomed of the Lord shall return, and come to Zion with songs and everlasting joy upon their heads: they shall obtain joy and gladness, and sorrow and sighing shall flee away."

He stopped, for it was the end of the chapter. He wished it was longer, for he wanted to communicate more to them while they lay there apparently unresisting. And there was something peculiarly powerful about the words, the note of the promise coupled with the strange authority that went with Holy Writings.

"The wilderness shall blossom like a rose," Ida Randolph repeated, and there was that certain gleam in her eyes now of real expectancy. "And streams in the desert . . . it's as though God were saying that to us. . . ."

Her lips began to quiver some again, either in the emotion of new hope the words gave her or in the sudden self-piteous contemplation of their condition. Sebastian turned to look at Sparks, but the radio operator's eyes were closed again, and he was very still.

"I do not wish to disparage the words," Brelsford said,

then, and he was smiling as if to provide cover for what he was about to say, "but Isaiah there is talking about the future millennial age, isn't he, Sebastian?"

Sebastian looked back at the chapter, sensing again that Brelsford did not intend to allow the center of wisdom to slip away from himself, even if it meant challenging the appropriateness of the scriptural reading. "Yes, he is talking about that," Sebastian said, feeling too that dissolving sense of not being adequate to Brelsford's sharp sagaciousness even in the matter of spiritual things. "But you can't deny the very real nature of God who can produce as much now as He will in the future. . . ."

"Well, all I'm suggesting, Sebastian," Brelsford cut back, "is that you go to a more appropriate passage, one that brings Jewish history to bear on more immediate circumstances. Try Genesis 26:19 and see if you don't come closer to the immediate condition. . . ."

Sebastian noted that Barbara Churchill had turned now to face him, and Dennison had rolled back to lean on his elbow and was staring back at him with some intensity, and Eaton lifted his head to watch, as if Brelsford's challenge had suddenly lent credence to the Scripture.

"You seem to know it so well, Mr. Brelsford," Sebastian returned, not wanting to look like a Sunday-school child doing the bidding of a teacher, "why don't you tell us?"

"Glad to oblige," Brelsford chirped. "It says, 'And the servants of Isaac dug in the valley and found a well.' Now that word for valley in Hebrew is *nahal*, Sebastian—do you know what that means?"

Sebastian didn't know Hebrew. He had studied only New Testament Greek. Brelsford waited, as if sure Sebastian didn't know, allowing the silence to have its effect.

"Well, what is a *nahal* or whatever it is?" Eaton asked impatiently, his head sinking back on the rock again.

"It means a wadi, Eaton," Brelsford sang back, his body seeming to puff up with the bloating power of superior knowledge, "the very thing we are in right now. Isaac dug a wadi like this and found water—now doesn't that cheer you up, Miss Randolph?"

Ida Randolph didn't know how to answer. She looked from Brelsford to Sebastian, almost demanding that Sebastian contradict the statement.

"So you are confirming the goodness of God," Sebastian answered, "in the same way I have with Isaiah."

"Not exactly," Brelsford replied, a crafty smile canceling some of the fierce image the adhesive strips gave to his face. "You see the Old Testament is a book of Jewish history—it records how man used his scientific, engineering, and technological skills and instincts to reshape his environment. They dug for those wells, Mr. Sebastian—they didn't wave a magic wand over the desert sand and wait for God to do a miracle."

"Then how do you explain Moses' rod getting water from rock?" Sebastian asked, not wanting to go on with this because he knew Brelsford had developed this argument before, well-founded on scientific principles.

"Simple enough," Brelsford retaliated, and he stood up to make his stature loom over all of them as he launched his crusade, which apparently was a life-long fixation for him. "Moses but cracked through a water cistern preserved from a former advanced civilization. I can tell you of the scientific mastery of a number of civilizations such as the Middle Bronze I of Abraham's time, of the engineering of the Neolithic people of 6000 B.C. . . . and even across this dry waste we're on right now there once moved the great Nabataean civilization with water storage programs around 2000 B.C. . . ."

"So what does it really matter anyway?" Ida Randolph said, still smarting at having Brelsford command scriptural authority and seemingly wrest the spiritual momentum from Sebastian's grasp.

"Ah, dear lady," Brelsford countered, glad for the challenge, "it means considerably more than you realize. For there are two ways you can follow to get the water you need to survive—go Mr. Sebastian's way, the way of

Isaiah, the pray-all-night-and-wait-for-the-miracle way, which I must say in all fairness will leave you quite dead; or you can follow the scientific way, take from the Bible what the Jews have left us, namely that to live you must use science to tap the patterns of natural universal law. . . ."

"If you know so much about the Bible," Ida Randolph pursued indignantly, "why is it you are so profane in your manners with God?"

Brelsford made a great display of shock and incredulity. "Profane?" he said, lifting his hands in appeal to the rest of them. "I cannot be profane about that which I do not believe in, Miss Randolph. All I'm saying here is that we have the fortune of finding water here because of the perpetual law of the universe, and we don't have to depend on the whim of a Deity whose acts are not consistent with His being. And if Mr. Sebastian wishes to inject hope for us even from his Sacred Book, he should choose that which will bear on our immediate condition and offers hope based on practical demonstrations of man's ability to shape his own environment. . . ."

There was a heavy pause, and it was up to Sebastian to form an answer to that. Miss Randolph looked steadily at him, so did Dennison, and Eaton's head came off the rock once to turn his way. Miss Stockton was suddenly busy with something in her handbag, but she was probably waiting too. Only Miss Churchill sat outside the periphery of the exchange, her back to them, but he knew that she was just as mindful of the tension of the moment as any of them.

For Sebastian, it was the moment of total paralysis. Brelsford's argument was strong, well-documented by his own scholarly world view, and pointedly and deliberately earthy. He had never had to face a challenge like that before in Nashville. He now had neither the intellectual equipment nor reasoning powers to counteract the weight of the argument. More disturbing still was the fact that Brelsford had forced the issue now—he had planted the choice in the group, between his own proven scientific way of life and the uncertain, nebulous way of faith. None of them perhaps realized it yet, but subconsciously they had already been convinced by Brelsford and were only waiting now for Sebastian to say something that would alter their judgment.

Sebastian cleared his throat, knowing he had to say something if for no other reason than to protect his own right to be a clergyman at all. "There's a point of extremity that even science has to face eventually, Mr. Brelsford," he said, trying to sound as categorical as Brelsford. "Every man must sooner or later come to the impossible where reason has to yield to faith—when that time comes for you, only then can you determine if Deity is inconsistent with His being."

"Bravo!" Brelsford bellowed with a laugh, and the mocking tone of his voice was like an ugly spear flashing in the sun. "Let it stand, Sebastian, that you at least rang the cracked bell of your religious faith, feeble as that sounds!"

"There's your wind, Mr. Brelsford," Miss Churchill suddenly broke in, rising as she did so and moving across the circle of the camp, between Brelsford and Sebastian as if she were attempting to cut the exchange in that way.

Sebastian felt the puff of the late afternoon desert breeze stroke his burning cheeks, and he wanted to stand up and say something more so that Brelsford would not have the last word again. Instead he felt Sparks' hand on his sleeve, and he turned to look at the radio operator who had a trace of a smile on his puffy lips.

"I'm sorry I passed out, Yank," he said in a half whisper. "That . . . what you read about the highway . . . that was good . . . I don't want you worryin' about my soul, Rev'rend . . . my Scottish mother told me all about that highway when I was a wee lad at her knee . . . I ain't had a jeweled life since . . . nothin' to be proud of . . . but I don't think God will forget me when the books are opened . . . do you?"

"If your name's written there, Sparks, He won't

forget," Sebastian assured. "But maybe now's the time to make sure. . . ."

Sparks smiled weakly. "One thing I don't cater to and that is tryin' to get insurance in the last minute life . . . I'll have to go with the policy I took when I was six, Rev'rend . . . I hope that won't make ya feel like you fell down on the job. . . ."

For Sebastian it was like taking a man within sight of the goal line and leaving. Yet it seemed that further argument or persuasion was not in place.

"All males over twenty-one, Mr. Sebastian!" Brelsford called to him as he, Dennison, and Eaton started out on their explorations for water in the wadi below.

Barbara Churchill came up to him then and leaned over Sparks.

"I suppose I should thank you for your usual on-stage appearance right on cue," he said to her, finding it difficult to keep his voice from reflecting the personal indignity he was feeling.

"I felt the wind," she said, reaching for Sparks' pulse. "Besides, you might as well know, too, that I don't particularly like philosophical wars developing in a survival group like this. I'd suggest you refrain from any more incidents of Bible reading that will give Brelsford his opportunity."

"I said I would do as the moment and need dictated," he insisted, keeping his voice level and conversational for Sparks' benefit. "I don't intend to neglect my spiritual duties for the sake of Brelsford or your so-called philosophical war."

"In most cases it wouldn't mean a thing to me," she replied. "But this kind of thing is belittling you, especially since it appears that you are losing in every one of the bouts. And when you lose, the strength of the airline command loses, and we can't afford to let Brelsford get too much power lest he take control of everything, the water, the course of our march—everything. . . ."

"I may not have lost," Sebastian tried gamely to reclaim

his dissolving spiritual authority. "If you hadn't come in when you did, I think I could have met Brelsford handily enough . . . anyway I don't think I'm on anyone's side here in quite the final way you put it. . . ."

"You're already committed if you didn't know it," she argued, and she examined Sparks' shoulder again. "As far as the others are concerned, you are airline, like Sparks and myself. And in that light your ministerial duty will have to take second place."

"I don't remember declaring myself for the airline," he protested.

"When you took those water bottles, you became airline," she returned in that flat, factual tone of voice.

"That's right, Rev'rend," Sparks cut in then, his eyes a little more glazed again by that peculiar cloud of encroaching pain. "You're airline now . . . like Barby says there isn't much you can do about undoing your stand . . . and you might as well as know about Eaton too. . . ." Sparks coughed, and Sebastian helped him up to ease the congestion in his lungs. He glanced at Barbara Churchill for some explanation of what Sparks meant.

"What about Eaton?" he asked, addressing both of them. She hesitated a moment, as if she didn't want to say anything about it, but when Sparks couldn't seem to get the words out, she began:

"Most everyone who's lived in Palestine for any length of time knows that Eaton is an ex-Nazi . . . his real name is Heinrich Zimmerman. He was a general implicated in the crimes against Jews at Auschwitz. He was found after the war and tried in Jerusalem. Since the evidence was not totally clear against him, he did not get the death sentence—instead he was offered the opportunity to work as an engineer for the Jews or take life imprisonment. Zimmerman chose engineering, changed his name to Eaton, which is not uncommon, and began working on road development. . . ."

"As much as he hates Jews, he would accept that?"

"It's better than rotting in prison," she replied.

Sebastian waited a few seconds to let this new revelation filter through. "So now he's running away?"

She shook her head. "Probably not. He's got freedom probably to go to other countries for engineering meetings, I suppose . . . he can't go far anyway, he knows that, without being found again and perhaps getting a worse sentence."

Sebastian turned back to Sparks. "Sparks, why is it so important to you that I know about Eaton anyway?"

Sparks gave a half smile, and his lips trembled some now with the effort. "When you juggle, Rev'rend, it's important . . . you keep all the balls in front of you where you can see them . . . you got to know their size, shape, and how they'll act . . . you know just about everybody here by now . . . you ought to know about Eaton . . . I don't think he's ever got that super race out o' his system . . . man like that can tip the scales either way in a showdown . . . and mostly he'll try to do it his way . . . so you ought to know. . . ."

"Mr. Sebastian?" Brelsford's voice sounded from down the wadi, "are you with us?"

Sparks gave a half grunt and tapped Sebastian weakly on the shoulder. "Old Sir Thomas Browne once said, 'lead thy captivity captive and be Caesar within thyself' . . . you got more goin' with you, Rev'rend, than Brelsford . . . just remember that. . . ."

And what about Eaton? Sebastian wanted to ask that too—was Sparks trying to tell him that Eaton was more of a problem to him than Brelsford could ever be? What did the radio operator really mean? How much did he know? Did he have as much knowledge of this Agent Christopher thing as Miss Churchill?

But Sparks gagged again, and Sebastian put him down carefully on the blue blanket. "One thing more," she said, looking at him, "Dennison's got a concussion that's getting to him . . . watch him, he may wander off from you or go off a cliff. . . ."

"Are you sure you've told me all?" he snapped at her,

not bothering to keep the testiness out of his voice now. "Maybe it's time we had a little skull session again, so I can be sure who's who in this macabre game."

He thought he saw a slight smile tug at the corners of her mouth and perhaps just a trace of apology cross her gray eyes. "You've got all that you need for the moment," she said. "Now you better be off. . . ."

"I wonder if I can be of any assistance?" Miss Stockton said, and her voice coming so close from behind them startled them both. She was standing over them, and they didn't really know for how long, for she was half-hidden in the shade from the rock overhead. Sebastian looked quickly at Miss Churchill, asking the question as to how much the schoolteacher had really heard.

"You might help with the baby, Miss Stockton," she said calmly, "and thank you. . . ."

Sebastian got up and walked down the rocky path to where Brelsford, Dennsion, and Eaton stood waiting. "Be Caesar within thyself." If any man ought to be automatically without being told, it should be he, a man of God with the Holy Spirit indwelling him, and yet he couldn't help but feel now the overwhelming sense of total failure, the smallness of himself and of his God in the full picture here. He had gained nothing for the spiritual world thus far—in fact, he had lost. He had been reduced to the least common denominator, as Eaton implied, among them—and even Sparks seemed to sense this by his attempt to give him some new confidence. Perhaps it was true then—he could never feel any real strength unless he was among those of like calling. Cut off from his vestments, the society of fellow saints, he was at sea. The revelation did little to build new fiber for what was ahead now—perhaps Miss Churchill was right, he should avoid deliberate injection of the spiritual at all here, especially with men like Brelsford and Dennison who were vastly superior to him, even in their knowledge of biblical truth. He was walking among giants, three of them now, two whom he was already well aware—and now the third,

Eaton, or Heinrich Zimmerman, cast into a new role, a new pressure, a new profile to contend with who could be, perhaps more than any of them now, the true Christopher.

"But God hath not given thee the spirit of fear. . . ." Well, then, it was but to control the adrenalin, to stop the draining of the precious sweat that formed like grease on his face . . . fear sweat, the kind that stuck to him and smelled different from the honest salt of courage. . . .

"I trust your punctuality and alacrity of movement is more evident in your church life, Mr. Sebastian?" Brelsford greeted him in his usual saturnine way as he walked up.

"Neither punctuality nor alacrity has any relevance for a soul trying to get ready for a timeless eternity, Mr. Brelsford," Sebastian shot back, smiling as he did so to keep the exchange from getting too heated. "Though you have little sympathy for it, there are some yet who get some solace from making their peace with God. I will be glad to give you as much when you are ready. . . ."

"I have been ready for death since the day I was born," Brelsford countered with a proud lift to his head. "I doubt that I will need any holy incantations said over me. Now pay attention to what I say so you know how to look for water."

"Proceed," Sebastian said, and as his eyes shifted from Brelsford's, he noted Eaton peering back toward the far horizon again. Why hadn't Barbara Churchill told him about Eaton? Why, really, was Sparks so anxious to let him know? Sensing Sebastian's scrutiny, Eaton's eyes darted back and locked with his for a brief moment. Whatever was there in those fiercely glowing greenish eyes, there was certainly now all of the defiance that went with his background. Perhaps that was what he had felt about Eaton all the time—that superior, challenging kind of air that went with men who once had destiny in their fists, who once stood astride the world, who had for a moment tasted the glory of universal supremacy. But there was something else there too, something more readily identifiable now—that look of secret knowledge, of cunning device, of a man who was looking down on people far inferior to himself of what he knew or was and a glitter of secret triumph that flashed without pretense. Eaton did not obviously have much use for clergymen either, and though he was less vocal than either Brelsford or Dennison, there was in his eyes that which represented a way of life totally and unequivocally at war with every vestige of godliness.

Sebastian dropped his eyes back to the wadi, and he felt the slight palpitation across his heart again so that he coughed and cleared his throat—and the greasy taste of sweat was on his cracked lips as Brelsford began pointing out their course of exploration.

* 7 *

They moved down into the canyon after Brelsford pointed out the method of exploration. He and Eaton would take the right slope of the cavern, while Sebastian and Dennison would take the left. It was simply a matter of checking every crevice and hole they came across and where there appeared a sign of green moss or weed, they were to signal the others.

Sebastian moved up the left bank of jagged rock behind Dennison who, like Brelsford, was anxious to make the first discovery. The climbing was not easy. Though the slope was not necessarily steep, the rocks were either too rough and uneven for climbing over or too smooth to get a decent footing. The afternoon wind that had refreshed them on the higher camp area was not reaching them here either, the high walls of the wadi shutting off the normal flow and rerouting it to higher altitudes before winding down to the desert beyond them.

Dennison's soft grunts of complaint were the only sound as they moved up the slope. Now and then he stopped to stare into a dry hole or sweep the thorny black rocks for some sign of greenery. There were times when he just stood blinking at one spot for a long minute in a pose of preoccupation or as if he were remembering something he had forgotten to do at some time. At other

119

times, he would stand and simply shake his head as if he were trying to clear his mind of some dangling cobweb thought that didn't seem relevant. It was clear that the man wasn't really focusing properly on what he was doing, and Sebastian, knowing he was suffering from possible concussion, felt that he should stay close to him lest he actually fall here and tumble down that murderous slope with its jutting spears of rock.

But while they were stopped halfway up the slope, Dennison turned to him, stared at him for a long minute as if he had suddenly realized that Sebastian was behind him and said, "We won't find what we're looking for hanging together like this. Why don't you go on down a few yards, and I'll take the upper area. . . ."

It was not a request, but a command. Sebastian hesitated a moment, wondering if he should suggest taking the upper slopes instead. But Dennison's pose was one of truculence, his eyes were steady and unblinking now as if his sense of superiority over Sebastian gave him a feeling of clarity and purposefulness. Sebastian turned and walked on down without a word and began his own exploration, now and then shifting a wary glance upward to make sure Dennison was not working himself into a dangerous position.

After a half hour or so of slipping and sliding over the razor sharp rocks, Sebastian found himself a good fifty yards ahead of Dennison. The man was spending a great deal of time just staring at rocks as if he felt water were actually locked up inside, and that any minute it must come bursting out. There appeared to be no reason to fear Dennison's falling since he had worked his way up to the upper ledge that appeared easy enough to negotiate.

Sebastian went on then, faithfully checking every possible break in the rocks for some sign of water. He tried not to think of his own thirst or the rubbery swelling of his tongue and the painful lips that he could not close over his teeth without opening fresh lacerations that filled his mouth with the salty taste of blood. He ignored the slashing wounds the rocks made on his hands and on his knees and shins and most of all the mocking voice from somewhere that told him this was all foolishness. That he was only going through the motions before death anyway, that the best thing to do was to lie down back at camp where the wind was still cool and let it come. He tried to fight that off by quoting Scripture verses from memory, picking out all the promises he could remember in the Bible as to God's faithfulness. But this soon began to sound like Sunday school memory time in his own church. . . . "Let's see if we can say all ten verses now, boys and girls, without looking and that'll put another star in our class flag. . . ." He tried instead to pick out one verse and stick to that, but as his mind ran through the ones he knew, he found he couldn't settle on any one that would fit what he felt or that which would be more relevant to what he was experiencing.

"The heavens declare the glory of God and the firmament showeth His handiwork," he said out loud, not knowing why that came out now. And as he slipped over a sharp outcropping of rock, he landed on his back, his eyes open to the slamming metallic sky. And he laughed, so that it surprised him. Look at Your handiwork, God! Look at this bleeding, frantic handiwork of Yours! Behold Your soldier of the cross who hunts for life with the panic of a child in search of his mother! Look at Your firmament, Lord, this bone yard of rock on which hangs Your servant like meat on a hook . . . or are You there at all, God? If You're not, I don't blame You . . . You belong in cathedrals with high altars and communion tables wrapped in white linen . . . You belong with Easter lilies and with roses on the pulpit "presented this morning in memory of . . ." You belong to the smell of Bible paper and Morocco leather and freshly varnished mahogany pews . . . You belong to the sound of coffee cups and spoons stabbing cream cake at the Ladies Knit for Missions Club . . . You belong to tranquil organ notes in the evening and militant piano marches in Sunday school . . . You belong to stained glass, velvet carpets, maroon choir robes . . . You belong to men whose hands are soft, whose suits are just out of the cleaners, who speak with the gentleness of fathers to their children at bedtime . . . there is Your rightful firmament, God, where You belong, for which Your glory is declared . . . but not here, not in this valley of death, this bone that sticks in Your throat, this ugly wart on the beautiful face of Your creation . . . this accident produced by the mixture of the sulphur from hell and the acids of nature's bowels . . . You don't belong here, nor do I . . . for the heavens declare only the perpetual hell that is mine and the firmament only says that dying won't be easy . . . so if You're not here, God, I don't blame You. . . .

And he felt himself wanting to cry . . . for the shame of what he thought, but also for the mocking truth of it . . . but when his mouth worked around the sob, his lips pained him, and the shock of the hurt snapped him back to his circumstances . . . and from somewhere far out in the hollow cave of his nightmare, someone was yelling.

He saw Brelsford below him, waving his arms up to him and pointing at something beyond that led up to a fortresslike mound of rock. Beyond Brelsford about fifty yards, Eaton was coming down from the far slope in answer to the call. Sebastian looked back up the slope to where Dennison was, standing high on the ledge and looking down in that same pose of concentration at rocks and whatever else he saw in his own tortured brain. Sebastian yelled to Dennison, who slowly turned to look, and Sebastian pointed to Brelsford. "He's found something, Dennison!"

And he felt the dilemma now as he got up and worked his way down the rocks. He wanted to find that water now, for life hung on it so finally, but he didn't want to find it like this with Brelsford and Dennison gloating over their scientific instincts. There was a genuine fear in his heart now that such a discovery might cancel out totally any sense of spiritual relevancy the others might have felt up to now. Water would mean life, and for that he prayed, but it would also seal out God in their lives, for if man's scientific instincts could be substantiated here in this hopeless situation, then where did God fit into the universe of their lives at all? He could hear Brelsford crowing about it already and feel the tremendous weight of his argument—and what answer could he give then? The fear was not only in what it would do to them, but what it would do to himself—for he needed one moment of vindication, one stroke of heavenly intervention, something that would give him articulation, something to lend credence to his faith and raise him to a level that would put dignity back into his profession and restore sinew to his shriveled-up spiritual fiber.

He got down to the canyon floor as Brelsford was beginning to ascend a kind of narrow dirt path that led to a fortresslike outcropping of rock. He waited at the bottom for Brelsford to announce his findings, and glanced back once to see Eaton still back a good thirty yards and moving up. Brelsford had finally mounted a hilly mound of hard claylike sand and stood to peer over what appeared to be a parapet of rock.

"It's here!" his exultant high-pitched voice rattled off the canyon walls. "Water! Lots of water! Water to drink, water to float a battleship!"

Sebastian kept looking up at Brelsford who continued bouncing up and down off his heels, the yellow nylon scarf around his head catching the late afternoon rays of the sun and turning him into some kind of strange madonna, while his aluminum walking stick waved in salute to his own discovery. And as Sebastian watched, Brelsford did a little jig, his boots pounding into the sandy mound and stirring up clouds of dust so that for the moment he was shrouded in it, the only thing showing being the incongruous yellow turban.

Then it happened. The whole scene jarred suddenly into violent movement. There was the booming sound first that smashed off the canyon walls sounding as strange and out of place as a jackhammer in a graveyard. The sound repeated through the rocks, and it had hardly dissolved before another was added to it. At the same time, Brelsford suddenly flew off the sandy mound as if he'd been jerked backwards, sprawling flat on the path and sliding down head first. Over that terrifying booming sound, Brelsford's voice came screaming above it all: "No! We're friends! We're friends!"

Sebastian stood there not comprehending the roaring in the canyon nor the peculiar pose of Brelsford on that path and the strange yelling that came from him.

"The fool's bumped into a wild band of Bedouins," he heard Eaton yell from what sounded like a long way behind him. "They shoot first and ask questions later!"

Sebastian still didn't understand. He could only watch with some mounting sense of terror as Brelsford got up again and started moving back up the path, yelling, "We're friends! Put away your guns! We're friends!"

"They'll pop him again if he sticks his head over that mound!" Eaton's voice sounded again, and it was more a commentary to himself or to Brelsford than to Sebastian.

Sebastian turned to look and saw Eaton crouched down behind a small barricade of rocks. "What do they think we're after?" he yelled back at Eaton.

Eaton raised his head to look back at Sebastian, not knowing if the question was worthy of an answer at this point. "They're protecting that water hole," he finally shouted back. "They probably think we're out to steal it from them. . . ."

By now, Brelsford, after slipping and sliding on the path, was standing erect and trying to run up the path to the sandy mound like a defiant opponent who was bound on becoming king of the mountain. There was another booming sound and the sharp whine off the rocks. In that instant, Sebastian lost all sense of right or wrong. There was no sense of value that shifted the balance, unless it was the instinct of his own profession that had been drilled into him since childhood. For a long moment he hesitated, waiting for Eaton to make some kind of move to alter the situation. But nothing happened. And then all he saw was Brelsford fighting to command that mound of sand again, to make his miserable entreaty to people who obviously were not to be entreated. And what he saw was a man who perhaps was the only real hub around which their survival hung, that if there was to be a logical, reasonable way out of this hell, then Brelsford was the man to plot it. So then maybe that was why he did what he did now. And even as he sprang forward and started the low crouching run up the path toward Brelsford, everything in him squealed the warning and made him give off with a low sob that sounded like an unintended battle cry or the terror-stricken protest of one who didn't really want to die this way.

He hit Brelsford just below the knees with his right shoulder, just as the man was about to climb the last step to that sandy mound and murderous rifle fire. Sebastian heard him grunt, and then he came down backwards, his weight crushing over Sebastian and knocking the wind out of him. Sebastian felt the dust and sand in his nostrils, and he fought the blanket of suffocating darkness that came down on him. He managed after what seemed a long time to grope back down the path, forcing his eyes open, trying to get hold of Brelsford. But Eaton was there now, gripping Brelsford by the collar of his khaki shirt and dragging him down the path as he would a dog. And all the time Brelsford was yelling: "Tell them we're friends, Eaton! Man, it's our only hope! Tell them. . . ."

But there was more rifle fire and more sounds of high-pitched whines as the bullets bounced off the rocks around them, and Brelsford's yelling was lost in it. Sebastian saw then that there was a widening black spot on Brelsford's right side above the belt, and it was obvious the man couldn't get up to walk. He picked up Brelsford by the legs, and Eaton followed suit, pulling him up by the shoulders. They began to run with the heavy weight, stumbling under it, their breaths audible as they fought to get out of range of the rifle fire.

They were not more than fifty yards down the canyon when they ran into Dennison. He stood in the path blinking rapidly at them, not comprehending, looking at Brelsford with some alarm and then beyond to the booming sounds.

"Go on back, Dennison!" Eaton yelled. "It's wild Bedouins!" Dennison didn't move. "Get out of the way, then!" Eaton shouted, and Dennison finally stepped out of the path slowly. When Sebastian and Eaton moved by him, he began walking on toward the sound of the firing.

Sebastian stopped and let Brelsford's legs drop to the ground. It was obvious that Dennison was not thinking clearly. "Go back for him, Eaton," he yelled. "I'll try carrying Brelsford in."

Eaton dropped his end of Brelsford and went back toward Dennison. Sebastian got the dead weight of Brelsford on his shoulders, but he was a good thirty pounds heavier than Sparks. He lost his balance and fell with Brelsford on top of him. His hand brushed the wet spot on the man's shirt and when he took it away he saw it was blood. He rolled out from under him and said, "Brelsford, can you walk at all?"

"Tell them we're friends," Brelsford mumbled, his eyes pleading. His face had turned ashen gray, and his eyes began to glaze from the shock.

Another shot bounced a bullet only a few feet from him, and Sebastian looked back to see if Eaton were coming. Eaton was having his problems with Dennison, who seemed to ignore Eaton's reasoning. Finally, Eaton's right hand shot out, palm flat, and caught Dennison full across the face. Dennison stared at Eaton a long minute, and then he lifted his fists in the air as though he were going to come down on Eaton with his full weight. Then, as if he suddenly walked out of a dream, he dropped his arms slowly and looked around. Seeing Brelsford on the ground, he came walking back swiftly, leaned over and lifted him by the shoulders. Sebastian lifted the legs and they started out, half running, but mostly staggering with

126

the ungainly weight between them. The rifle fire continued, smashing ugly sound into the wadi, and bullets reached out among the rocks for them, coming so close at times that chips of rock stung Sebastian on the arms. They stopped only long enough in the long mile back to camp to alternate in carrying Brelsford. When they were sure they were out of range of the Bedouin rifles, they still kept up their desperate pace, mostly under the prodding of Eaton who was sure the Bedouins would be on their heels soon.

When they got to the foot of the escarpment that led up to the camp area, Barbara Churchill was waiting.

"What happened?" she asked, bending down to touch Brelsford's blood-soaked shirt.

"Wild Bedouins," Eaton said simply, his chest heaving from the exertion of running and carrying Brelsford. "There isn't time to talk now. We've got to get up in those rocks out of sight."

They carried Brelsford up the slope and set him down carefully. Ida Randolph and Mabel Stockton wanted to know what was going on and what all the shooting was about. No one answered them. Eaton sat down, pulling his knees up to lean his arms on them, his head hanging down, trying to get his wind back, his shoulders and back heaving with the effort. Sebastian sprawled out on the rocks that burned from the sun, drinking the light wind, hoping it would assuage the liquid heat in his lungs. Dennison simply sat down a few feet away, next to Brelsford, more concerned now for his fellow scientist.

"Brelsford found the water all right," Sebastian finally said to Miss Churchill, "but these Bedouins were guarding it. They shot him before he had a chance to explain who we were. . . ."

"Bedouins?" Ida Randolph said, holding her face between her hands as if she couldn't take another crisis, a look of both fear and hope coming across her pointed features at the same time. "But—Bedouins . . . they're people . . . they could guide us out of here . . . and if they have water, why can't we reason with them? We're not their enemies!"

Her voice began to rise to that key of a near sob, and Mabel Stockton moved in quickly to comfort.

"Best thing to do is wait," Miss Churchill said, her voice reaching out to soothe. She had bent down to cut away the shirt around Brelsford's wound, and she didn't look up when Ida Randolph began to cry in choking gasps as if something had broken inside her. The sun had turned to a deep orange of early dusk now, flashing its nearly crimson fingers on the scissors as she cut away the cloth and revealed the ugly bluish hole in the fleshy bulge of Brelsford's side.

"It went through," she said, relief in her voice. "But he's lost a lot of blood. We'll have to shore that up and hope for the best."

She cut up bandage and strips of adhesive from the medicine kit, Dennison watching her every move intently. She did a good job as usual, but Sebastian wondered if it would be enough to hold. What Brelsford needed was a few days to rest to give that wound time to heal.

"What about Sparks?" Sebastian asked her then.

She didn't look at him, nor did she answer. She finished up the bandage, and then she handed him the familiar blue and gold cap. "Before he died he said you should have his cap," she said tonelessly.

Sebastian felt a peculiar numbness come over him. He thought he had been ready for this. He fondled the cap in his hands for a long minute. This was all he had left of a life that had slipped through his hands, a good life, a life of quiet strength and genuine humor. A life that should have gone on to an eternity with God—a life that he, a minister of the Gospel, should have guided in with firmness. Instead he could only hope that Sparks had made it—on the strength of a childhood profession, made perhaps in ignorance and lost undoubtedly in a life spent in unholy enterprise. He should have taken more time for Sparks

128

. . . but this place, this hell of a place offered no time to dwell on God, to throw life lines to sinking souls . . . time only for the struggle to stay alive, to engage in foolish forensics with science, to fight off the mocking solicitations of the Devil, to strain to find something wise and holy to say that would keep God alive in this world of death. . . .

Brelsford's rasping cough cut into his thoughts, then, and he watched as the yellow-turbaned scientist rolled his head back and forth, fighting to get back up for another round. He lay back, only his eyes rolling around the circle, trying to place who they were and where he was. Finally, with his eyes looking up back over his head toward Eaton, he said, his voice rasping in pain and weakness, "Eaton . . . you got to make . . . contact with them again. . . ."

Eaton lifted his head from his arms slowly. "They'll be looking for us now," he replied listlessly, "since they know we're not shooting back and are easy game. . . ."

Brelsford coughed, clutching his side as he did so, his head waving side to side to contradict Eaton. "It's . . . it's our only chance, Eaton," he insisted, and he was shaking now as if all the vehemence of his desire bottled up inside was fighting for outlet.

"Our only chance is to climb those ridges when it gets dark," Eaton replied flatly. "They'll be prowling around here about then. . . ."

Brelsford fought his way up shakily, pushing Miss Churchill's restaining hands aside. He rolled over on one elbow, so he could face Eaton directly. His face was greasy and as pale and yellowish as the adhesive strips. He was breathing hard with the exertion and swallowing gulps of air. "Those Bedouins . . . they're not warlike," his voice croaked through the whistling gasps from his lungs. "Do . . . do you understand, Eaton? Show them . . . we're friendly . . . and they'll be friendly in return. . . ."

"Brelsford, I know that no one comes into the Negev this far south unless they're armed to the teeth," Eaton replied bluntly, his eyes shimmering green and black at Brelsford. "And I'll tell you why: because of the wild tribes who, one, are first-class bandits and, two, very particular who stumbles on their precious water holes. When you stick your head into their camp again, they'll blow it off and pick you clean, leaving you as bare as when you came into the world. . . ."

Brelsford fell back in defeat, and it was obvious he was taking it personally, that his moment of near triumph had reversed to leave him helplessly a victim of events he had not counted on. It wasn't just the water and what it meant for survival. It appeared that he felt he had lost the opportunity to prove what that discovery would have done to support his philosophy of life.

"He's right," Miss Churchill chimed in lightly, and Brelsford's eyes opened again, and his look at her was almost venemous.

"You . . . you think I . . . don't understand Bedouins?" he demanded in that hoarse, grating voice.

"I'm sure you do," she countered, "but not some of these you often find in the Negev, Mr. Brelsford. In fact, between here and Ain Ghadyan are probably more wild Arab tribes who are ready to rob you of your gold fillings."

"If you knew that, why did you insist on going this way, leaving the wreck?" Dennison cut in now, picking up the battle for Brelsford.

"I hoped we'd miss any encounter with them," she replied in that coolly factual voice. "There are certain times of the year when their activities are less mobile. I had hoped this was one of them."

"You're suggesting we don't try for Ain Ghadyan?" Brelsford asked pointedly.

She didn't answer immediately, and the group was very quiet now except for Brelsford's breathing, which was more from pent-up anger and frustration than from his wound. Even Ida Randolph held her hand over her mouth to stifle her sobs. Only Eaton seemed indifferent as he went back to leaning his head on his arms.

"What I'm stating as fact, Mr. Dennison," she said then, "is that our chances of running the renegade Bedouin gauntlet to Ain Ghadyan are one in a hundred."

"That leaves . . . that leaves only one crazy alternative," Brelsford broke in again, lifting his head off the blanket that served as a pillow under his head.

Miss Churchill put the dressing materials back into the medicine kit and nodded. "That's right, Mr. Brelsford, only one alternative—south."

"South!" Dennison roared, and his voice echoed in the rocks like the clanging of a bell. "Do you know what you're saying?"

A gasping kind of laugh came out of Brelsford then, and again he seemed to take a big breath as if he were getting ready to dive under water for a long time. Only now he was building it up for one long tirade again. He pushed himself up on one elbow to lend emphasis to what he was going to say, his face puffy with the incredulity of what she had suggested. "Then . . . then you better tell these people what . . . to expect out there, lady . . . no water there because no wadis . . . nothing but sand . . . hills of sand . . . miles of sand . . . tell them what it's like . . . to die of thirst out there . . . it's long and maddening . . . better to face the Bedouins than that torture chamber of the South Negev . . . tell them that, Miss Churchill. . . ."

"And I know what wild desert tribes can do to their victims, Mr. Brelsford," Miss Churchill shot back. "Would you like a description or two of that?"

"Oh, my God," Miss Randolph moaned and sank limply to the rocks, her body shivering with the new agony of fear.

"Then it's a decision someone has to make," Dennison said, while Brelsford coughed on his thwarted attempts to go on with the argument.

"That's right, Mr. Dennison," she confirmed, giving him a quick smile as she would a child who had come up with the right answer. "Someone has to make that decision. . . ."

131

The silence was heavy now. Dennison stared at her, daring her to reveal who, and Eaton had looked up now with definite interest. Sebastian went on twirling the blue and gold airline cap between the fingers of both hands, keeping his eyes off them, but feeling the rising tumult in his own heart.

"Brelsford's been leading thus far," Dennison insisted. "He's still sound enough to make decisions for us."

"Mr. Brelsford made one costly decison today," she countered keeping her voice polite but steady. "That could have cost us all our lives . . . besides, he is not physically able, that you can see for yourself and so can he."

A painful smile came on Brelsford's mouth then, and he said, "Then, I'm sure the decision maker will have to be yourself, Miss Churchill?"

"Perhaps," she replied.

Again it was very quiet. They were waiting like people watching a high point of a drama, waiting for it to break one way or the other. Sebastian was conscious that the airline cap twirling between his fingers was as predominant as a glowing pinwheel in the sky. He looked up quickly and caught Dennison and Brelsford looking at him steadily, and even Eaton's fierce glowing eyes held on to him with a penetrating intent.

"Behold the man!" Brelsford let out with a choking derision, and he laughed again, clutching his side as he did so, a laugh of bitterness with pain riding the crest of it, so that it was condemnatory, more than a direct statement could have ever been.

"You can't be serious," Dennison challenged her, his eyes blinking rapidly, his body going tense.

"Mr. Brelsford made the assumption," she replied coyly.

"Well is he, or isn't he?" Dennison demanded.

"When the time comes for decision you'll know, Mr. Dennison," she snapped, her voice gone brittle now.

"There's no one else here stupid enough to let the

decision be anyone's but Brelsford's," Dennison said with a snarling tone to his voice.

"If you want to die without a fight, then join the ranks of the stupid, Mr. Dennison," she returned tartly.

"And what do you know about deserts, Reverend?" Dennison sneered at Sebastian, putting a sarcastic emphasis to "reverend." "Do you have any idea of where you're heading once you start south? How many miles to the nearest outpost, Mr. Sebastian?"

"Bir Milhan," Brelsford croaked again, "Bir Milhan, Sebastian, do you . . . do you know where it is?"

Sebastian looked at Miss Churchill helplessly. She threw a quick glance at him as if to say she had no answer for him, but at the same time warning him not to try to meet Brelsford's or Dennison's arguments on their terms. He wasn't even sure that going south was the right decision anyway—in fact, he was more tempted to let Brelsford have his head, for he had already proven his ability in finding water. But there was also the desire of Miss Churchill—and he had to swing her way for no other reason now that the fact that she was making choices on the basis of the other problem of Agent Christopher.

"Mr. Dennison, I'm not looking for the decision-making power here," he said. "I'll do what I have to do when the time comes . . . right now I have a man to bury, rations to distribute . . . if you don't mind, I'll get to it."

Again Brelsford gasped a raking laugh. "Carry on, Sebastian, and perform thy tasks—but let the work of men to the men!"

"You can stop your cat-bawling any time, Brelsford," Eaton cut in then, "There's movement down in that valley and they're going to hear you in a minute. . . ."

The sun had slipped behind the far horizon, and the broad strokes of purple closed in fast. They all peered down into the canyon, not wanting to see anything, but intent on discovering what their chances were.

"It's time we moved higher," Miss Churchill said to them quietly.

"Let them come," Brelsford's voice rang off the rocks again. "Then we'll see how wild our Bedouins are. . . ."

"Shut up," Eaton said, his voice quiet but deadly, so that they all looked quickly at him, not at all accustomed to the dapper man making such a statement with such authority. Brelsford was startled by it as well, and he could only stare back at Eaton from his blankets, peering through the misty purple of evening as if he wanted to be sure it was Eaton who had spoken.

Nothing more was said, until Sebastian spoke up. "I'm going to read over Sparks . . . I would welcome all of you to pay your respects. . . ."

No one replied. They moved around quietly, preparing to climb to the higher ridges. The cold had come again, and it added to their feeling of heavy depression. The baby began to cry a little in gasps, and Miss Churchill's voice sounded in the dark, giving assurance to her. The moon that was already high during the day, and turning flat on one side to indicate that its robustness was near an end, began to cast weird shades of lime as the daylight was all but spent. After awhile the moonlight was bright enough to force the silent sentries of rock into silhouette, but visibility was only a matter of a few yards at the most. Later, when the stars turned up to full brightness, the glow of the heavens would add some, but for now it was comforting to know that those wild Bedouins had no clear vision of the higher ridges.

When Sebastian started to read over Sparks from his Bible, all of them were there except Dennison and Brelsford. After he had read the promise of the Lord in 1 Thessalonians, he added a few words of his own, glad to be hidden from them in the half-light so that they could not see the torture on his own face, the agony of committing a man to the uncertainty of eternity: "This man was a good man," he said. "As a child he made his peace with God—of his adult years, we know nothing. But we do know that God Himself will judge." He felt that he ought to preach to them all about preparing for eternity for he

134

wasn't sure when he would have them quite like that again. But then the baby started to cry again, and he felt Miss Churchill stir for she knew she should try to quiet her before the sounds got back to the canyon floor. So he had to finish it quickly with words that seemed to have no meaning for him. "As we hope for this man's soul to rest in the bosom of the Father, let us also quicken our hopes on the life we still have . . . for it is in the darkest hour that the light of God shines the brightest, the movements of God are surest, the concern of God beats the strongest . . . according to your faith, be it unto you. . . . Amen."

He and Eaton lifted the blanket-covered body into the shallow crevice in the rocks and piled the loose rocks on top. Then quietly each of them moved away, not anxious to linger over death. He stayed back to fuss with the rocks, to fill in the gaps in the mound. After awhile Mabel Stockton and Ida Randolph came back to help him, and finally Miss Churchill.

She worked with him, the two women on the side. Then as she leaned over quickly to stop a rock from rolling down the mound, a metallic clink sounded loudly in the deathly silence. The moon and the stars together were giving off a kind of greenish-yellow light, and the gold, cylindrical instrument shone brightly in that glow. He stared down at it for along minute, even as he was conscious of her reaching out with one hand to quickly retrieve it. He gripped her wrist before she could pick it up and held it while he reached down for the object. It was a good six inches long, shaped like a fountain pen, tapering off at one end but fat and bulky at the other. He looked up at her and wanted to say something, but the warning in her eyes prevented him. The two women were busy with the rocks and apparently hadn't noticed. Quickly Sebastian slipped the instrument into his belt and released her wrist. She pulled it back slowly, rubbing it with her other hand, and he hadn't realized he had gripped her so hard. But now he felt no sense of apology if he had—suddenly he was confronted with another contradiction in her, a serious one this time, and all he could do was stare at her as if he was seeing someone in a totally new light. She, in turn, stared back at him, but there was no look of embarrassment at having been discovered, no appeal in those eyes for understanding—there was that same honest, detached, steady gaze void of emotion of any kind. Then she went back to piling rocks on the grave, and he got up and walked away, following the path that led to the upper ridges, feeling the dizziness from fatigue and the lack of water and food. But on top of that was the flooding sense of confusion, of shame, of indignation—and of real loss.

When they were all accounted for on the higher ridges, he broke out the rations. The water for each of them was only a trickle now. The food was a quarter cracker and only a sliver of sardine. He served it deliberately, then took time to work over the child with more care. He gave her more water than the others, for her skin was hot and feverish again, and the little mouth was covered with blisters. He knew they watched him, and he felt their animosity rise without their having to express it as he robbed them of their precious supply to treat this smallest bit of life. But he paid no heed to them now—he felt detached from them, their feelings, their prejudices, even their needs. He was suddenly concerned only with doing what he knew was right, and there came into his being a kind of careless demeanor, the movements of a man who had lost all sense of value in others, who had suddenly decided that what measure of justice might have prevailed or whatever human quality might have existed, it was gone now—so what did it matter?

When he served Miss Churchill, he dared to look once more into her face in the hopes of seeing something there that might indicate appeal. But her face was hidden in the shadows from the overhanging rocks, and she did not bother to come out of that covering of anonymity. All of which but confirmed to him that she had no intention of apology or appeal and that what the gold fountain pen radio transmitter said of her was true—and he was left only with the weight of how to reconcile her treason with her other strong virtues that had appeared to be so genuine.

When he had packed the meager rations back into the bag, he hoisted it over his shoulder and mounted the rocks to where he had encountered Eaton earlier that day. There he sat down and stared across the glowing tombs of rock, feeling the crushing load of being forsaken, betrayed by man and God, all motivation for life draining out of him as from an open wound.

After awhile he knew she was there without turning to be sure. He knew that when his pulse quickened, or his heart gave off the peculiar tripping ripple, she was close. But the strange exhilaration he felt at other times, the sense of anticipation, the feeling of wanting to stand tall when she came into his presence, was gone now.

Only a strange sadness gripped him, together with a sharp thrust of indignation at being betrayed.

* 8 *

"You still don't trust me, do you?"

She was behind him, probably making sure she didn't have to look at him while she built her defenses. Her voice remained its usual dry, businesslike tone. She knew how to play the agent role, he thought, every scene straight, without emotion.

"I'm not sure it matters anymore," he said, caught between a rising head of indignation within and the weight of both sadness and exhaustion that prevented him from making his voice sound as hard as he would have liked to. "Anyway, we've gone over this too many times already—right now I'm not sure there are any balances here that can be trusted in weighing good against evil."

"You'll have to continue with those you have."

He gave a half-grunting laugh that didn't come off very well. "Why? Is it so important to continue to be contradicted?"

"I haven't the time to convince you on that," she countered. "But I can tell you that that transmitter is not mine."

He lifted his hands skyward in a gesture of resignation. "So it isn't yours. I have to believe you—what else is there for me to do? I'm caught on the barbed wire, and every time I try to squirm loose the tear gets bigger."

"You sound whiny like a whipped dog," she jabbed him.

"I feel both whiny and like a whipped dog, if you want the truth," he retaliated, trying to keep his voice light as if it really didn't mean anything to him one way or the other. "And don't bother trying to goad me to go charging out for the second half—I've decided to fit into this wild drama only in terms of what my profession demands, nothing more."

"Brelsford's got you on the run I see. . . ."

"Brelsford, maybe, and a few other people. And while we're on the subject I think the man makes sense . . . going south is a bit ludicrous, to put it mildly. We've got about as much chance out there as—as diving off a fifty-foot tower into a wet hanky."

"So you're going to just fold up the tent and call it a day, are you?" and there was a cracking sound to her voice now, a different tone from anything he'd heard from her. "You think you can simply decide when to back out of a situation like this, and to use your analogy, when to yield to barbed wire or fight it? You think you can pick and choose your role in life out here like you do back in Nashville, Wisconsin? Do you think this is some kind of lawn game we're playing where we can substitute freely or just drop out when we get tired or feel the pinch? Well, I'll tell you one thing, Mr. Sebastian, you can't get off the barbed wire right now because you've got to prove to yourself that you are more than a biblical band-aid panhandler . . . you've got to prove to yourself and this miserable bunch of suffering humanity here that God exists in the proportion that you've been preaching most of your life from the sterile, antiseptic, safe pulpits. . . ."

He swallowed once, hard, as if he'd just gulped a chunk of red pepper—he felt the burn of the tirade rush through him, and it left him even more perplexed, because he never really thought she had any such strong feelings about ministers.

"I suppose I should thank you for that," he managed to

say finally, "but there remains my own inability to classify you right now. And though I can't be quite as colorful in my description of you, I can at least say that you appear a rather sickly gray to me right now, very blurry as far as consistence and character is concerned. . . ."

"I'm not Agent Christopher," she said with finality and some exasperation now. "You'll have to accept that."

"Why should I? Especially with the evidence you carelessly dropped in front of me an hour ago?"

"If you'd let me explain first and judge second, it might not be so painful."

He winced, because the rightness of that cut deep. He sighed and looked down into the canyon. "Say on, dear lady, say on," he tried in a mocking tone, and pulled out the gold-colored transmitter and laid it on the rock beside him. He felt her movements behind him and from the corner of his eye saw her sit down ten discreet feet away. For a moment they could have been anywhere admiring the view, two people who had casually met and were enjoying what the universe had to offer while their spirits fused toward one another. But here every action of intimacy—intended or unintended—was cut short by the cruel clippers of circumstances and surroundings, and, in her case, the contradictory image that now so hung over her and grated on him with irritating relentlessness.

She said that she had found the transmitter that same afternoon just before he and Eaton returned with Brelsford and Dennison. "When I heard the first shot I went down to the canyon below the camp site. While I was standing there, I caught the sun's reflection on it."

"Why would our man Christopher just throw it away like that in such a place so close to camp?"

"He didn't throw it away . . . the power unit failed on him. So he did the next best thing. He wedged it between two rocks, with the pointed end eastward to Ain Ghadyan. There's enough power left to give off a signal for a radio fix by his friends. They could follow it in, see the

140

obvious direction to which we were headed, and assume where we were going."

"But Ain Ghadyan is out now . . . Christopher must want to get that transmitter back now that the Bedouins are forcing us to alter course. And if it's one of the men who were out with me today, he probably saw that it was gone when we came back. And if he knows it's missing, then he knows one of us knows he's among us."

She nodded. "That's a possibility."

"Why haven't his friends come in here on the run after all that shooting?" he pursued again, wanting to cover every loophole now to make sure of her, hesitating for fear he'd catch her in a trap, but relentless in his insistence because he wanted her to be anything but guilty.

"They're not sure what to do, I would think," she replied, meeting his every probe with her eyes steady on him so that he could see that she was not trying to evade, and each time he had to look away for he found her eyes always disturbing. "They're waiting for his transmission to tell them what to do. I would think that his power ran out on him unexpectedly today, so it means they'll be coming in here soon to find us when he doesn't send."

"Tonight?"

"I'd say they were overdue, that's why I'm pushing on the time."

"Okay, are we better or worse off with Christopher out of touch with his friends?"

"Depends. So far he's been holding them off, for what reason I'm not sure. Now that he isn't sending, they're going to get excited. On the other hand, he's out of touch with help—so it gives us a break, perhaps we can even hope that his friends will stumble on those Bedouins and fight to a draw."

"I still don't get why he didn't call in his friends when he had the opportunity."

"I don't think he's really sure of them," she said in a kind of soliloquy, as if she had been thinking about that for some time. "It could be he doesn't want to chance it with whoever is out there. They could be Egyptian agents who would kill him, take the film and use it for their own offensive on Israel. Nasser would like nothing better than to topple Israel on his own—think of what that would do to his stock in the Arab world?"

"But Christopher has the gun . . . he can make his move any time he wants to."

"Of course. He wants to make it out of here without help from anyone, but he will do anything he has to if he finds himself cornered. And he's not sure which of us is the Israeli agent—he'll play it out as long as he can."

He was satisfied for the moment. Her answers were sure, steady, factual. He felt the inward relief in the knowledge that he had probably jumped to hasty conclusions about her. But the power of logic was not difficult for her in any case. He had to accept her on that, he had no choice. And, anyway, he wanted to.

He stood up now and stared at the far horizon to see if there were some sign of enemy camp or pursuit. There was none.

"I want to ask again about going south," he began then, stuffing his hands into his trouser pockets and continuing to stare out into the quiet night. "I told you before that I think Brelsford's right. Going south is a mighty big jump to nowhere . . . but if you insist on doing it, then I think it's time you took the lead. Why don't you now?"

"I told you. Because I am a woman," she replied. "It would be easier for Brelsford to swing the party his way if I told them to go south rather than you."

"All you're asking for, then, is for a man to lead."

"The right man," she corrected him, and he looked back at her steadily now to detect any look of contradiction on her face. There was none.

"I think our friend Eaton could do it."

"Why him?"

"He seems to know what he's doing. I'll wager he fought with the Nazi Afrika Korps in the desert too. He's got a good sense of direction, a feel for command. Both

Brelsford and Dennison respect him."

"And what if he's Christopher?"

He turned to look at her suddenly, for he hadn't considered that.

"He doesn't seem fit for the part."

"I think he fits perfectly."

He knew he couldn't win that argument, so he shrugged it off and turned to look back into the desert night. Then he said, "One more contradiction that needs explanation—I don't understand how you can have such a low opinion of me as a clergyman and still continually project me into a role of a general."

She got up from where she was sitting and faced him directly, her arms folded across the bulky gray sweater. "What you did for Brelsford today in that canyon is one reason why," she said crisply, and he knew she hated to spell it out for him, as though it were an embarrassment for her to admit anything positive about him.

"How'd you find out about that?"

"Mr. Eaton filled me in after I cornered him about it."

"I'm sure Eaton wanted to hand me a medal," he said with a half grunting laugh.

"On the contrary. He thought you were a fool for what you did. Eaton's concept of life doesn't reach that far. He spit into the dark and said that all you did was add another wounded man to our company, which means slower going and a waste of water. . . ."

"And what about your concept of life—as an agent of a national power, how do you view the value of the individual?"

"Mine is not much higher than Eaton's—that's why I'm trying to get you to understand why you are important to the survival of this group."

"Well, don't get any ideas that I'm a hero just because I threw a tackle at Brelsford," he reminded her sullenly, although he would have liked her to believe it, or even express it. "What I did was probably more selfish than anything. Brelsford was the only hope I could see for our survival, that's all there was to it."

"I'm gambling you'll do it again," she replied. "When the time comes, if it does. What drove you to do that for Brelsford may be what we'll need again."

"I'm trying to accept that as a compliment."

"I'm not giving any. I'm merely analyzing you in terms of the immediate situation."

"I may disappoint you," and he didn't know why he kept cutting himself down before her.

"It's probably what I expect," she shot back. "But I'm counting on the surprise, that you'll deliver what we need when you have to."

"And it's got nothing to do with my being a minister?"

"Whatever it is, I leave it to you to determine."

"It's costing you a lot to admit that I have anything of value, isn't it?" he probed then, seeing that she stood unusually stiff before him as though every word were a painful surrender.

"I haven't seen too much of value in the church, no," she admitted. "I've given you more than I thought I could ever give."

He cleared his throat in the ensuing silence, wondering what it was that had shaped her thinking of clergymen, and why she couldn't even yield a little under the circumstances.

"What if they choose to follow Brelsford or Dennison?" he asked then.

"Then you have failed," she said simply, "and so have I."

He waited a long minute, walking back and forth on the flat rock, fighting to lay hold of conviction, clamping down on the same rising force of indecision within.

"How long will it take to Bir Milhan?" he asked.

"If we move well, no more than four days."

"And what about water?"

"We might make it on what we have—or we could run across friendly nomads farther south."

"Four days with next to no water—in this heat? I know

144

the body can take punishment, but not that much. And with Brelsford—and the child?"

"The decision is yours now," she said with finality. "You can go Brelsford's way and try those Bedouins, but even if we manage to get by them and to water, we still have the open desert east where Christopher's friends will catch up to us. Your decision is simply to decide which way you'd rather die or which way you'd rather try for life."

She stood there looking at him a long minute. He didn't know what her look meant. It was kind of measuring combined with some serious doubt of him. Then again it was almost commiserating, as if she knew the pressure she was putting on him. All possibilities passed across her face in rapidly changing moods, and then it froze into the same impassive detachment again.

"I'm going around this ridge and back to the canyon floor to replace this trasmitter where I found it," she said. "You better get back to the others and get them ready." She walked back to the overhang of rock where she had stood when she first came up. She stopped over and picked up the blue and gold airline cap, then tossed it to him. He caught it with his right hand. "You left that behind. You might as well wear it—who knows, it might help."

"One thing more," he called softly to her. She paused, waiting, her eyes on the rocky trail in front of her. "You don't have much use for the church, especially ministers—but you seem to have a pretty good knowlege of us. Did you get that in your training?"

She waited a long time as if debating whether to answer. Then she turned her head slowly to him, and her eyes fixed on his face. "I had plenty of time to study all about ministers—my father was a missionary to the Jews."

He stood there on the flat rock until she had disappeared over the ridge, the swirling mixture of cross-currents numbing his senses. He wanted to laugh, because suddenly the whole situation had become bizarre in a tragic kind of way. And he did laugh. It came up in his throat and cracked his lips, but no sound came. He let his lips tremble with it, and his throat ached under it—and it could have become a kind of gasp if he held it any more. So he forced it down, and the laugh became a gag in his throat.

He stood there a long time looking down at the rock under his feet. "Lead thy captivity captive and be Caesar within thyself." "Now thanks be unto God who always causeth us to triumph in Christ," he said softly. But did that apply to all situations? Triumph over temptation, over self-indulgence, cheating, lying, stealing, fornication—but did it apply here, was it supposed to? Triumph over the feelings of inability to become a field general, a tactician, a strong leader of men, a genius in desert survival? Did God make the situation and then create the man—or was it the other way around? Did it mean he could dare walk into that camp and tell them he was taking them south—SOUTH—and then in taking them, lead them through what was even obvious to him an impossible journey? Paul was talking about imprisonment for the faith, stoning for the faith, beatings forty times with a club for the faith—but did he mean triumph over circumstances like these? It wasn't a question as to whether God was able, but whether God expected him to take on a role that wasn't in keeping with the immediate spiritual frame of reference. Perhaps he was demanding more of God than he was supposed to.

He stood there in the quiet, looking up at the brilliance of the heavens with their incongruous gaiety, almost mocking him as they kept winking at him as though this was some kind of big bad joke they were enjoying at his expense. He wanted to hear a voice, the thunder of God as it was for Moses on Mount Sinai. He wanted something, a vision, anything to break this silence that only aided in his indecision.

"I think they're gone now," came the voice, and he

gave a quick start and turned quickly. . . . Eaton was standing there looking at him solemnly.

"What?"

"The Bedouins, I think they're gone . . . they'll probably be back. Whatever we're going to do, we better make up our minds now. Where is the girl?"

"Off on some duty," he said quickly. And then he almost asked Eaton what he would do in the situation. And it was as if Eaton knew. He stood there waiting, almost expecting the question. Sebastian moved off the rock and up the path to go by Eaton.

"Did you see them?" Eaton asked.

"Who?"

"Whoever is out there."

Sebastian looked into Eaton's face which was only a few feet away. The moonlight caught the traces of pen scratches on his face that appeared like smudged creases from carbon paper. The eyes as usual were half-hidden in the dark sockets, hard and glowing like hot coals in the dark bottom of a furnace bed.

"I don't know what you're talking about, Eaton," he said curtly.

"You and the Jew girl," Eaton returned with some intimation in his voice. "You have much to talk about . . . or maybe you know they are there too. We should wait to find out."

"Miss Churchill is airline, Eaton," Sebastian said, but he didn't know why he should have to defend himself to Eaton. It was as if the man had taken on a new personality, as if his leading remarks were almost on the level of accusation and demanded explanations. "I'm part of that airline by the rations I carry—there's nothing more to it than that. If we wait around here to see what you think is out there, we'll die."

"We'll die either way, certainly no better out there."

There was a swinging thud to the statement, as if it were a prophetic utterance. Sebastian felt he couldn't leave it there, it almost seemed essential to put a chip in the superior, impenetrable block of the man's dogmatism.

"In America, Eaton, we have a saying in baseball for the player who strikes out—there's no shame in swinging. But to stand there with the bat on your shoulder and get called out—my friend, that is shame."

And to add emphasis to the remark, Sebastian pulled on Sparks' airline cap and tugged it down firmly on his head. Eaton's mouth twitched a little as if a smile were coming up, a smile of mockery and disdain. He looked at Sebastian as an SS trooper might have viewed the bold but asinine gestures of a Jew putting a prayer shawl on his head as a defiant act of resistance. Sebastian hadn't intended to declare himself for command quite like that in such a simple but dramatic and final stroke. But he didn't wait to say anymore—he turned and went down the rocks to the place where the others waited.

He could have wished for more divine anointing for what he had to do. He could have waited for some sign from heaven, put out the fleece, prayed it through. But all he had now was a Scotsman's philosophy about Caesar, the words of Scripture that he wasn't sure he could draw on or had the right to draw on in this situation, and the clever ad writing from a souvenir baseball score card—these were strange fragments to fit into the marching orders for a preacher. But it was all he had now. If there was a moment of truth for him, this was it. He had come thousands of miles on a spiritual quest—it had to begin now.

"Mr. Sebastian!" Brelsford's voice rang out to him as soon as he got down to the camp site, and it had the usual rising challenge to it.

Now then—"rise up, oh man of God, and put thine armour on. . . ."

✳ 9 ✳

Brelsford was having trouble with the dressing on his wound. Blood had soaked through, and the dressing now hung loosely, the adhesive tape too damp to hold. The right trouser leg down to the thigh was soaked. Sebastian got the first-aid kit and set to work.

"You and the girl talk a lot, don't you?" Brelsford growled, but his voice was not strong enough to crest over a hoarse, grating sound.

"It seems to bother you and Eaton," Sebastian replied, cutting out a new strip of bandage.

"We don't like to be left out of it, especially if it concerns our future."

"Well, to include you I'm afraid would only hike your blood pressure, Mr. Brelsford," Sebastian answered.

He removed the bandage and looked at the wound in the dim light of the moon. It was not closing or clotting as it should, The blue, purplish hole kept oozing out Brelsford's life.

"Where is she now?" Brelsford insisted.

"Probably doing some meditating of her own, I suppose."

There was a pause during which Sebastian laid on the fresh bandage, and then Brelsford reached up with his right hand and gripped Sebastian by the front of his sweater, pulling him down so that he could make sure no one else heard what he had to say. There was a fierce glow in his eyes that seemed to match the color of the bright yellow scarf around his head, and his body had grown taut as a spring. The strength of his grip was surprising, for he still looked no better than earlier, although the shock had worn off some.

"I know what you have in mind, Sebastian," he said, his voice just above a whisper and the words coming out through his clenched teeth. "You think your God is going to hang a star out there in the heavens like that fairy tale of the virgin birth . . . you think He'll do it again and lead us straight to water. . . ." Sebastian tried to pull out of his grip, but Brelsford dug in tighter, twisting the cloth as he spoke. "I know your kind . . . I lived with a stupid, fanatical father who thought he could pray for healing and rain and bread for the table . . . I know the suffering he put us through. . . ." He coughed harshly, but he wouldn't let go of Sebastian's sweater. "So now we're pawns in your desperation to prove God the same way. . . . Well, I don't intend to be the sacrificial lamb again, preacher . . . go if you want to, but I reserve the right to stay here and die if necessary or hope for those Bedouins to find me. . . ."

Sebastian was stunned by the sweeping invective of the man, shocked too by the ugly experience Brelsford had had with religion. The vehemence of the words made God sound like a monster in the universe. He could not recover quickly enough to retaliate.

He pried the bulging fist loose from his sweater, was about to say something to counter the raking denunciation, and then Brelsford suddenly flopped back on the blanket unconscious.

Just then Barbara Churchill came up from the lower canyon and moved in to check Brelsford, as did Dennison, and the two schoolteachers. Only Eaton remained outside the circle of concern, as if he knew all that was going on anyway.

"Loss of blood," Miss Churchill said simply.

"He can't travel in that condition," Dennison snapped, offering proper excuse now to remain where they were as Brelsford suggested earlier.

"Stop making a bloody nuisance of yourself," Eaton suddenly cut in, and they all paused to look back where he stood, again surprised at the biting tone to his voice. "He'll travel or give us all trouble—when those Bedouins find him they'll make him talk and tell where we are. . . ."

"You suggesting we go south too?" Dennison snarled, and he got up now, ready to do combat, his body bristling with intent. Eaton was ready to oblige, for he took one long stride forward to meet the onslaught.

"We'll go where we have to to stay out of those Bedouins' hands," he retaliated, and his own voice had turned very quiet. "And if it means beating sense into you, then let's have it your way. . . ."

Sebastian saw then that it was going to be a fight to the finish. This was the beginning of the first seeds of anarchy in the group. He saw that there was no time to let the two men battle it out here, to say nothing of the devastating effect it would have on all of them. He was conscious of pressure mounting in the quiet night from outside the group as well as within, and though he had no sense of certainty in taking command and going south, yet he knew now that some decisive action would have to be taken if the total deterioration of the group was to be prevented.

"Hold it," he said, then, driving some sense of authority in his command, and Dennison turned suddenly to face him, ready to take on Sebastian, too. "We're going south, Dennison," he said with finality, and handed the scissors to Miss Churchill so she could finish the job of dressing Brelsford's wound.

"Don't be such a stupid fool!" Dennison hurled at him, and so harsh was the statement, that Ida Randolph sucked in her breath, either at the vehemence of Dennison or the shock of hearing any man address a minister so crudely. Dennison, meanwhile, had tensed up to the point that his body appeared ready to spring at Sebastian. "Leave us a water ration, and we'll take our chances here, Brelsford and I!"

"This ration is intended for all of us," Sebastian returned mildly, forcing himself to keep his eyes off Dennison lest his own inner trembling show in his eyes. "I don't intend to split it. We've got enough to keep us going for another day or more. If we keep up the pace, we can get to Bir Milhan alive."

"With Brelsford half dead?" Dennison howled, the heat of his breath touching Sebastian's cheek and offering a strange contrast to the icy cold of the night. "With a small child who keeps demanding more and more water all the time? That's murder! And I'll see to it that it sticks, Sebastian! I have it all down in my record, just in case I don't make it out of here—when they find us out there, they'll find the book and read how you deliberately ignored the logical course of action for the crazy fixation you have for some kind of religious experience. . . . If I die, they'll know, Sebastian, they'll know. . . ."

"You won't die, Dennison," Sebastian said, keeping his voice steady even as the battering ram of Dennison's fury ripped into him. "And we won't let Brelsford die either, that's a promise. . . ." And he caught the warning look from Miss Churchill, as if she were saying that he was sticking his neck out too far for Brelsford. But ignoring the look, he rose to face them all, including Eaton who stood back viewing it all with his usual pose of sniffing indifference and disdain. "And that goes for all of you . . . none of us is going to die, and the sooner we get that fixed in our minds the better our chances will be." Nobody said anything. Dennison just blinked at him helplessly, his eyes wild with a fury that couldn't be expressed. Even Ida Randolph managed to keep from crying as she stared at Sebastian as though he were some kind of strange apparition. "Now, we don't have much time left; if we're going to make time, we've got to take advantage of this darkness. Dennison, you help Eaton carry Brelsford. . . .

We'll spell each other every hour. When it gets daylight, we'll lay low out of the sun. . . ."

"Sun?" Dennison yelped again. "There's no shade out there, you fool! Not like here! You'll roast and curl up like a barbecued onion!" Again there was that wild laugh; it bounded off the rocks back to them, as if the Negev itself laughed, the laugh of death that had followed them every painful, torturous mile thus far.

"Those Bedouins are down there again," Eaton called out from his position overlooking the canyon.

"All right, let's move," Sebastian said, and he waited to see what Dennison was going to do. Dennison continued to sit there on his haunches, and for a moment it appeared as if the man might do something as foolish as Brelsford had done earlier. But then Eaton was there waiting for Dennison to help him with Brelsford, and Dennison reluctantly moved to comply with the order.

Sebastian didn't look back as he picked his way up over the encircling rocky ridge looking for a way down the other side. He wanted to convey to them that he was sure they would follow, that there was no uncertainty on his part about them. Though he felt the turmoil of his decision, of taking command, and of half wishing that he had stayed back there and taken his chances with the Bedouins, yet he was committed now—and everything depended on how well he showed confidence and assurance in what he was doing.

After an hour of slipping and sliding down the jagged rocky escarpment, they reached the flat prairie floor that spread out before them into endless miles of nothingness. There seemed to be more sand here and less rocky surface. It was just as Brelsford had warned. It was a fine sand blown in from the million years of wandering wind, the kind that was produced from rock cremated by the flaming magnesium sun, lifeless sand that poured freely as salt but which could feel as heavy as cement on weary feet.

It worried him some, that sand. It could drag their progress considerably, alter even Miss Churchill's close reckonings of how long to Bir Milhan, instead of four days it could be six or more. That could be disastrous. Unless he pushed them on, never allowing any rest, moving night and day—but they couldn't take that either. Already they were showing signs of the debilitation from lack of food and water.

He turned his head to look back to make sure they were following his change of direction to the left. They came in as much a confused line of march as they had under Brelsford. They were moving more under the pressure of possible pursuit behind them than because he was dangling out promises of survival to them. Dennison and Eaton were stumbling along with Brelsford who hung between them, his buttocks almost dragging the ground. Eaton had his head up, holding Brelsford's shoulders in his hands in a pose of apparent ease—that would be Eaton, never allowing the strain of the moment to show. And it seemed that his eyes were on Sebastian, watching, and maybe he was smiling . . . smiling at the uncertain leadership of a clergyman who he probably knew didn't really know what he was going to do next . . . and back of him Barbara Churchill, her athletic stride as purposeful as always, the smooth coordination of her movements mocking him again, reminding him that she knew he wasn't really up to it, that her experience with preachers of his stripe had already left her with bitter memories of inadequacies and failure . . . and maybe she was smiling, too. Was she, after all, secretly enjoying his faltering but desperate attempts to prove himself? While using him for her own ends, was she really watching and waiting for the moment when he would fold under the pressure? Was he to be the final dot for the "i" and the cross for the "t" that would underscore her experience with her missionary father, and thus prove that what had happened to him to make her so bitter was not a fluke, but characteristic of all men who wore the cloth? And what was the sturdy Mabel Stockton thinking of him as she walked along carrying the jelly-pulp of Ida Randolph? She walked so ramrod straight even yet, head high, her glasses winking in the moon-light, one capable arm around the frail stick of a woman, dragging and half lifting her along as though she were a child not wanting to come home. Quiet, meditative, hardly moved—Mabel Stockton—who never expressed an opinion, or showed an emotion, but who moved on in the ponderous attitude of a fatalist accepting what came as part of a universal destiny established at birth. What did such a woman, who ran her life probably on a schoolroom schedule with its certainty of accomplishment, think of him who was linked with the many possibilities of a faith that could see no certain end in any certain way? He would like to know what Mabel Stockton thought about anything—God, baseball, hot dogs, sex—for she was yet the one least open to appraisal, for she had said no more than a half dozen words in the whole trip thus far. But she would be thinking too—watching him, probably thinking how thin the straw is upon which to lean for life. "Well what did you go into the wilderness to see? A reed shaken in the wind?" he wanted to shout back at her even as Christ asked the mob about John the Baptist, only the answer for himself would have to be: "You indeed are seeing a reed shaking horribly in the wind and just pray it doesn't snap in two. . . ."

And as for Ida Randolph . . . well, even in the blind relief that the very vestments of a man of God could command the supernatural, even Ida Randolph would have to wonder now . . . for she was the kind who could be pursuaded from east and west, who wanted to believe the best of God but could become suspicious by the domineering arguments of a Brelsford or Dennison. How many did he have like Miss Randolph in his Wisconsin parish? Those who swallowed his sermons as truth on Sunday but became a bit doubtful when his commands for healing did not raise people from the sick bed? Those who enjoyed the security of the sanctuary and considered him next to God until the tornado ripped off their roof—and suddenly he was a powerless, anemic man reduced to the level of common, weak, victimized humanity as they were? He knew the Ida Randolphs the best . . . and he carried them every day of his ministry like Mabel Stockton carried her now, nursing them along, assuring them, dragging them weeping and terrified down the rugged trail of life, now and then shoving their nose into New Testament promises to show them it wasn't as dark as it seemed. But even in knowing them, he feared them . . . for their loyalties shifted, their support was contingent upon safety and security . . . when pressed, they could make unreasonable demands of God . . . and if conditions got worse here now, Ida Randolph could be the first to crack and her first target would be him . . . the man of God who was supposed to do miracles. . . .

Well, it was too late now . . . and somehow the moment right then seemed to dredge up peculiar voices from other times and places, all adding their own derisive commentary to his position now.

"Football isn't the game for you, son," his father had said. "It's got blood and savagery in it . . . you don't have to run over anybody to prove yourself. . . ."

"You let that old man get beat up out there by those two bullies . . . and call that Christian?" the pretty brunette hurled at him on that campus a long time ago. But she didn't understand—blood and savagery was not his way. . . .

"If you believe in what you preach, then go on down to that city council meeting and tell them your church takes a stand against all that pornographic smut flooding the news stands," Carol had jabbed him that horrible night of rain and thunder. "If you don't, I will!" But she didn't understand either . . . he had to be careful he didn't get involved with political problems. It could get messy fooling with the city bosses . . . the church could get caught in the middle . . . so she had gone, driving that sports car in a mad race to the city hall, he pursuing . . . and then all he saw was the flashing pinwheel of her headlights going over and over . . . and all he had left of her was what came out of that smashed-up car that looked like a ball of tin foil in the ditch . . . a grim, torturing reminder of his pathetic plea for understanding that he was only a man of God. . . .

And suddenly he stopped, and for a moment the rumbling sound in the night was like the thousand voices shouting at him for the failures of his past. Then he heard it again, and he knew it was gunfire, coming from the wadi they had only recently fled from.

He noticed too that the others had stopped and were looking back. He walked back quickly to them, wondering how he should explain that firing or how Barbara Churchill would do it. When he got there, Eaton and Dennison had put Brelsford down on the ground and were bending over him. Now and then their heads would bob up and face toward the strange sounds in the distance.

Brelsford was still unconscious, but he kept moving his head back and forth as though he were hunting for air.

"What's that?" Dennison asked of Sebastian, indicating the sharp staccato of thunder claps that tolled down to them. Sebastian deliberately busied himself with checking Brelsford's dressing, leaving Miss Churchill to explain.

"More Bedouins fighting over that water," she said coolly, but her look at Sebastian said enough, that it was actually Agent Christopher's friends who had run into the water hole and were fighting it out with those Bedouins.

There were a few more dull, paper-bag explosions, then a long volley of continual slamming sounds—and silence.

Sebastian noted that Brelsford's wound still wasn't closing as it ought to. It kept oozing dark blood. He redid the dressing, building more pressure on the bandage and wrapping the adhesive around Brelsford's waist to make it firm.

"We've got to move on, or we'll be run over by them in a minute," he urged then.

"You'll kill him," Dennison challenged, turning back

from his study of the back trail.

"He'll die here just as well."

"We could have had a chance . . . back there!"

"Why argue about it, Dennison? You can hear what's going on back there, and it doesn't sound like a U.N. peace team. We've got a chance to get out of here if we get a move on."

"Do you have the foggiest notion of where you're going?" Dennison snarled turning to cut deeper into the tender nerve endings of Sebastian.

"As much as you do right now, Dennison," he replied, conscious of how the others watched him to see how he reacted to the continual swiping diatribes like this, not really sure of him either.

"And God's given you the compass, I suppose?"

"I follow the Big Dipper, Dennison, and that's as scientific as you can get."

"Ha!" Dennison coughed a gagging kind of laugh as if he'd caught a fly in his throat. "Bir Milhan is about the size of a wart in this desert—you wouldn't hit it even if you were a bird with a bombsight!"

"Perhaps you ought to have this," Eaton cut in then, and extended Brelsford's long aluminum shaft. It was Eaton's own brand of uncomplimentary humor. He and Dennison had no love for each other, but they shared a mutual contempt for God and religion of any form. Eaton's face remained its usual mask of unreadable wrinkled beach sand, and the eyes burned more fiercely as if his head were a Halloween pumpkin with a candle inside.

"I don't think I'll need that," Sebastian fought back doggedly, "I work miracles with both hands free, thank you."

He didn't wait to see what effect that had on Eaton—he knew it wouldn't register anyway. He turned back to Dennison. "Dennison, if you want to do something for Brelsford you can take the first turn carrying him on your back. . . ."

"He's not even conscious, how do you expect him to

158

ride in that position?" Dennison sniped back, not exactly sure if he wanted to go that far for Brelsford.

"He's coming to a little now," Sebastian said. "But to make sure he rides, we'll tie him aboard with adhesive strips."

He didn't wait for Dennison to argue further. He asked Eaton to help get Brelsford up on Dennison's back. Breslford, coming to now, began to mumble, "I won't follow that star . . . I won't follow that star. . . ." They got him up on Dennison's back, tied him on with the adhesive wound around Dennison's shoulders and back. Brelsford was firmly held on like a strapped-down pack.

"Eaton will spell you in a half hour, Dennison," Sebastian said and they moved out again.

There were very few protective hills or wadis now. They were exposed to the scrutiny of sky and moon or whatever or whoever else was there with them. For Sebastian there was only the sound of the water tinkling hollowly in the bottom of one of the aluminum jugs, giving off a mocking lyric, reminding him that when they stopped in a few hours to yield to the sun, there would only be water enough to wet their tongues—that was about it. He didn't want to think about that—visions of what lack of water could do to reducing men to animals was fresh in his mind from all the reading he had once done as a boy. And he didn't want to think about his own nagging thirst, the heaviness in his legs, the flaming swollen tissue in his lungs that kept gagging him even in the cold desert night air. What bothered him most was the honest feeling of terror at the thought of failing them now. . . .

Then he realized that he had come to a line of sand that was humped up like a snow drift, not more than four feet wide and two feet high. He wanted to move his legs through it, but he stood there looking at it, sensing that it was an unusual design in the monotonous flat prairie of sand.

He was about to make his first step into it when Eaton's

voice cut sharply into him from directly behind: "Wait!"

Sebastian paused and turned as Eaton walked up, the long aluminum shaft of Brelsford's in his hand. This then would be Eaton's challenge . . . it had come earlier than expected.

But Eaton moved on a few steps in front of Sebastian, poked the long aluminum shaft in front of him and dug deep into the peculiar sandy ridge. There was a low rumbling sound like the muttering growls of some wild beast, and the sand hill suddenly disappeared with a sighing whisper into a crevass of rock. Sebastian could only stare at the hole where the sand had gone, wondering where he would have been now if he had stepped on it as he intended.

"A million years ago perhaps an earthquake did that, and the earth never healed itself," Eaton explained simply. "It is common in a desert like this. That crevass probably runs a mile with the sand just covering it over in a very flimsy bridge." He paused and then handed the aluminum shaft to Sebastian, "Now, perhaps you really ought to have this."

Sebastian took the shaft without a word, wondering why Eaton didn't let him go down into that awful chasm in the first place. "Thanks," he said, still a bit bewildered by it all, conscious of the ohers behind him, staring at the crevass, watching, wondering, waiting.

Sebastian pushed on then, finding another way around the crevass and proceeding, not even turning to see if the others followed, his mind confused again by the peculiar gesture of Eaton's that didn't really make sense.

He led them for another half hour without a break in stride. He was angling for a small shoulder high outcropping of gray rock when he saw them. There were four camels and on each a white-robed rider. They were not more than fifty yards ahead and off to the right, cutting across their line of march and heading eastward and south. He saw them at the same time that the two schoolteachers were coming abreast of him on his right. Beyond the two women was Dennison laboring under the weight of Brelsford who by now was asking to be put down so he could walk. Sebastian was about to tell them to fall behind to maintain the order of march lest they stumble into another crevass. Now seeing the camel driver, he snapped out at them in a low voice, "Hold it!"

The schoolteachers stopped immediately as if they'd been jolted, because the sound of a human voice in the terrible silence was as electrifying as a peal of thunder. Dennison half staggered to a stop and painfully turned to face Sebastian for an explanation. Eaton moved up next to him, and then Barbara Churchill stopped a little behind them.

"Stand still and don't move," he called to them softly. As long as they stood like that with the gray rocks behind them he had no fear that the camel drivers would see them. And he didn't want to be seen—he had no certainty if they were the same renegades they had encountered earlier at the water hole or more friendly. But the look of the rifles across their saddles said enough.

They stood quietly waiting. Each of them had now probably seen the camels themselves. Sebastian tried to keep his eye on Dennison while watching the camels at the same time. But then, without warning, Dennison made his move. He broke out of the line of protecting rocks, rushing down across the sand, hoping to catch the attention of those camel drivers and make one more attempt at bidding for rescue. He ran with penguinlike waddles, the weight of Brelsford more difficult now. Brelsford, meanwhile, tried to adjust to the new jolting movements, long feet hanging down making him look as hysterically funny as a tall man on a burro.

But Dennison hadn't gotten more than ten yards out before Eaton jumped forward, his movements gliding across the moon-splashed sand. He hit Dennison from the side—Dennison's grunt was loud and protesting, added to by Brelsford's sharp cry of pain as he went down under Dennison. The movement and sound was enough to attract the camel drivers. Their rifles flashed yellow orange, and the thundering sound smashed the night, rolling in long waves across the empty wastes.

Though the shots were wild, Sebastian felt the bullets hit the rocks behind him. He yelled to the others to get down, and immediately Mabel Stockton pushed Ida Randolph to the sand, and Barbara Churchill crouched low, giving the child the protection of her body.

Another volley of rifle fire threw up sand around them, and Sebastian felt a glancing blow on his left side. It spun him out of his crouch into a sprawling slide on his back into the sand. He rolled back over and lay flat, wanting to be sure what the men on the camels were intending to do now. He expected to see them turn and head toward them, firing as they did so. Instead they moved rapidly in the other direction, and it was obvious that the drivers were afraid of what they had stumbled on in this no man's land.

When the thundering sound of the rifle fire died in the cavelike acoustics of the desert night, Sebastian got to his feet to examine himself, not wanting to attract any attention from the others. His left side was a little numb—also very wet. He found no wound, however, and suddenly with a sharp jab of panic realized that the wetness was water. The bullet had gone through the ration bag, and even now the last of the water was leaking out of the container. He felt inside the bag, and his fingers touched the jagged ends of the bullet hole in the flask. He shook the flask once. There was no familiar tinkle anymore.

"Sebastian?" and it was Eaton's voice calling to him from where Dennison and Brelsford were still lying on the sand. As he moved, his mind began to compute rapidly under the fresh stimulus of this new crisis. Those shots in the night had undoubtedly already attracted Agent Christopher's friends—if they were still alive and out there somehow chasing the false lead toward the east and Ain Ghadyan. That meant they'd be changing their course too and heading after them—sure now that they'd been following a dead trail. And now the water . . . how was he going to tell them about that?

He came up to Dennison who was lying holding on to his right knee, for once having nothing to say. Brelsford lay quietly in the sand, a few feet away staring up at them as if waiting for someone to dare a few words of wisdom in this new situation.

"Dennison says he's twisted his knee," Eaton said without feeling. "He got off easy at that. . . ."

"Get up, Dennison," Sebastian said. Dennison didn't move. He lay there staring defiantly at Sebastian, his dirty white bandage around his head offering sharp contrast to the heavy black beard on his cheeks.

"I can't," he said finally, truculently.

Sebastian felt the flush of impatience and irritation then, and his voice took on a strange kind of barb that surprised even himself.

"Dennison, I'm just one hair away from letting you and Brelsford lay right there. If you want your wish now to sit it out and wait for rescue, then I'm all for it. Now for the last time, get on your feet and test the knee!"

Brelsford began to giggle, and it became a torrent of laughter that forced him to grip his side again. "You're out of character, preacher . . . you're beginning to lose your ministerial halo, my friend . . . what'll God think of you talking like that?"

"Dennison?" Sebastian jabbed again, ignoring Brelsford. Dennison waited, not sure if the challenge was serious or not. Then, slowly, he got up, pushing Sebastian's helping hands away. He stood a moment, put his weight down on the knee. "Okay, try walking on it. . . ."

Dennison took his first few steps with shaky, hesitant moves. It was obvious it was painful, but it wasn't seriously crippling him.

"You'll feel better after you walk awhile," Sebastian said.

"We're going on?" Ida Randolph asked from behind,

her voice shrill from the shock of the new encounter with the camel drivers.

"We've got to go on," Sebastian said simply, "We've nowhere else to go right now. . . ."

"Then . . . could I have just a drop of water, Mr. Sebastian?" she pleaded, her voice going into that whimpering appeal of a child.

"Not now," Sebastian said gently. "We have to watch every drop . . . we'll need it more tomorrow." He didn't figure that was a lie. There was perhaps a bottom cover in the flask that he was going to hold on to for the child.

"We need water," Dennison said then with menace in his voice, and there was an added note to it indicative of the burning madness rising in him. "If you want to keep us moving, then we've got to have something to wet our mouths . . . you've been holding out long enough."

Dennison moved limpingly closer in toward Sebastian. His body was tilting forward, his hands coming up, the bandaged one swinging ahead like a club. Sebastian stood waiting, a lump of fear rising in his throat, for the moment was close now, the moment when their animal drives took over from their weakened dying human instincts.

"Dennison, don't be a fool," he tried, and at the same instant Dennison made his lunge. He tried mainly for the water bag, but his body hit Sebastian hard in the ribs, and he went down. He fought to hold the ration bags, but Dennison's clawing, animallike desperation was too much. He felt the bags ripped off his shoulder, and as he fought to get up again he sensed the confusion around him. Through the dust and blurring image of shadowy figures moving against one another, he caught Eaton there throwing Dennison aside as if he were no bigger challenge than a kitten. Mabel Stockton was fighting to hold on to Ida Randolph who was screaming to get hold of that water bag herself, and Barbara Churchill was standing next to her holding the child close as if trying to keep this horrible sound and sight from the infant.

Sebastian stood up and saw Dennison sprawled a few

feet away, the aluminum flasks turned spout down in his hands—the little trickle of water that was left falling into the sand. Hungrily Dennison tried to get his mouth under the spout—but there wasn't enough even to make the effort worthwhile.

Dennison held the two flasks up in his hands, waving them for all to see, turning them upside down to emphasize the disaster. "No water!" he screamed. "Not a drop left! You were stringing us along all the time! You've got us out here now without one drop of water . . . you've taken us five miles away from it, and you knew all the time there wasn't enough!"

"Look at the flask, Dennison!" Sebastiam tried cutting into the rising hysteria of the man. "It's got a bullet hole in it—I caught that in the last barrage from those camel drivers. We had enough for another ration or more up to then. . . ."

"Shut up!" Dennison railed back, and he threw the flasks at Sebastian, but they sailed on by harmlessly. He got up and made another lunge toward Sebastian, but his knee gave away and he sprawled out in the sand. He lay there, his body shaking with the sobs that were muffled in the sand, and the sight of a grown man broken like that left them all numbed, bewildered, and silent. Ida Randolph's jerky, moaning gasps rode above Dennison's, and then the child began to whimper in coughing cries, and it was like hearing the torments of hell to Sebastian.

Then above it all came Brelsford's piercing laugh, strung up on the new octave of madness that was peculiarly Brelsford's in this hour. "Why don't you pray, preacher?" and his voice carried a note of triumph as if he were crowing in the face of their hopeless condition and the defeat that was so resoundingly Sebastian's. "Go ahead—we'll wait, preacher! Now's your time to produce the miracle! Make Him listen to you—that is, if you can find Him! Or maybe He isn't there, Sebastian . . . maybe He's nowhere at all. . . ."

Brelsford began to cough and his loud, challenging

165

invective died in his throat. But it hung in the air nevertheless, mingling with the smell of gunpowder and the broken spirits of Dennison and Ida Randolph and the mournful pleadings of the child, It was there, hung out for them all, and Sebastian felt the weight of the questions they were undoubtedly forming for him, questions he couldn't answer.

Sebastian waited awhile, giving them time to let the jarring notes of the raging action dilute themselves in the quiet of the desert. They sat around listlessly, each of them reflecting on the meaning of their condition now without water, projecting perhaps into the future hours or days when their own bodies and spirits would break like Dennison's.

After awhile, then, Sebastian asked Eaton to help get Brelsford tied on his back. Eaton did as he was told, lashing Brelsford on Sebastian's body with the adhesive strips. Sebastian tried to think of something to say to encourage them to press on, but everything that came to mind sounded so empty, especially in the light of Brelsford's howling commentary on the hopelessness of even expecting God to do anything.

So they walked on, stumbling after him only because it was better than sitting there to face death. "And the parched ground shall become a pool." Brelsford's mocking whisper sounded in Sebastian's ear as they walked. "And the thirsty land springs of water; in the habitation of dragons where each lay, shall be grass and reeds and rushes . . . don't forget that promise of Isaiah that you read, preacher. Don't you smell the humidity? There's water someplace—only a few hundred feet down maybe . . . all you got to do is follow your star . . . right, Sebastian?"

And it went that way for the slow, agonizing steps Sebastian walked, his mind trying to shut off that grating ridicule. He tried to answer Brelsford with Scripture of his own that spelled promise—but the pressing weight of the man on him shut off his breath. He was a helpless victim of Brelsford's contradictions, of his own wandering spirit and the build-up of dreadful circumstances that had only one design—failure.

And he was hearing something else too . . . when Brelsford's voice lapsed . . . just faintly . . . and he stopped several times to listen, turning once to watch the others to see if they heard it . . . none of them apparently did . . . except for Miss Churchill who looked over her shoulder . . . but it was there all right, and only the ears of the two of them would catch it for they were expecting it . . . the sound of motors, growling far in the distance and traveling over the sharp, cold aerial of the desert air . . . pursuit was there, closing fast . . . men in mechanized equipment, armed men who would kill to protect their own interests in search of Christopher . . . they who would perhaps mercifully end it all and spare them the future agony at the hands of this relentless desert. . . .

So now, oh, man of God, product of thin clay that is crushed in light breezes, which way shall you die? It was that simple. And he turned to look back and caught Eaton directly behind him, and he saw the thin smile on his face, the smile of awareness . . . yes, Eaton knew too, about pursuing vehicles and also the vanishing vestiges of leadership that Sebastian was feeling now. . . .

So which way shall you die? And take with you the bitter bile of your company and the horror of knowing that God is not here. . . .

* 10 *

The moon was well past its zenith, hanging frosty bright in
the blue ice that surrounded the Negev at night. Sebastian called a halt when he stumbled over a small rise of
sand and found a jutting mound of fortresslike rock forming a kind of half circle. Off to his left was a long line of
jagged, sawtooth mounds that pointed like stalagmites
toward the sky. "That's the end of Wadi Iqfi," Brelsford's
voice mocked in his ear. "That's your last hope . . . beyond
that is a long valley of death, the South Negev. . . ."

The rest of the party had already shown their gradual
surrender to the debilitation that the Negev exacted. It
was three days since the crash, and they were stumbling
wearily, unable to hold up from lack of food and from lack
of the water this desert seemed to demand relentlessly.
Ida Randolph was continually falling to the sand, and it
was getting harder for Mabel Stockton to help her up.
Even Barbara Churchill's usual confident, strong stride
was beginning to shorten, and there was some hesitation
in her movement as though she weren't able to make each
step fall into line. Only Eaton walked strong and deliberate, as if all this were but child's play, and even when he
had Dennison leaning on him, he made it appear that he
could carry the group and not miss a step or falter in the
least. It was such demonstration of strength that was

bringing Eaton to a center from which they could draw extra energy and will. It was Eaton's determination, too, that forced Sebastian not to wilt even though he carried a horribly wearing burden in Brelsford. It was suddenly very important that he did not yield now—and it was for this reason he saw the need for rest to gather his own dissipated energies.

They all dropped quickly to the sand behind the small rocks, lying sprawled out in various poses, pulling their blankets around them, and moaning softly in their agonies. Sebastian let Brelsford down carefully after Eaton ripped off the binding adhesive straps. Then he broke out what food he was able to salvage from the ration bags, but none of them took it with any enthusiasm. It was water that was preoccupying them now—the fish only seemed to add to their thirst. Sebastian urged them to take it for the strength it could give them. He noted their lips now, all swollen, blackened by the lack of water or else cracked open and ulcerated. Their eyes, too, showed the dull glaze of people who were already giving in to the inevitable. There were no arguments now, no points of advice, no questions, no indication of their will to survive. They were sputtering candles trying to keep the flame alive on already melted wax. It was going to be harder now to get them up again.

He checked over the child and found much to his dismay that there was not much to be done for her. She lay in her blankets feebly giving off hoarse whimpers. The tender skin on her face had been cruelly bitten by the sun leaving large welts that oozed jelly-like fluid. Her mouth was puffed up and red, and the little tongue reached out for some touch of wetness. Sebastian didn't look at Barbara Churchill. He knew what he would see there—that the child had only a matter of hours left without water. And Brelsford likewise was a case study in agony. His wound, though clotted, had drained off what precious body fluid he had in reserve—now he could only lie there, his mouth hanging open, his tongue swollen and almost black looking, flicking out now and then to try to wet his cracked lips.

As for himself, Sebastian felt the thousand jabbing spikes running through his aching muscles from the long haul with Brelsford on his back. Burning shafts up his back from his groin when he tried to walk, and when he tried to focus on anything he found that there was either blurred or double vision.

He ministered to them as best he could, saying nothing, for anything now would sound irrelevant or ridiculous in the light of their circumstances. After he had finished, he walked up to the rocks and climbed over them to sit on a small sand hill that overlooked the way they had come. He sat there, his arms folded against the cold, staring out into the silence of the night. There was no sound of motors now. That was strange. But he didn't try to figure that out, it was far too much to even think about in the light of his own preoccupation with survival.

He finally pulled out his Bible and in the dim light of the moon thumbed through the Old Testament record, picking out verses that might emerge as God's direction for the hour. He read about Isaac and his wells, and Hagar who had a well of water appear before her eyes in this same desert. He jumped from one passage to the other, trying to draw from each some assurance, some hope, waiting for God to illuminate by His own miraculous way. But the more he read the more he became convinced that it wouldn't come this way. He felt like a dying man running through the promises in the Book, hoping to use one as an argument to God for life.

He closed the Bible and tried prayer. His soul cried out, but no words came. Something would form way deep inside him, but would not rise to his lips. It was as if everything framed in his thoughts was not applicable, and he suddenly felt himself totally cut off from any sense of God, any presence, any contacts at all that might diffuse new hope within himself. All he felt now was incrimination of his past, his years of ministering in the noncritical areas of life, of pontificating on those safe and sure postulates that never demanded proof. And he knew then that his prayers couldn't form on his lips because they were words that were trite, meaningless, words addressed for the God of the comfortable, safe, and sure way of life he had in Nashville. He knew nothing of the God in crisis, the God of the Negev, the God of the impossible—he had reshaped God to his own form of Santa Claus and Easter bunny who could deliver gaily wrapped packages and chocolate eggs but who couldn't be counted on to alter the agony of the human condition. How then could he pray to God here, a different God in his own mind altogether, a God he had never tried, proved, or seen work anywhere?

Suddenly he felt another presence with him, and he looked up to see Eaton standing there a few feet away. He would have chosen anyone but Eaton right then, for there was no real way to cope with the man's overpowering sureness. And Sebastian knew too what Eaton had come to say.

"You see it too?" Eaton said, and Sebastian looked up, following the line of Eaton's finger across the purple lavender and pale lime of the desert. At first he saw nothing, but then the winking flickering strip far out became a solid ball of orange, glowing with consistency.

"It's a fire," Sebastian said, knowing full well now who that had to be out there.

"Of course," Eaton said confidently, as if he had built it himself. "The same people who have been following us for days—would you say so, Mr. Sebastian?"

"Wild Bedouins don't give up easily," Sebastian said, feeling himself slowly becoming impaled on Eaton's attitude of command now.

"It may be . . . but I suggest to you, Mr. Sebastian, that Bedouins do not build fires that size in a night so filled with mystery. . . ."

Sebastian stood up then, wanting to meet Eaton's challenge and dissolve it in the shortest time possible. He did not think he could win on a long encounter with the German. There was too much truth on his side already.

"Look, Eaton, I know that you are Heinrich Zimmerman," he began then. "Sparks told me all about you before he died. He thought I should know because he felt you'd be a key factor sooner or later."

This time Eaton actually tried a smile, but the lips only curled back across the teeth as if the corners of his mouth could not respond or as if the ability to smile genuinely had been dulled by years of unuse. "He is quite right. I am the key. I say that with honest self-appraisal. I fought with Rommel in the Libyan frontier. I served in the Afrika Korps three years. I know this kind of battle, Sebastain. . . ."

"Okay," Sebastian said with a sigh. "Now you've come to offer me your leadership, right?"

"It is obvious you cannot make Bir Milhan this way. . . ."

"So what is your way, Eaton? Dump Brelsford, Dennison, and the child? Lighten the load for the sake of a few? The old Nazi way, General Zimmerman?"

"I have considered that . . . they will die anyway, Sebastian. There are five of us who could make it. This is more like a military operation—sacrifice the weak for the strong. It is a principle I have used when situations call for it."

"Yes, well, Auschwitz and Buchenwald will testify to that all right. . . ."

"I had nothing to do with that!" Eaton snapped, suddenly bristling with defensiveness.

"All right, all right," Sebastian said. "Well, let me tell you right off that I don't accept your leadership. I don't intend to change horses at this point in the stream. We'll all go out together or die together. I may not be a general or know all about deserts, and I wish I did, but right now I'm getting a kind of stubborn streak that tells me we're going to get out of here. And even though I know you can do it better, Eaton, I know that once you get the lead the real

Herr Zimmerman of the Nazi world view will take over, and I would not even wish that on that wild, renegade crowd of Bedouins out there. So as long as I have two feet under me, Eaton—General Zimmerman—you'll fall in behind me like the rest."

Eaton stood in silence a long minute, his eyes shining their usual mocking green challenge. "Of course, words do not count for anything here, Mr. Sebastian. You can sound brave and make big, bold statements—but when it comes to action it will be different. Your sentiments as a clergyman blind you to the facts, Mr. Sebastian. You cannot make such sentiments work here where men become animals," and Eaton's voice began to rise with the intensity of his argument. "The love of God and appeals to common decency do not work here! It is the harsh facts of life that I have learned when you were yet a boy—these people must be treated on the level that their environment dictates, which demands an emerging personality who must lead with ruthless power and authority. And sooner or later I will emerge—I will emerge! I am trying to spare you the pain and ignominy of being removed by them—when their desperation drives them to hurt, kill, destroy! I know men in deserts, what lack of food and water can do. . . !

"So I should thank you, Eaton," Sebastian replied, feeling the smarting dig of the words that were more true than he was willing to admit.

"We cannot make it under your leadership!" Eaton snarled in a low, raspy voice.

"Then you'll just have to wait until I'm removed, Eaton," Sebastian retaliated. "Because I don't intend to yield to you or anyone else. Is that understood?"

He waited a moment staring hard across the gulf between them, as if really not sure Sebastian had refused him. Then he was gone as quietly as he had come.

It had left him shaken, so that he gripped his cold hands tighter together to stop their trembling. He stared at the flickering fire across the desert, almost mesmerized by it now as his mind began to clear and something strange began to take shape.

He felt Barbara Churchill sit down a few feet from him, but he didn't look at her immediately. He kept his eyes on the fire, feeling out into depths of thought he hadn't dared to contemplate and which now struck him with a shaft of both revelation and some terror.

"You heard what went on?" he asked then.

"Yes."

"And you see the fire?"

"I saw it at the same time Eaton did."

"Well, is it Bedouins?"

"No," she said with a weary sigh, as if it didn't matter anymore. He had never seen or heard her yield in that way before. She rested her arms on her drawn-up knees and put her chin down on them to stare at the fire as though she were taking a specific sighting of it like a navigator. It was strange to see the normally defiant tilt to her head now bowed under the pressure. "Eaton is right," she added. "Bedouins wouldn't build a fire that size for any reason."

"So it has to be our friends then—and they're really trying to make a point with that fire, or else they've got a lot of marshmallows. . . ."

She didn't even acknowledge his attempt at humor, if she heard it at all. "It's obviously a signal to our man Christopher—letting him know they're there."

"Yes, Eaton seemed to know when it was going to come too. He came up here and pointed it out before they struck the first match. I think Eaton's our man all right." He waited for her to confirm or reject it. When she didn't, he went on, "And it bears out why he wants to run this show. He wants to step up the pace, get ahead of those people out there, for some reason only he knows. He doesn't figure he can do it with me in charge worrying over Ida Randolph or fussing over Brelsford. . . ."

"Then why doesn't he just go on by himself?" she asked, her voice almost dreamy as if she'd been chasing around these same thought corridors for some time and coming up with no positive answers.

"Because he's not sure he'll find Bir Milhan either," he added, "and because he can't find these. . . ."

He pulled out the packet of airline navigational charts wrapped in plastic that Brelsford had had on him, held them up for her to see. She turned her head, her chin still resting on her knees. She looked at the charts, then at him, and for a moment she appeared interested in the fact that he was thinking and acting on his own. "So he's stuck with us," he went on, driving home to her the significance of it all as if she didn't know. "And as long as he is, he's going to try to move us along, to stay ahead of his not too friendly friends. Now does that make sense?"

"You can build a similar sensible pattern around any of them," she warned. "I'll wait to be sure."

He paused, wishing she would concur more positively. And, then, feeling it was time to give vent to his slowly building decision, he said, "Apart from Eaton's possible role as Christopher, he said some things that make sense."

"Like what?"

"I think you know what I mean—the group won't follow me any more unless I can hold out a better promise of survival or drive them beyond themselves. I think you realize it too. And you've had enough experience with your clergyman father to know that I can't get that ruthless. . . ."

"You answered Eaton well enough on that point," she allowed, but not with any real enthusiasm.

"What would your father have done in a case like this?" he tried then, trying to find a launching point for what had to come now.

She lifted her head off her hands as though he had lightly touched an exposed nerve. "He would not have gotten this far," she said, keeping her eyes on the fire in the distance.

"He would not think so."

"But you would. . . ?"

"Yes, but I don't think that concerns us now."

"Then why did you think I would go so far?"

"I didn't. You were all I had, I told you that once. I never believed you would actually go this far."

"And you don't think I can go any further?"

She waited a long time before answering. "We haven't much choice," she said.

"You have an amazing capacity for evading direct questions and answers."

"Perhaps it's my way of trying to be kind," she shot back at him, her voice rising to a sharp edge now. "Anyway, where is this senseless chatter getting us?"

She was right, of course. They'd chased each other long enough around this same philosophical pylon. He waited a moment, and then he said, "How many vehicles do you figure they've got out there—Christopher's friends, I mean."

"Two or three, I suppose," she answered, going back to her study of the fire.

"And how many men?"

"Maybe a dozen." Now she lifted her head and turned to look at him. "Why?"

"Well, let me sum it up again," and he was glad at last that he had her waiting for him rather than the other way around. "One, our man Christopher, who is probably Eaton, is going to pull that gun on us pretty soon and demand these navigational charts, because he figures we can't get out of here alive now. Two, when daylight comes those agents out there are going to be right on top of us, and that's the finish of us. Three, we can't go another step with this group in the shape we're in without water and some form of transportation. How's that for deduction by a way-out minister?"

"If you are thinking of running into that enemy camp and walking off with their water and transporation, you are acting like a man suffering sunstroke." And there was actual incredulity in her voice.

"Well, it's what we're going to have to do," he said with finality.

"What chapter and verse did you get that from?" she flung back at him, and she made no attempt to cover her feelings for what he represented now.

He gave a half-grunting laugh to admit the point. "Well, I was doing just that awhile ago, running through the Book as if it were a bag of miracles, looking for the one that fit. You know, as you called me once, a biblical band-aid peddler, although I still wouldn't put it quite like that. Only I didn't get any magic directions to a water hole or a drive-in. All I got was Eaton running up here and pointing to that fire—and just like that it was as if that were all the glimmer I was going to get, and maybe that's all I can expect."

"It's not enough," she returned bluntly. "What do you expect to do, walk into that enemy camp and tell them you're a minister and say 'please give me a cup of cold water and a Land Rover in the name of God'?"

She was swinging at him now with sharp, verbal jabs, as if all her bitter experiences with her father had forced her to the point of total exasperation.

"I don't know what I'm going to do," he admitted, keeping his voice quiet but firm. "But I don't think it will be that way."

"What other way is there for you?" she demanded, and she half leaned towards him to put emphasis to her words, acting like a mother would with an impractical child who couldn't see why sand castles had to dissolve on seashores. "Those people out there aren't pro-God, my friend. They are ruthless killer machines who know how to protect their property and don't mind who they chop into confetti in the process!"

"Every man is capable of a little more when he has no choice," he reasoned doggedly.

"Every man?" she challenged, and she stood to her feet now as if sitting down would not do justice to all that she had to say. "I beg to differ with you there."

"We ministers may not be as bad as you think," he tried lamely.

"I don't question the desire," and she allowed some modification which didn't help much, "but I doubt the will and the necessary ingredient that will put you far enough over the line to actually affect our percentages in pulling it off."

He paused, because he had no direct answer to that. He didn't know if he had the necessary ingredient either. He hadn't really thought that far ahead.

He finally stood up himself, because it was important to face her directly with this, and it was certain he could get no confidence sitting at her feet at this point.

"You once said back there that you'd gamble on my willingness to try another life-saving operation with Brelsford. Well, I'm saying now that I'm ready."

She turned her back on him then, to stare out into the desert night, trying to dismiss the rest of his argument or hide her own mounting emotions from him.

"It's not the same. Let's be honest," she chided, her head lifted to the stars. "What you did for Brelsford and what you're suggesting now are two entirely different situations in depth and degree."

There was finality in her voice. And truth. He felt uncertain again. She had no intention of sanctioning what he suggested on the slim margin of success that he offered by his way of life. There were certain limits within which she would expect some performance from him, and at that she would have to prod him into it. She was a bit taken aback by his daring proposal, and perhaps this was why she chose to keep her back to him . . . to keep him from detecting her bafflement about what he suggested. Still, it did not alter her own conception of his ability or the actual commitment to accomplish it.

"I intend to try it with or without you," he declared, putting final resolution in his voice.

"Just to prove you can get involved?" she whipped back at him, not allowing him to build up momentum for his position. "Just to prove something to Eaton, to me, to the rest? Isn't that a bit selfish?"

"Perhaps it is," he countered, fighting to cut through her bristling command of the situation, and perplexed that she would fight him so hard on this when it was undoubtedly obvious to her that this was the only way. "But I'm thinking of survival too—I'm thinking of the child, of Brelsford. . . ."

"Brelsford?" she cut back with a snort. "Don't force charity to that extent, please. . . ."

"All right, don't ask me for all the definitions about my feelings. There isn't time," he said, snipping off her desire to build on that incongruity. He waited a moment to gather himself, to pick up the thoughts that had been pounding deep into his soul since the crash, but more lately since he had led them south. "I know how you feel about the church . . . you apparently figure all preachers are like your father, people incapable of rising to the crisis situations that demand involvement with the blood and exposed membrane of suffering humanity. You figure us to be made of cheap china anyway, people with low breaking points. And maybe you're right. But the fact remains that the dye is cast. You cast it yourself. You shoved me up front to be your prop, for what reasons I can only surmise. Now the whole thing is out of control."

He moved up behind her now so that he was staring at the nape of her neck, and he noted the deep tan of her skin, the contrast of the golden, luminosity of her hair against it. He felt a sweep of tenderness towards her, and he wanted to put his hands on her shoulders to try to reach her with his deep feelings right now, to try to pour some balm on her hurt, to get her off that spear of bitterness upon which she was impaled.

"For you see now, don't you, that I've got to follow through with this. Because to the rest of them, I'm it. Even Eaton knows that. They don't like it, they don't even want it—but I'm it just the same.

"I'll admit something else too—something you probably detected way back there at the wreck that first night when I tried to get off the hook, remember? Up to this point I've not been much of a minister—I've played it safe in the clutches, demanding nothing of God and expecting nothing in return. I was representing a Christ who died a neat, sophisticated death on a church steeple with the organ playing, rather than one who died on a garbage dump to the sound of a cursing, vile humanity. So I've come all this way to find out what it smells like, tastes like, to share that suffering. It's taken me awhile to realize that there won't be any quick seminary solutions to this one, and I know that I can't expect any miracle from God bigger than what I'm prepared to do to be a practical solution to this problem. So I've got to do it, because my whole spiritual life hangs on it—and I'll be honest with you, again, I don't even know what I'm going to do when I get out there among those people, except maybe die, and I'm not sure I can even do that very well."

He waited for some response to that—a change in the ramrod, defiant stiffness of her body, that resistant tilt to her head that said she was remaining adamant in her position. After awhile her head dropped from its upward angle of pride and defiance, and he thought it was the first indication of yielding. But her voice was gone flat, toneless, as though she had suddenly become disillusioned with everything.

"We can't disappear without arousing suspicion," she said, and it was one last attempt to head him off.

"Eaton's the only one we have to worry about," he replied. "And I doubt that he'll move without those charts or water. And what's more he'll probably be content to sleep it off, waiting to take his chances with his friends in the morning. How much time to daylight, do you figure?"

She didn't answer for a long time. She stood there as though listening to something a long way off, perhaps that which echoed back from her past, maybe to a like conversation, to other moments of encounter like this with her father.

"About four hours."

"Well, that's a good margin to work in."

She turned then and faced him, and he saw the warning signals flying in her eyes, the flash of new fires that had erupted during the exchange. She had it controlled all right, to a steady even heat, and he felt it, and he knew then that whatever experiences she had had with her father had left her with deep prejudices and smoldering resentment.

"I will only add one condition to that so-called glimmer of inspiration," she said in that clipped, precise manner that was characteristic of her when she was angry. "Any fool can go out there and die. That's an easy way out and a kind of cheap demonstration of involvement as far as I'm concerned. I don't intend to follow you out there to witness your voluntary crucifixion so that you can make up for your shoddy past. If you want to prove anything to this group, then you'll have to go out there and come out alive. If you think on that for a minute, maybe you'll want to change your mind!"

He blinked at her, awed by her almost vehement, slashing words. He wasn't sure he caught the significance of them, but as he let it filter down through his tired brain, he began to catch something of the reasonableness of the intimation. She knew it was impossible for him to try this and live, since he was neither schooled or conditioned for this kind of action, and this only made it more serious for her. For if he did fail and died out there, that would put her and the others in worse shape than they were now. And it also meant she would probably die or be taken prisoner—and that meant failing her assignment in getting either Christopher or that film or both.

He was conscious of her eyes holding on him as he waited for him to respond. He turned once to look at the fire beckoning like a bold pennant in the distance, catching the winking derisive commentary of it too. Perhaps she was right—maybe dying was easier than trying to live through it. But the contemplation of it didn't paint any promises for him—he wanted to live as strongly as she.

"I don't make good martyr material, God knows," he said, "and I want to live as strongly as you want that film back from Christopher."

The honest admission didn't seem to do much to cut her defiance. She turned her back on him again, as if to say that was not enough either, an attempt to dismiss his whole suggestion too. And it was then that he knew that it had to be something else. It didn't make sense that she should dig in so deliberately, running cross-grained to the way she'd prodded him into leadership all this time, and suddenly demur when the big step was before them. There were ghostly shapes of the reason in the back of his mind, and he wanted to articulate it, to be sure of her, to confront her with the double image he had of her that was so profoundly visible now.

He paused to rub a shaky hand across his forehead that was strangely hot in the fierce cold of the desert night, debating whether to say it, to probe this delicate channel—whether there was really time or whether he was ruthless enough to pursue it, because he did not want to hurt her. But looking at the hard, adamant rigidness of her back, he didn't have the heart to thrust into it with any words that would bend her. And anyway, he wasn't sure—it was only a speculation. If he was wrong, it could alienate her—perhaps for good. If he was right, she would never forgive him for clipping the chords of her pride, humbling her, adding to her already heavy responsibility the shame of having been found out.

"Well, as Sparks said, be Caesar within thyself," he said, putting that tone of lightness back into his voice. He picked up Brelsford's aluminum shaft and started out for the fire in the distance. He was aware that she did not follow, and he felt that she was probably waiting for him to change his mind or debating whether she should share this with him.

But after awhile, he felt her even, rhythmic footsteps in the sand behind him. But she did not come up to his side.

She stayed a few feet behind, as though she were unwilling to be a partner in this, but merely coming along to prove him, to be a kind of detached observer, to fill in what he needed—nothing more. It was not a time for detachment—he needed all he could get in terms of comradeship, unity of purpose, and action. And the night had suddenly grown colder, the prospects of the coming encounter and violence even darker.

"But whatsoever thy hand findeth to do, then do it with all thy might. . . .

"O, God, strengthen these hands, these trembling, palsied hands. . . ."

* 11 *

They walked in silence, the sand sounding like the swish of silk under their feet. Now and then Sebastian paused to test the sand ridges ahead of him with the aluminum stick to make sure there were no hidden crevasses. He would have liked to talk to her about other things, her own life, her father, her spiritual beliefs, what she did for relaxation, if she liked classical music, sports. Because violence was soon to be on them, and while he would like to declare himself sure of living through this, he could not assume the same for her. In fact, the more he walked the more he realized that they might both die, because those people out there, as she had warned, were not particularly anxious to make it any easier for them.

But there was no natural opening to her at all. There never really had been. But now it seemed that she was even more deliberately removed, more detached, almost completed in her isolation from him. It was as if she were sure he was going to die, and she didn't want any intimate remembrances to carry back with her; or else she was finding it difficult to do anything else after the way she had raked him back at the camp. Then again it could be that their mission now offered no platform on which to meet casually. It was hardly the time or the place to engage in meaningless conversation. So he let it go at that—and tried concentrating on what lay ahead.

As they drew nearer to the fire, he became aware of the fact that a sentry would have no problem spotting them a mile out. There was no cover, and the sand was white in the moonlight so that they offered a perfect target against it. But there was nothing to do but go on, trusting that the night watch would stay by the fire rather than out in the icy night of the desert.

Now, as they drew within a few hundred yards of the camp site, he saw the sharp rock silhouetted against the fire. That would help. He needed some way to approach the camp.

When he crossed over the crevass that Eaton had saved him from earlier, he dropped down on one knee to survey the ground ahead. He felt her hang back, waiting. He wanted to ask her a few questions because of his uncertainty at this point, to feel a sense of involvement from her, even to honestly get her opinions. But he knew he wouldn't and couldn't. He had to call this his way now, and she was deliberately impressing him with that fact.

He took the time to get his strength back. His knees felt as soft as putty, and his hands trembled where he gripped the aluminum shaft. He tried not to think of his thirst and that painful throbbing knot deep in the pit of his stomach. His mind had difficulty fixing on any one thought, and he knew he had to start forming some line of action for that moment when he got to the camp site.

"I think we better crawl in from here," he said, half to himself, half to her. She didn't answer, so he got down on all fours and began the slow, awkward journey sometimes on his stomach, at others on his hands and knees or a low crouch. Now and then he felt her movement behind him, and once she touched his feet as he crawled. He stopped to look back, but she only stared back at him without saying a word. He turned and moved on.

When they got to the foot of the rocky mound that arched up over them to a height of twenty-five to thirty feet, he turned to motion her up beside him. She came,

185

moving in those same gliding motions on her stomach, and he marvelled again how her body could be so well coordinated even after the ordeal of the desert.

"We might as well move up together and take a look," he said softly to her. "I don't think there's a guard here anywhere—he's probably by the fire." She gave a curt nod in response, and he turned and slowly inched his way up the sandy incline, feeling against his palms the scrape of the rock that jutted up underneath. When he was at the crest, he waited until she was next to him and said, "Okay, let's have a look see. . . ."

The first thing he saw below him was the fire, shooting up out of a large barrel that must have been used for fuel at one time. Dirty black puffs of smoke came from it in jerky spurts as if from the stack of a steam engine. Undoubtedly they were feeding the fire with gas or oil, judging by the smoke, and that was the reason for its rising to such gigantic heights earlier.

His eyes shifted around the fire, trying to count the still forms in the brown woolen blankets. "I count six," he said to her in a half whisper.

"Eight," she responded after a few seconds, her breath now warm on his right ear. "Over there . . . two of them across the fire near the Land Rover. . . ."

He shifted his glance quickly, saw the other two sleeping forms lying near the olive green vehicle.

"The guard," she said, then, touching his arm, and he followed her quickly extended forefinger and saw him sitting on the small packing case beyond the fire, a rifle across his knees. He was dressed in the brown woolens of the Middle Eastern military, with a heavy jacket wrapped close around him and a khaki hood over his head. Now and then his head jerked as he fought to hold off sleep.

"He's about out," Sebastian said. "Suppose he's the only one?"

"There ought to be another one somewhere," she replied, and even in a whisper her voice didn't sound any more interested than if she was giving a guided tour and

186

pointing out the sights. "They wouldn't trust to one guard with those Bedouins around."

They waited, watching, looking for some sign of the other man, never really knowing if he would come on them right there from behind and below. After five minutes or so, during which he sought out some plan in his own mind, which had gone blank in this entirely new and strange arena, she touched his arm again. Another soldier came walking in from the farther direction, blowing on his hands. He came into the arc of the fire, kicked at the dozing sentry who jerked awake and swung his gun up with flashing movements. There was an exchange of conversation which Sebastian did not understand.

"Arabic," she said, anticipating his query.

They waited while the second guard lit a cigarette, warmed his hands over the fire, then walked back to whence he had come. He said something else to the guard on the packing case. They both laughed.

"He said that when light comes they'll have something to shoot at," she explained.

"Meaning us, I trust?"

"Undoubtedly."

"Humm—and just when I was thinking they didn't really look so bad after all." She didn't comment, and he added, "I can't figure how they know we are out here, so close to them. . . ."

"That will explain it," she said and pointed to a small boxlike object about four feet high half covered with canvas.

"What is it?"

"A seismographic sonic detector," she replied, "if I see it right. . . ."

He swung his head around to look at her. "A what?"

"It's a machine the Russians perfected in their work in finding underground streams in the Siberian peninsula. We captured one from the Egyptians on a night patrol a few years back. It can pick up the sound of a cat on sand five miles away."

He turned back to look at the boxlike thing, letting that sink in for a moment, realizing afresh that he was dealing with people who were taking no chances on Christopher getting out from under them—or for that matter any of them in the party. He felt a shiver of apprehension as the night, building with complications, bore heavily down on him. It was time now to come up with something. And fast. Every second they stayed there lowered their chances of success.

"What's that machine over there?" he asked, pointing to another bulkier, awkward-looking vehicle on the opposite side of camp, on top of the gradual hill facing out where the last guard had gone.

"Half-track—it's built for rugged terrain and has rear tractor treads for better traction in sand."

"Would that be better for us?"

"Too complicated to get started, and it's in the wrong position for a quick getaway."

She kept giving him the answers in those same crisp responses, her voice up but under a whisper. He wanted to think there was some sense of mutual adversity coming through from her, a sense of comradeship, some indication that she could at least forget all her bitterness and pride in this moment that brought them closer to death by the second. But all that came through was her inflexible bond to duty—she was not seeing men, feeling relationships, or considering percentages. She was performing within her duty as an agent of the Israeli Secret Police—and she was making that more obvious now than she ever had.

He swung his gaze back to study the Land Rover to the left, then back to the right where a dozen jerricans sat on the lip of the small sand crater overlooking the camp.

"Those cans," he said, "water or gasoline?"

"Petrol without a doubt." Then, after a pause she took up the initiative of interrogation for the first time, "What are you thinking?"

For the moment, he wished he could just lie there with

the warmth of her body close to his, her lips not far from his ear, pretending this was a beach and he had nowhere to go, and if he thought long enough he might hear an ocean surf, smell the wetness—and maybe even allow the exhilaration of her nearness to sweep through him offering the pleasurable deviation from the pressures of the moment.

"We better try for the Land Rover," he told her. "Is it Egyptian made?"

"Looks more like Czech to me," she replied.

"What about ignition?"

"It's got its own built-in switch. You don't need keys."

He nodded. That was a big problem out of the way.

"All right," he whispered, giving off with a sigh as he made up his mind, "this is the way we'll play it. You go around back of those gas—petrol—cans. The fire is low enough for you to get in close enough to uncork one. Pour out the petrol down the rocky crest there toward the fire. You'll have to pour fast enough so it won't sink in the sand—but if you do, when it hits the bottom of the barrel where the draft holes are, the flames will shoot back and ignite the rest of the dump. That should create enough uproar to allow me to get that Land Rover started and moving. . . ."

"It's too risky," she stated conclusively.

"For me or the Jewish nation?" he shot back, hoping that it might be the former.

She ignored the remark. "How are you going to get into that Land Rover, crank it up, and get moving with those two soldiers sleeping ten feet from it?"

"That's my problem," he replied, knowing full well that it did look like a very long shot.

"Then let me do it," she insisted, "I've had more training at this kind of thing."

"You're also too valuable to the cause," he countered. "If anyone is going to get hurt or even killed, it might just as well be me. You've still got Christopher to think about when this is over. . . ."

189

"So if you fail, I'm no better off," she reminded him curtly.

"Well, if I fail, you can try for the half-track. There'll be enough confusion for you to get to it and make a run for it. But be sure of one thing—when you see me move that Land Rover out, you get back around this rock and be ready to jump aboard. I don't intend to stop that thing once I get it started. Now—let's start counting off to a slow three hundred when I give the word. . . ."

"What about the half-track?" she cut in, concern and urgency in her throaty whisper. "Are you just going to leave it there for them to follow us?"

"I certainly don't intend to abandon those men down there to the desert," he said mildly. "I'm not in the business of deliberately taking life, even though I know it's hard for you to understand that. . . ."

He turned to look at her. She kept her eyes on the camp, the light of the fire reflecting its leaping, fitful pulse, answering the sparking coruscation of the flames in her eyes that were fed on her own mounting impatience and distrust of him. She was avoiding his look deliberately. If she wanted to say anything to him or convey anything of Godspeed or good luck or whatever it was she would say, it wasn't about to come.

"Don't forget," he went on quietly, "when I say the word, start counting off to three hundred—when you hit two-hundred-fifty start pouring the petrol. I won't make my move out of there in any case until that petrol hits the flames. . . ." He waited just a few seconds, and then he added, "Well, we brought nothing into this world, and it's certain we can carry nothing out. But it's been nice having such intimate contact with the Jewish cause." She didn't respond. "I don't know if you believe in prayer, but I'd be glad to say one for both of us now. . . ." She looked for a moment that she might say something. Her dry, bruised lips moved just a fraction. But nothing came. "Okay," he said, "start your count."

She made a quick roll over on her back from him, then

slid quietly down the sand embankment and began crawling her way around the camp to the right in those same easy movements. It almost appeared as though she was running from him, afraid of staying alongside another second or yielding to his invitation to prayer since she had ruled God out of her life a long time ago. For one second he almost yielded to the pressure to call her back—but the urge passed and he turned instead to the strong pressure of the immediate. He waited until she disappeared around the rock facing, and then he rolled down the incline cautiously and began making his way around to the left of the camp area, counting slowly as he went.

He knew that he had not allowed enough time. As he inched his way toward the Land Rover, he had to stop frequently as someone stirred in his blankets within the camp or else the sentry yawned loudly. The fire in the oil barrel was fitful too, sometimes shooting up on fresh, unburned bulk fuel and lighting up the area with exposing brilliance. Though he was keeping the Land Rover between him and the camp as much as possible, he was also forced to descend the gentle slope to the vehicle itself. This put him in perfect view of the people sleeping beyond the fire and certainly of the guard if he should rouse himself and look up. There were times when he had to stop, press himself close to the sand, to lie very still. All this was taking time, and he had no more than a hundred count to go when he reached the Land Rover itself.

What was important now was that she did not move too early, and since they were both running on the same inaccurate time, it could very well happen, the explosion catching him yet outside the vehicle. He needed the time to get in, find the ignition switch, and familiarize himself with the gear shift.

He paused once as he heard a faint tinkling sound. That would be her removing the cap off one of the gas cans. There wasn't much time, then, and he would have to put caution behind him now.

He was at the door of the Land Rover, still lying prone on the sand so that he could look under the vehicle and see the entire camp. He reached up and turned the handle. Much to his relief it was unlocked. Very carefully, biting his painful lips in the tension, he pulled on the door. The squeak was as loud as a trumpet in the still, cold night air. He looked quickly under the vehicle. The sentry was awake, looking around groggily, not sure.

"Two hundred forty . . . two hundred forty-one . . . ," he kept counting in the back of his mind. "O God, what am I doing here?"

The sentry went back to his doze. Now to give the door a good pull, make sure it doesn't squeak like that again . . . he had it half open, enough to crawl up inside.

Then came the voice. It was close, demanding. He dropped back on his elbow to look again. One of the soldiers sleeping nearest to the Land Rover was sitting up and directing his words to the sentry by the fire. The sentry came to attention, answered and then got up quickly, putting his rifle at the ready. He walked over, his voice sounding as if he were assuring the man in the blankets that all was well. But the assurance would not suffice. Now all that could be seen was the sentry's hard boots and the other man's back. Then those boots began to come toward the Land Rover.

This was it then. Sebastian threw himself up into the cab of the Land Rover, trying to make his moves as quiet as possible. But in the back of his mind he knew that he couldn't possibly make it now. . . .

"Two hundred seventy . . . two hundred seventy-one . . . this game is not for you, son, it's got blood and savagery to it. . . ."

He was up in the cab, debating whether to try hiding in the back or jump for the ignition switch wherever it was. The sentry was not ten feet away now.

"Two hundred eighty . . . two hundred eighty-one . . . if you believe what you preach, then why don't you go down to that town meeting and take a stand. . . ."

The sentry's eyes were almost close enough for Sebastian to tell the color . . . and then the flash lit up the night with sudden, blinding brilliance. It was followed by a soft, puffing sound—and then the night was filled with the thumping cannonade, sounding like firecrackers going off in a rain barrel. One jerrican of gasoline after the other went up into the air, trailing orange-yellow flame like the blazing streamers from a roman candle. The sentry had stopped, turned toward the spectacle, frozen for a long minute by the rocking display of it. Then he started running towards it as if he thought he could stop it just by waving at it. The camp was in a confusion of bodies and voices shouting commands—but it wasn't going to be long before order set in.

Sebastian knew he hadn't much time to dally here. His eyes raced over the instrument panel looking for the starter. All the knobs looked the same. He pulled, shoved, turned—nothing happened. Then, when it looked as though there wasn't an ignition, he found it. He pulled it once. The motor began to grind. Something smashed into the body of the vehicle just then, and now there was shooting, but he wasn't sure if it was all at him or some of it at Miss Churchill.

It seemed an eternity before the engine caught. When it did, he threw the gearshift into what he figured to be first gear, for he had to have full power to jump out of this sand and get up that small slope. But when he let out the clutch, the motor stuttered and threatened to quit. He slammed the gear up toward the seat yelling, "O, God, make it grab!" This time the vehicle shot forward, and the sound of bullets slamming into the metal body was a steady staccato. Even as he got to the crest of the slope, the windshield disappeared as a volley of rapid fire blasted it to bits. He felt the slashing sting of glass on his face and the wet pasty feel of blood almost instantly, but he kept the motor going and roared up the incline, blinking and squinting against the feel of glass against his eyeballs. He cut down the other side, hoping Miss

Churchill had time to get back and half fearing she might have gotten shot.

She was there, and he felt his heart jump with relief. He slowed just a little, and she caught the door frame with both hands, vaulted herself up into the cab in the same movement, falling hard against him as she sprawled in. He gave the engine full power, and they shot across the sand, angling on a course to the left of the crevass.

They said nothing for a mile. He wanted to shout his jubilation, his triumph at her. He was alive! But his own breath was already coming out in shaky gasps, and he doubted he could say anything to her without sounding like a highly nervous after-dinner speaker.

"Are you hurt?" she yelled at him above the roar of the wind rushing through the blasted-out windshield.

"No, I just insist on getting eighteen shaves on one blade," he yelled back, unable to resist one stroke of bravado, but she didn't smile or respond. She turned instead and looked back at pursuit.

He kept pushing the Land Rover now, not too sure of the handling of the vehicle, but finding it necessary if he expected to gain on his pursuers. He saw the familiar rock line of his own camp ahead, then, and he cut into it, slammed on the breaks and shouted to her: "Get the ladies moving! I'll see to Brelsford!"

None of them could shake themselves out of their stupor fast enough to comprehend what was going on. Sebastian pulled Brelsford up out of his blankets and threw him over his shoulder, running for the vehicle almost in the same motion. "Where did you get this vehicle?" he demanded as Sebastian dumped him ungently into the back seat. Meanwhile, Mabel Stockton, who seemed to be recovering the fastest, practically dragged and half carried Ida Randolph to the Land Rover. She prodded and pushed her into the back seat with Brelsford without the usual tender loving care. Dennison, blinking in disbelief at the new turn of events, made his moves in a kind of daze, but he needed no one to tell him what four wheels could do to relieve the situation.

It was Eaton who stood back and hesitated, as if not either comprehending or else finding this too much beyond belief. Or else, as Agent Christopher, he was indeed suddenly thrown off balance and did not know exactly how to move.

"It won't take you anywhere standing there, Eaton!" Sebastian shouted at him, and Eaton simply turned and looked back where the headlights of the pursuers flashed very near now. He gave Sebastian one cursory glance as if to indicate he knew now why all the haste and ran for the Land Rover.

"What and whom are we running from?" Brelsford howled again as Sebastian got the Land Rover moving, heading out into the uncharted territory, making the wild attempt to head for Bir Milhan, the pursuing headlights almost on top of them. No one answered Brelsford, although the rest of them were probably waiting for either Sebastian or Miss Churchill to say something. Sebastian's main concern now was to stay ahead of that half-track. He didn't think they'd be shooting now—they'd be afraid of hitting their Agent Christopher. But it was going to take a lot of skill to keep the Land Rover ahead in this sand— even now it shot into the pockets and managed to get through on four-wheel drive, but still it slowed and careened as the sand sucked on the wheels.

"Don't take it out of second!" Barbara Churchill warned him. "She won't pull!"

"I demand to know who is chasing us, Sebastian!" Brelsford's high-pitched voice sounded again. No one else chimed in. They were concentrating on the driving with Sebastian now. And they were still trying to come out of the shock of suddenly becoming mobile, that in the middle of their nightmare they were suddenly racing through the desert in a weird kind of drama, the target of some very insistent pursuers for what reason they couldn't imagine. But they held to silence, for what mattered was that they were moving, and they didn't want to deter Sebastian from his intense deliberation at the wheel.

"I'll have to head for that rock line!" he yelled at Barbara Churchill next to him.

"It's all tangled erosion!" she shouted back.

"It's the only way to lose them!" Sebastian replied. He turned to look in the back seat to see if they were all holding on, and then he yelled, "Where's the child? Who picked up the baby?"

Ida Randolph cried, "I thought Miss Churchill went back for her!"

Barbara Churchill shook her head, and he saw in her eyes the first indication of genuine feeling, a look of horror at having committed the oversight, a look that came out through her usual successful attempts at cover. Ahead of them Sebastian saw now a jutting island of rock in the sand, a good fifty yards or so in width. It was a wild risk, but now he was bent on doing it.

"All right! Hang on! We're going back for her!"

He felt a heavy hand strike him hard on the right shoulder, and Eaton was shouting now, "Don't be a fool! You can't go back with them behind you!"

"I said we're all going out together, Eaton!" Sebastian hurled back at him, and switched off the headlights as he made the sharp turn around the rocks to the right, bounced jarringly over outcroppings, felt the axles take the brutal pounding and fighting the vehicle as it threatened to overturn.

"You can't sacrifice six lives for one child near death!" Eaton tried again, and his voice was berating, filled with the incredulousness of what Sebastian was attempting and almost pleading in terms of his own sense of priorities.

"He's right!" Brelsford chimed in, coughing on the clouds of dust that rolled into the vehicle now. "You've no right to do this, Sebastian!"

Even Barbara Churchill was staring at him in question, perhaps wondering if he had suddenly gone mad in this whole exploding, bobbing night.

196

"Well, you've got no choice!" Sebastian said. "You can hit me over the head if you like—but then you'll be splattered all over the desert! Hang on now, we're almost half way back!"

The sudden turn around the rocky island and the cutting of the lights put off pursuit for the moment. But after a few seconds, Barbara Churchill yelled. "They're on us again!"

Sebastian hit the accelerator to the floor. The dust rose in the cab so that they were all coughing now, and Ida Randolph was beginning a low moan of terror that was rising like an air-raid siren. Brelsford yelped like a dog in pain as his wound shot stabs through him with every jump of the Land Rover. And Sebastian clamped his teeth down harder against the ache in his arms as he tried to fight the balky machine from tipping or plowing too far nose down in the sand. He caught the flash of headlights in the rear mirror again, and he knew he couldn't outrun them forever. It was a question now of whether he could get out of the trap he was creating for himself.

When they shot into the familiar camp area, Miss Churchill jumped out before Sebastian had braked to a full stop. She was back in seconds with the child in her arms. He swung the vehicle around to head back the way he had come, but he knew he was faced with the problem of getting by the pursuing half-track. He cut out his own headlights and waited, watching the bouncing lights of the approaching vehicle close in.

"The man's gone absolutely mad!" Brelsford piped up with insistence. The rest of them probably agreed, but they all sat and waited, watching, feeling dwarfed by the rising mountain of uncertainty. For Sebastian everything was hung on quick action, surprise moves, and those small margins that a lighter, more maneuverable vehicle could accomplish. He knew all this was a long risk, but his mind, seeming to be much clearer now and capable of making rapid calculations, was measuring each situation in terms of those sudden, dramatic moves he knew he was not capable of but which he had to attempt to execute anyway.

Now he waited as the half-track dipped down in the gulley just beyond them, his hands feeling greasy from the sweat where they gripped the wheel—and then as it came over the rise right on top of them, he threw on his own high beam lights. The stabbing shaft of light hit the windshield of the half-track, and the big vehicle swerved to the left as the driver tried to avoid what must have seemed a head-on collison.

In that same instant, he goosed the Land Rover so that it shot by the half-track and out into the open desert again. They had the advantage but not for long.

"I demand to know who those people are!" Brelsford shouted his high-pitched protest again.

"Lawrence of Arabia, who else?" Eaton trumpeted, and Sebastian thought how strange for Eaton to try humor, but Brelsford said no more.

Sebastian looked in the back seat again to check on them and saw Dennison lifting a water bottle to his mouth. "Dennison, put that down!" he yelled. "You'll spill it all out trying to drink on a run like this!"

It was Eaton who finally wrestled the water bottle from Dennison, but only after overpowering the man who had suddenly gone beserk over the few swallows he had managed to get down.

Satisfied that that was under control, Sebastian aimed the Land Rover for the line of rocks that constituted the last of Wadi Iqfi. His only hope now was to find some hide-out, though their chances of doing it were slim. It was either that or be caught by the more powerful machine behind them, and there was no hope of beating them into Bir Milhan. Not in this sand. As he drove, he wished he were a more experienced driver, for he did not have complete confidence in himself when it came to opening up in the stretches. But even then, he felt a strange exhilaration in what he was doing. He had no fear at this point. He was in a perfectly legitimate contest. He was battling for the lives of people in a different dimension than he had from the pulpit, but he was doing so here in a much greater sense, at least in terms of risk and ultimate results. He knew he could die here at any moment, and yet that thought only made the desire to win more intense—and though he hadn't much time to think about it, this after all was perhaps what he needed most.

Now he was heading down into the narrow wadi. He threw on his high beams. There was jagged rock and jutting boulders that reached out with ugly fingers to pluck at him as he passed. There was a narrow passage, enough to let him through, and he shifted down to keep from hitting the rough terrain too hard and bouncing them all through the canvas roof.

"Are they following?" he asked Barbara Churchill.

She looked back. "No," she replied. "They won't move in here with that bigger vehicle. They'll wait for you to come out the other side!"

It was necessary then to try to get through the wadi before they got there, or else turn and head back, doubling back out of the wadi and swinging around them again. He gave gas to the engine, made a quick angling turn and then saw too late that he couldn't negotiate the turn properly. He spun the wheel hard, but the vehicle tipped and slammed into a wall of rock on the left, then again on the right, dropped off a six-foot incline and fell with a clattering crash into a gulley below. There was a scream of pain from Ida Randolph and yelps of protest from the others. Sebastian felt the steering wheel slam into his chest, and he slipped into a velvety kind of darkness.

He woke to the feel of cool water on his face, and his swollen tongue reached out hungrily, desperately for it, and the feel of it going down his throat almost made him cry.

Then he opened his eyes, and Barbara Churchill came out of the murky fuzz. "You know you'll be getting a mother complex if you keep on nursing me like this," he said, and he got up holding on to his aching ribs as he did so. She stepped back from him, holding on to the water bottle.

"You're all right, nothing more than a bruised rib cage," she said in a clipped tone.

"Right, who needs ribs?" he joked again, biting against the stabbing pains through his chest. "Well, let's have a rundown on the others. . . ."

"Miss Randolph has a broken collar bone, Mr. Brelsford is unconscious from banging his head on the roof spar, Mr. Dennison is sitting over there staring into nothing and humming 'Waltzing Matilda,'" she said to him dryly. "The rest of us have survived—including the child—at least I think survived is what we can call it."

"How about supplies—water?"

"We have about two gallons."

"Food?"

"Dry bully beef—enough."

"Did you give them a drink?"

"They've all had it."

"What's that?" and he pointed his toe at a small wooden box on the ground.

"Grenades."

He looked up at her quickly. "Well, those boys meant business, didn't they?"

"We'll probably need them before long," she said flatly.

"No, we won't, Miss Churchill," he contradicted her. "This is still my show, remember? And there's nothing in this script that calls for the bombing of the enemy."

"Unfortunately, those people hunting us don't have the same sentiments," she reminded him.

He didn't bother answering her. He looked around. "How bad is our transportation?"

"It will run," Eaton's voice suddenly cut in, and Sebastian peered forward to a small overhang of rock where only Eaton's legs showed in the moonlight. "Apart from a dented radiator and maybe a cracked undercarriage, there is no more damage." Sebastian wondered what Eaton was really thinking right now, but before he could venture some probing questions, the sound of motors came loud to them, and a long stab of light shot down towards them from the desert above, like an exploring cat's paw feeling for a mouse in its hole.

"They will come now," Eaton called out the warning, "whoever they are, Mr. Sebastian!"

Sebastian got into the Land Rover, turned the ignition switch and ground away at the engine. When it finally started, the loud clacking noise indicated that the fan was probably bent against the radiator. He put it in reverse, but the steep incline of the vehicle against the rocks and the greasy rocky surface under the wheels kept it spinning on the spot.

"All right, Miss Churchill," Sebastian called, "you get in and drive . . . the rest of us will try pushing from the front. . . ." Suddenly the probing light went out and the canyon was smothered with pale black again. It could mean they would really come now, and Sebastian yelled, "Come on, let's not dally!"

And suddenly Miss Stockton was there, her spectacles seeming to be energized by moonbeams as they sparked and flashed like fitful arcs of electricity. "I'll be glad to help," she said, and before he could say anything, she moved to the front of the Land Rover and waited there beside Eaton.

Again the light switched on from above, and this time it caught them, freezing them in their pantomime. A shot boomed into the rocks, and a voice followed over a loud-speaker. "They say to come out," Miss Churchill explained from her place behind the wheel.

"Or they will shoot us," Eaton added from his crouching position in front of the Land Rover, and there was a strange kind of grimacing smile on his lips as if that was some kind of mean joke he enjoyed.

"All right, we've got to make one big push together!" Sebastian yelled to them. "Dennison!" Dennison looked up blankly at Sebastian from his position a few feet away. He was sitting there with his back to the large slab of rock, his knees drawn up under his chin. He stopped humming "Waltzing Matilda" waiting for Sebastian. Sebastian went over, took him by the good hand and led him to the front of the Land Rover. "Push now when I tell you," he said. Dennison looked confused, but he placed his hands on the front fender where Sebastian indicated. "Now, Miss Churchill, start giving it slow gas when I tell you!"

Somewhere in the back of his mind he heard the shot from above again and the loud thwack of the bullet bouncing off the rocks near him. "Now—everybody heave!" and he threw his weary back into it, hearing the desperate, coughing gasp of Mabel Stockton next to him as she threw her bulk into it as though it were her dying act.

* 12 *

They fought the Land Rover with their meager strength, not having to be told that their lives hung on getting the vehicle moving again. They groaned, giving out audible cries of anguish as they strained, feeling the machine move by torturing inches as the wheels spun to get traction on the slippery rock, the clack of its fan against radiator a peculiar mocking laugh rising to a hilarity all its own as Miss Churchill fed more gas to the engine. Now and then a shot from the desert pinged against the rocks, and chips of it sprayed them. But it only drove them harder, for they knew instinctively that time was of the essence, that those bullets being bounced deliberately over them would soon reach down to pluck at any one of them with finality. They weren't questioning Sebastian now or making their effort contingent on what knowlege he could give on just who the enemy was and why they were so insistent on getting to them. Except for Dennison, they were humans now with cognition factors, driven more by the will to survive than an intellectual satisfaction of who was the executioner. Brelsford, of course, was still sprawled out cold under a protective rock shelf, and Ida Randolph could only crouch in fear near him, peering at them with wide eyes, her face pinched in that usual vice of pain and terror that distorted her features to the point of grotesqueness. Her mouth remained in that fixed curl of a child ready to cry, as if every second she expected to be swallowed up by the peculiar goblins that perpetually made up her paranoic world view. But the rest of them were as one, welded at last into their first act of mutual consent, sensing the dissolving vestiges of life with every passing second and fighting gravity, steel, and emaciated body and spirit with intensity that was far beyond them. There was a point when Sebastian, hearing the sharp grunts and groans from Miss Stockton next to him, lifted his head to tell her not to strain so hard, for this was no job for a woman. But when he looked towards her, he saw the teeth bared by the effort, the face twisted in the agony of determination, the glasses moist from her sweat—and it was the first indication of humanity in her that he had seen during the whole journey, so he forgot what he was going to say and treasured the possibility that Miss Stockton demonstrated the latent strength they all had to fulfill the ultimate goal.

Then came the awful seconds when the few thousands pounds of dead-weight Land Rover hung uncertainly on them, spinning its wheels uselessly so that the tires gave off a high whine, and the smell of burned rubber joined the smell of gas fumes and human sweat—and it was in that second that Sebastian realized that they could be crushed like bugs if the Land Rover won now, for they would have no time to jump out of the way as it came back down on them. There was that horrible moment when he felt that he had no more muscle to give, and his shoes began to slip on the rock, and the moaning of all of them testified to waning ability to hold and push at the same time.

And then Eaton suddenly called to them, sounding like a field general that he was, his voice cracking hard over the roaring engine, "Push! Push or we die!" And from somewhere Sebastian rose to it, and even Dennison caught the challenge, and his arms bulged as he gave new leverage.

And then they fell, all of them. Sprawling out on the rock as the Land Rover shot back up over the ledge and left them pushing on air. Sebastian fought the overwhelming, powerful desire to lie there and get his wind—he knew that above all this were people waiting and watching and for all he knew already coming down into the wadi.

He jumped to his feet, noticed that the Land Rover was now back behind a protective wall of rock, away from the insistent searchlight and the sharp deadly fingers of the bullets.

"Get Miss Randolph," he yelled at Mabel Stockton, and at the same time ran over to pick up Brelsford. The searchlight jumped with him, trying to pin him with its beam. The shots this time came rapid, the same kind of sound that had ripped out the windshield on the Land Rover earlier. The smashing, tearing sound of the bullets was terrifying now. There was serious purpose in the firing.

He found Brelsford was coming around, his eyes opening and closing in the wonder of his surroundings. There was no real damage to him apart from a sizable knot on the top of his head where he had hit the roof spar, but the man was yet too dazed to make it by himself. Sebastian looked around for Mabel Stockton, but she was nowhere in sight. He saw her finally when the light stabbed back toward the Land Rover, sitting by the rear wheel, put out of action by her straining effort earlier or else refusing to expose herself anymore to the parasitic Ida Randolph.

Sebastian turned back to her. She sat pulled up against the rocks looking like a trapped animal, cowering there, trying to get away from the insistent, probing light. He couldn't handle Brelsford and her too, so he said to her, "Miss Randolph, it's only fifty feet to the others . . . you can make it easily. . . ."

But she only shrank back further against the rocks, and little whimpering, puppy sounds began to come from her as she refused to face this violent world she couldn't understand and which practically had her out of her mind in fear. He turned back to see if anyone were coming, and he noticed now that the beam of light was focused on that fifty feet of open ground. They would wait for him to go back and open up on him as he did.

"Miss Randolph!" he snapped hard at her then, and she suddenly looked up, terrified, struck by the hard note of his voice. "If you won't run for it, I'm going to leave you here! Do you understand? I'll leave you, because I've got the others to think of! There isn't time, do you understand?"

"You—you can't!" she wailed, reaching out her long arms in appeal. "You're a clergyman—you wouldn't! Where's Mabel? She won't leave me here!"

"She won't be coming for you!" Sebastian yelled back at her. "Make up your mind, Miss Randolph—I'm going to go myself with Brelsford in a minute. Do you want to stay here, because I don't intend to risk anyone else's life or take the time to come back for you!"

Sebastian picked up Brelsford, then, and hoisted him on one shoulder. "Don't—you can't!" she screamed at him. "What kind of a man of God are you to abandon an adult when you'd risk us all for a child?"

"The child had no power of its own," he fired back. "You do! What's it going to be, Miss Randolph?"

He waited just a few seconds during which Miss Rnadolph began to tremble as if she'd suffered a severe chill and couldn't control it. Sebastian made his move to go—and then she was up on her feet clutching at him.

"I'll follow you!" she screamed at him.

There wasn't time to argue. That was at least better than nothing. So he started out, trying to dog trot with Brelsford heavy on him again, feeling her hands hanging on to his sweater, pulling on him, half demanding he stay there by her tugs, the other shoving hard into his sore ribs to urge him on. The firing reached out for them immediately, and he saw the creeping line of bullets from the far side of the circle, moving in exploding puffs of smoke and rock. He tried to get her around him and ahead, but she hung back, and finally stopped there—he could only swing around once to look at her, not able to do anything with Brelsford hanging on him . . . she stood there, her hands clutching her face, her mouth open to shape the scream of terror.

"O my God, help her!" Sebastian moaned, for in another few seconds she would be cut down by that creeping line of bullets, and he knew he could not live with the fact that he had forced her out there on her own. He kept walking backward with Brelsford, hoping she would keep on moving. "Ida!" he yelled above the smashing sounds of the night, and his voice was a half scream, hurting his throat.

"Put me down!" Brelsford suddenly yelled, and Sebastian felt the man squirm off his shoulder, land unsteadily on his feet and half stumble away from him toward the Land Rover.

Now Sebastian turned back to her, making his moves toward her like a swimmer heading for the surf, rising high on his tiptoes, preparing for the shock of it. But now the bullets were near her, kicking up rock, sand, and shrapnel at her. She screamed, as if stung by it, and she jumped forward, moving in terror, looking like a witch without her broom, flying by Sebastian like a ghostly apparition, her bony, pointed features looking like a bundle of twigs being hurled along by the wind. He spun around, a little shocked by her sudden agility and speed, jumping back as the bullets raked toward him, doing a quick skip-roping dance as he turned and landing in a sprawled heap over the rock ledge by the Land Rover.

"Let's go!" he shouted, getting to his feet, and they jumped for the Land Rover, even Miss Stockton who vaulted to her feet now with alacrity and without gentility shoved hard on Miss Randolph to get her moving into the back seat. Sebastian got behind the wheel, made sure everyone was aboard, including the child, and then looked ahead at the narrow passageway through the canyon, wondering if he could jump fast enough to get away from that big eye of the searchlight.

"I'm going to have to go through!" he yelled at no one in particular, but trusting someone would have a better idea.

"They'll follow you to the other end!" Eaton contradicted, his breath heavy with excitement and the peculiar tense jubilancy of the voice of an ex-general who was more in his element now.

Sebastian looked at Miss Churchill next to him, who held the child in her arms. "Is everything in—water, food?" he asked.

She nodded, "And the grenades," as if to remind him that they were not totally unarmed.

"Why didn't you leave them?"

"To land in enemy hands? Never!"

He didn't answer her on that. He watched the searchlight flash long, bony fingers over their rock cover, and then he shoved the gear forward and let out the clutch. He got through the sharp turn that had fouled him before, and the light crossed over him once, and the bullets pinged on the rocks around them. They were on the floor of the wadi then.

"There!" Eaton yelled. "See their headlights! They are heading you off!"

Sebastian noticed the line of lights that shot ahead of them on the upper desert floor. There was no way out there. He stopped, flipped off the headlights.

"I'm doubling back!" he said.

"You can't turn here!" Miss Churchill warned, looking at the narrow passageway and the long drop on the far side where he'd have to back.

"As you said, we simply have to choose our way of dying," he reminded her, and shot the Land Rover ahead, turning against the far wall of rock. Then he reversed. "Keep an eye out for me!" he shouted.

"You can't see!" Miss Churchill said.

"Then get out and go on back there, Eaton!"

Eaton got out obediently and ran back to the edge of the rock ledge. "Come! Come! Come!" he kept shouting as Sebastian eased the machine back. "Stop!"

They were at the edge, but Sebastian figured he had enough room now to jockey around. He slipped the gear in and let out the clutch, and spun around hard, just missing the rock wall as he turned, not sure where he was in relationship to that without his lights and not wanting to put them on yet to give away his intentions to the enemy. No one said anything now as he moved back up the passageway without lights, trying to keep his memory alive as to how it looked when he came down, not wanting to slide off the precarious trail, for to do so meant they would lose their vehicle and who knew how they would come out of it.

"Where are they now?" he asked, as they crept along slowly in the darkness.

"Their lights are still back at the other end," Eaton called.

"May I ask," Brelsford's voice sounded wearily again, "what this whole nightmare is all about?"

"Archaeological field trip, Brelsford," Eaton responded, and it seemed that Eaton was taking delight in countering Brelsford now, as if he were feeling gratification in combating a superior intellect. Again, as before, Brelsford had no answer, or else didn't want to answer for fear of getting more pungent returns that offered him no out.

The Land Rover scraped a rocky wall then and seemed to shiver as though it was balancing on uneven ground. Sebastian had to put on the lights, and he saw that they were back at the original turn where they had had the accident previously, angling again for that same precarious six-foot drop-off. If he had gone another foot in the dark, they would have gone off again.

"Now they come!" Eaton said in warning again.

"All right, get a hold of something," Sebastian called to them, "I'm going to open up the rest of the way!"

He smelled the overheating of the engine as he fed it full power, and the temperature gauge was well past the danger point. That would be the fan belt having trouble circulating the coolent or else they had a leak. How long he could keep running he had no idea, but he guessed it wouldn't be long. He was caught between the impossibility of outrunning his pursuers and the fruitlessness of remaining in the wadi. He felt a twinge of pity for the rest of them, for he saw them now only as the victims of a conflict they were unwilling and innocently a part of. Except for Eaton, perhaps, who sat forward on the back seat because there was hardly room for him and because he wanted to lean into the action like a bird dog, his usually unreadable face lit up now and then with the fitful flashes of lighting that came with the rising tempo of the drama. And Miss Churchill, who sat very alert in the seat next to him, the box of grenades open at her feet, ready as always to meet the emergency that her training had prepared her for. These two knew their business—for them he could only feel admiration.

But there was a warmness for them all as he pushed the laboring Land Rover up the last few feet of the wadi floor—he wished none of them were Christopher, for somehow they seemed plain, simple people who pulsed with individual emotion and feeling. He felt linked to them as he had never felt linked to any people in all his ministerial years, as if they were the only human beings left on earth. It was both a strange and exhilarating feeling to be identified with and committed to people in that way.

But he hadn't time to ponder the sentiments of the moment. He was suddenly coming into the unknown desert, and he had to decide now how he was going to make his run for Bir Milhan with the enemy ahead of him waiting for him to show.

"There they are!" Eaton yelled, and Sebastian saw the headlights of the vehicle farther up the wadi line, coming back slowly, the searchlight running hungrily around the wadi floor below.

"They don't know we're here!" Sebastian replied. He switched off the lights and cut out into the desert, running away from the wadi and heading for a lumpy protrusion of rock dead ahead that offered a point of evasion.

"Which way are you going?" Miss Churchill asked, shifting the child to Miss Stockton in the back seat who took the bundle without a word.

"I'm going toward that rock, cut around it, and force them to follow, I hope," he replied. "That'll give us some headway. . . ."

"Ha! Now they are on you!" Eaton shouted, and he sounded like a chess player applauding the moves of a colleague who was making it an interesting contest.

"Who are they?" Brelsford cried hopelessly, but nobody answered him now, not even Eaton who was intense on the new maneuvering.

Sebastian threw on his lights and gave the vehicle full power. Again dust rose up in the cab from the sand, and he could hear the sound of firing from behind as he cut around the rocks and headed directly south. The pursuing vehicle had followed blindly, instead of trying to head them off, thus putting themselves a good one hundred yards behind again.

It was then that the radiator cap blew off, and the geyser of steam shot up, spraying back into the cab with its hot wetness, bringing out a new cry of terror from Miss Randolph. Sebastian kept the vehicle going, ignoring the sound of an engine in the beginning stages of collapse. The Land Rover was getting sluggish under his hands, the headlights of the pursuing vehicle were growing larger, and there could hardly be time for good-bys now.

He pushed the machine up over a long, gradual slope of sand, noting Miss Churchill's hand going down to the grenade box. A rattle of gunfire sounded sharp behind him, and the bullets ripped into the roof of the Land Rover, scattering canvas scraps over them.

"Stop it!" Brelsford kept yelling. "Stop this insane business, Sebastian, right now!"

They were going down the other side of the sandy hill, and that's when Eaton suddenly threw open the back door and jumped out. It all happened too fast for Sebastian to make the right moves. At the same time, Miss Churchill went out the front, a grenade in her hand looking as big and ugly as a snake's head. She was not going to let Eaton get away, even with the enemy coming down on top of her.

Sebastian hit the brakes, but the Land Rover swung in the untractable sand, skidding around in a complete spin before sliding to a shaky halt, the sound of steam dying now and the engine choking on its own heat. He was out of the Land Rover and running back up the sand hill, fear gripping hard at his vitals, forcing him to cough, but it was not fear of the enemy coming over the hill but fear for Barbara Churchill. He saw them silhouetted against the lights for a moment as he ran, the larger bulk of Eaton higher up, the more slender one that of Miss Churchill not far behind.

He tried to call to her, to shout the warning, to check her mad attempt to get Eaton before he made it to his friends. She surely could see the futility of that now!

And then he fell once, and as he got to his feet, the explosion tore the desert with slashing sound. He saw the huge pillar of flame that was both blue and orange, and then the lights rolling over and over down the outer side of the hill where there was rock and deep gully. There was a long sound of clanging, muffled shouts, the soft, squishy sound of metal hitting flat—then there was another popping sound, and the flames shot up from the gulley below. He lay in the sand a long time, horrified by the rocking turbulence in the night, hearing the sounds like crumpling cellophane as the half-track burned below. He smelled gasoline and the acrid smoke that boiled up—and the burning flesh. He wept, even as he got shakily to his feet, not knowing why he wept unless it was the reaction of his own sensitive feelings to death like this and the realization again that somehow he was an accomplice to

this carnage. He stumbled up the hill, and he saw her standing there against the pale sky—and he ran up, grabbing her by the arm, wanting to be sure it was she.

"You—you did that?" he pointed down into the gully.

She shook her head. "I lost mine in the sand when I jumped out of the Land Rover," she said dully.

"Then . . . ?" he wanted to ask who, and she looked down quickly. It was Eaton. Lying there sprawled face up toward the sky, his mouth open as if he was trying to yell something, his eyes wide. The same ridiculous blue bow tie, looking as neat as always on the white shirt, the blue sweater in contrast to it. Sebastian dropped down next to the man, and he noticed the ugly marks of the half-track's cleats over his body where it had run over him.

"Eaton?" he tried, and slowly the eyes lost their wide staring and softened into recognition of life.

"You—you see, Sebastian . . . I told you I would emerge. . . ," and his voice was hardly more than a whisper, and the smile he tried was the same poor attempt, but now the corners of his mouth turned upward as if approaching death had relaxed the muscles and it gave him the look of a man telling a good joke. "It is the way . . . of a general . . . it is not your way, it can never be. . . ."

"Eaton?" he cut in, trying to reach him before the glaze came back into his eyes.

"Zimmerman . . . ," Eaton croaked, the smile still there. "General Heinrich Zimmerman, Waffen SS. . . ."

Sebastian looked back at Miss Churchill for an explanation. "The Waffen SS were crack officers in charge of concentration camps . . . some of them fought on the front lines too. . . ."

"I thought he wasn't admitting to concentration camps," he reminded her.

"He didn't . . . he is now. He's got nothing to lose and maybe he figures confession is good for the soul. . . ."

"You want to ask him if he's got the film?"

"No point. Obviously he wouldn't blow up his friends

and be stupid enough to get run over in the process."

He went back to Eaton. Perhaps there was still time. "Eaton—General Zimmerman," he began, "whatever your sins of the past, they can be forgiven by the blood of Christ . . . there's time. . . ."

"Forget it," Miss Churchill said from his side. "He's dead."

He stared at the smile still fixed on the mouth that was slowly relaxing as nerve and muscle melted. What strange attachments he felt now! The disdaining Eaton whose nervous contemptuous sniff had been so much a part of them, so driven by his own desires for mastery even here, but who even then wanted to commit one act of sacrifice for others. How could it be explained? What strange alchemy did the Negev stir up that forced contradition in all of them? Was Eaton trying again to make up for all the horror of the past he created or permitted in Auschwitz? By one act of sacrifice, did he expect to atone for all those crimes? How easy it would have been if he had had consciousness long enough to accept the atoning work of God Himself! But the Negev had its way of snipping off the string of time for any of them—cunningly it exacted the last breath, shut off the last moment of recognition, veiled the eyes from the glory of the Son of God! What hell is this? he cried deep within the hollow cave of his soul as he knelt there beside the crumpled, sinewy body of the once proud German who in his way had a peculiar drawing power by his compelling sense of strength. What spiritual no-man's land was this—or was it all the Devil's anyway—this endless track of waste, this chunk of volcanic ash still smoldering from the first cataclysmic collision in the universe, which God had to leave over for want of what to do with it? This hungry monster of a place that plucked life and soul in a twinkling, playing with time for a brief moment and then snatching them out with such eager, decisive moves!

He was conscious of the others standing there and looking on. "Now perhaps we can get down to explana-

214

tions," Brelsford snapped, and it was as if Brelsford were suddenly aware that his number one adversary, Eaton, was no longer around to so expertly silence him with well-placed barbs.

"That won't be necessary," another voice cut in, and for a moment Sebastian couldn't place the voice at all. He glanced up quickly, stood to his feet and stared into the ugly end of a gun that was held very steadily and surely in the hands of Mabel Stockton.

"Miss Stockton?" he said, half question, half fact, but unable to fully comprehend the enormity of the moment, the sheer ludicrousness of the image forcing him to disbelieve, for no one among them was at all less fitting the role of Agent Christopher than she—or wasn't that the way it always was?

"Ma—Mabel!" Ida Randolph gasped, and it was an explosion of doubt, horror, and total disbelief, shuddering from a woman who couldn't take much more without disentegrating completely.

"Shut up, my dear," Mabel Stockton said with a voice that was steady, polite, and matter of fact. She removed her glasses, threw them into the sand, and there stood before them a woman who suddenly did not look like a schoolteacher. Now her face, without the veil of the spectacles, was longer, her forehead high, and she looked younger in appearance. The surface look of intelligence Sebastian had detected two days ago behind those glasses had come out now, emanating from large, luminous brown eyes that were almost black in the light of the fire from the half-track in the gully below. It seemed suddenly that her drab brown dress was deliberately large to give the impression of a bulky, middle-aged old maid. Now she seemed to stand taller, and the lines under those clothes stood out as youthful, athletic, trim.

The transformation left them all silent in awe, and perhaps they were all like Sebastian, incapable of keeping pace with rapidly shifting action and personalities, their dull minds unable to function and their bodies unwilling

215

to feed any extra energy to perception.

"You waited a long time," Barbara Churchill said, then, and Sebastian looked at her, surprised that she didn't appear taken aback, and if anything there was a calm, unruffled poise about her that more than matched Mabel Stockton.

"I had to play it out," she replied, calmly triumphant, "because I could not trust those who were following, and I couldn't be sure of you, what you had to stop me if I played it too early . . . you are not very good at this espionage business, Miss Churchill, but you have a tenacity of purpose that does not die easily."

"Aren't you being a little melodramatic?" Brelsford bellowed.

"For you everything that doesn't fit your scientific computerized mind is melodramatic, Brelsford," Miss Stockton returned with preciseness. "That makes you indeed the most impractical man of any here, including Dennison."

Brelsford could only choke and fume on that, not finding the words to fit such blunt appraisal that came too close to argue against.

"But you kept in touch with those people for so long," Sebastian put in. "You acted as though you wanted them to come—you put that transmitter in that wadi back there to point them east—yet you didn't want them to get you. . . ."

"I had to play it either way, Mr. Sebastian . . . I didn't intend to hand over this precious film to the Egyptians if I could help it, and I didn't want Miss Churchill to get it either . . . so now Mr. Eaton has taken care of the situation very nicely . . . incidentally, it would take no genius to figure out who my counteragent was . . . Miss Churchill, you are a bit clumsy in your movements to say the least. . . ."

"Now there's only us," Sebastian said.

A ghost of a smile came across the marble of her face. "After such a Herculean attempt on your part, Sebastian,

I am sorry to have to leave it like this . . . but it is a grim fact of the business I am in . . . you can understand, I'm sure, that I would not come all this way and let you live."

"My God, Mabel!" Ida Randolph half screamed again. "You've been with me all this time! You ate with me, lived with me, shared my secrets since Boston. . . ."

"Since London, my dear, remember?" she countered with a sharp tone of distaste to her voice. "You were my only way of getting in to do my job . . . I must say I don't regret leaving your miserable self . . . I leave you gladly for the church to coddle from now on!"

"You will shoot us down like dogs?" Sebastian said, feeling the helplessness of the situation now, not wanting others to suffer for what was not their responsibility.

"I don't need to be as messy as that," she countered. "I have the Land Rover, the supplies . . . the desert will take care of you now. . . ."

"That machine won't get you far," Miss Churchill warned.

"Two gallons of water . . . one has already gone into that overheated radiator. It will take me the thirteen or so miles I have to go to Bir Milhan . . . the other gallon will go with me just in case. . . ."

"And leave us with no water or food?" Brelsford cut in again, his voice strangely subdued as if the seriousness of the situation was just getting to him. "Why don't you kill us now, it would be quicker. . . ."

"I can't leave evidence of violence here, my friend," she replied coolly. "When they find you they will assume you tried to walk out from the wreck and died of exposure . . . that keeps it as neat as possible. Now, the charts, Mr. Sebastian, please?"

Sebastian withdrew the charts from his shirt and threw them on the ground in front of her, and Brelsford looked a little surprised that he no longer possessed those charts and gave Sebastian an indignant look.

"Now, I shall be off," she said, backing slowly down the hill.

"What about the child?" Sebastian called. "Can't you leave enough water for her?"

There was no answer. They stood and watched her until she reached the Land Rover. She got in, gave engine to it, and drove off, a little wisp of steam hardly even noticable from the radiator in the murky half-light of dawn. They watched until she was gone far beyond their vision, the vehicle leaving a long trail of dust as crisply derisive as she had been.

No one said anything. Brelsford lay down wearily on his left side in the sand. Dennison's humming went on as he kept pouring sand from one hand to the other, his deranged mind carrying him beyond all this to some other time, some other place—and it was to be the most merciful end for him perhaps. Ida Randolph sank to the ground, still staring in the distance where the dust of the Land Rover had disappeared, her face framed by her usual scraggly shock of hair, a face that reflected the numbing shock of this horrible betrayal, a shock that could throw her completely into that same suspension as Dennison.

Barbara Churchill stood and watched too, her fists clenched tightly at her sides, her face reflecting the inner turmoil of seeing the nation of Israel disappear as factually as that dust.

"You want to get the child?" Sebastian said to her, wanting to arrest her attention, to get her mind off defeat.

She looked at him as if not comprehending, a long hard look that questioned how he could continue thinking about such lesser things in the light of the calamity just conceived. But then she moved, stiffly, uncertainly at first—and he watched her go down the slope, her steps heavier, her movements sluggish, her spirit dragging in the sand—and it hurt him to see that normally fierce glow of her person flickering its gradual surrender to the snuffing finger of defeat.

"Sebastian, would you mind *now* telling me what this is all about?" Brelsford's voice appealed, and Sebastian

218

sighed, walked over to where the scientist lay, and sat down a few feet from him. There was that same glowing intensity in Brelsford's eyes, for his brain would never quit working as long as there were mysteries that needed answering—it was important to Brelsford that every strange event have a scientific answer or at least an intellectually satisfying one.

"Well, Brelsford, it's like this. . . ."

* 13 *

He knew he had to get up. He was conscious of the fact
that the sun was already turning the sand to hot ashes
under him. He didn't know how long he had been lying
there. The last thing he could remember was burying
Eaton in that shallow sand hole on top of the hill near
where he had died. He remembered rolling the German
into it, pushing the sand in on top of him. He remembered Barbara Churchill and Brelsford adding their feeble, shaky efforts to his, while Ida Randolph tried her best
to add to it with her one good arm. Dennison simply sat
and sang his monotonous tune of yesteryear's glory.
Sebastian had read some verses he considered appropriate for Eaton, but there wasn't much he could read of
promise for a man whose destiny was uncertain.

Sometime later he had lain down with the others to get
strength back for their next move. The sky then was a
white vaporous color with the spilled red juice of the
coming sun running through it, turning the long table of
sand to a blurred, mucky strawberry milkshake. He had
slipped into a doze, trying to fight total surrender to it as
his body cried out for regrouping of its defenses worn
down now to a pitiful bastion of undernourished and
debilitated blood cells. His mind ran through troubled
patterns, mostly centering on the guilt he felt about

Eaton—that perhaps if he hadn't run off with that Land Rover and exposed them to the chase, Eaton might have lived. Or maybe he should have waited for those agents to catch up with them and trust to some other possible alternative than death at their hands. Maybe he'd been too bold, too adventuresome, pursuing a flimsy glimmer of leading that God may not have intended to be a leading. Perhaps he's made too big a leap from a minister of conventionality to one of erratic boldness—perhaps he'd pushed the pendulum too far the other direction so that Eaton and all those Egyptians cremated in the gulley would, after all, be on his hands. Perhaps he had let the Negev—the stark ugliness of it, the peculiar deathlike sureness of it—push him beyond sound judgment and force him to action that was hasty and now condemning. He thrashed over that as he slid further into the enveloping folds of exhaustion—and only the spinning pinwheels of the headlights of Carol's car followed him down, until they winked out. . . .

He woke to that. Never had that dream been like that before. Always those headlights had stayed large and hauntingly accusing—now they had dimmed out, as if the whole incident was gone from him.

He lifted his head off the hot sand, but the effort made him groan. He ached all over. His mouth was sore, like a raw burn that had blistered. His eyes couldn't take the glare of the sun on the sand that had turned caramel now and was almost turning into the color of salt in some places. He fought his way up out of the insistent arms that wanted to drag him back down, resisting the soliciting voice within that said he was too tired to go on. Yes, death never told you to lie down and stop functioning—it simply said to rest, take it easy, there's no hurry. . . .

Now he got to his feet and stood in the shaky world that spun before him . . . for nothing stood still . . . sand hills revolved around him, the sky looked like a carnival ride that did loops and dips, and he could almost hear the delighted screams of passengers. . . . there was not much to hold him up. . . . his legs did not register feeling, he might just as well have been standing on stilts . . . but he stood there hanging on, to what? And he giggled . . . and the sound of it shocked him . . . he felt embarrassed as though he'd laughed during someone's prayer . . . why was he getting up? As far as he could tell no one else had. And he turned to look around from his dizzy, fuzzy world—but all he could make out were the little mounds of rags that represented human life, laid out against the sand like the discarded playthings of a child . . . no one else bothered to rise to this mockery called day . . . they knew. Yes, they knew! They couldn't go another mile in their condition . . . not in this sun . . . wait for night, and by then they would have sunk lower to the demands of eternity . . . but why not? Better that way than to walk under the torch of the Negev, a lobster being dumped into boiling water alive . . . to walk across the live coals of this sand with that brass pan of the sky bouncing off its murderous heat, and all time cooking gradually until one's brains began to sizzle . . . . heat until brains crackle, then test with a toothpick . . . if firm, they're done . . . remove from the oven and serve while hot . . . and he giggled again, and the sound of it was strange in the muffled morning like an animal's growl . . . and he began to feel an attack of vertigo grip him so that he reached out with his hands, trying to force balance into his weaving body, to fix on some permanent, stationary target in front of him . . . his hands looked too far out, his arms too long . . . but he forced himself to keep his eyes on them until gradually, torturously the world began to stop its wild merry-go-round effect . . . and suddenly it stopped, its gears screaming against the brakes in his head. . . .

Now he could move, stiffly, uncertainly . . . his chest ached and the same stabbing pains from his ribs cut into his breath. But he moved anyway, toward Miss Churchill who was still lying in her blue blankets, unusual for her, for it was she who had always been the first to meet the sun. He stood over her shakily, looking down at her. Her eyes were open, but they were not seeing him. She was seeing the nation of Israel, slowly dying without water, forced to its knees by the Arab world, all because she had not met her responsibility. The heavy mask of exhaustion had turned her normally tan face to a paleness, and her eyes were brighter, even luminous, and it was like her features had taken on a peculiar glow. Her lips were puffy like his own, her skin drawn tight against her jaws and cheekbones. But even then she was beautiful, as if the draining process of the Negev had stripped away unnecessary skin and brought her features to a fine close sculpture.

"We have to go on," he said to her, and his own speech was slurred, thick with exhaustion and the cotton of his urgent thirst. Her eyes flicked over him then as though he were some necessary evil to be tolerated here. Her interest in facing the day was obviously gone. Her world had ended with the escape of Mabel Stockton.

But slowly she began to move out of the blankets in those same painful moves as he had. He wanted to reach out and help her up, but he knew that would only add insult to injury. When she got to a crouching position, she bent over the child, putting her mouth close to the child's mouth.

"She's alive?" he asked.

"Barely," she returned simply. "A walk in the sun today will do it . . . she hasn't got a drop of liquid left in her body."

He felt totally helpless. He sought for one flimsy straw of hope in the future day. What faith he had left was running a low amperage, for the pressure of circumstances, the unsuccessful attempt at running for life last night, had left him confused, totally disoriented and a victim of the beastial mockery of the Negev that put a solid exclamation point to this long sentence of complexities.

He walked over to Dennison who was sitting in the sand. It was obvious that the demented man hadn't slept. The dirty white bandage on his head matched the yellowish pallor of his skin that stood out in a sickly color against the scrub of black beard on his cheeks and chin. His eyes remained alive, but not comprehending time or place. They stared beyond to that distant land of war, perhaps, to the years of his youth and honor, to like experiences of suffering and death. In his eyes was the wonder of a child viewing an exciting play, now and then lighting up strangely as if he recognized a friend out of his past.

Sebastian reached out and took the brown hand in his and gently pulled. Dennison followed the pressure and stood automatically to his feet, and the humming sound came from him again as if he sensed it was time to march.

He left Dennison there and walked over to Ida Randolph. And it was like a hospital call again . . . go from bed to bed, say a word here, a word there, give suffering humanity some hope. . . .

She sat quietly in her blankets, the slashing lines of pain from her broken collar bone visibly etched in her pale, dull gray eyes. But she wasn't crying now or hiccoughing on her throttled emotions. She had vented her grief and now sat dried up of tears so that all that was left was resignation. The sling he had rigged up for her earlier from Eaton's shirt was still in place, looking as spotless as it had on Eaton.

"We're ready to move, Miss Randolph," he said quietly. She didn't say anything. With her left hand she pushed back her hair from her face and looked across the miles of smoking desert.

"You poor man," she said, then, and he looked up at her quickly from his crouch, astonished that she was actually attempting to sympathize with him instead of herself. "You must be forever true to yourself when the big lie is so real out there. So strange that God should forget you. I never thought of ministers who suffered with mankind as you have had to do here—what sins must you account for? I have mine that are real enough, but what are yours?"

He wondered how Job must have felt with the same question put to him. "We can't choose for ourselves either," he said to her, a little distracted by her blunt interrogation that came so close to his own tortured thoughts in the past few hours.

"You expect a miracle out there, Mr. Sebastian?" she asked again, not waiting for him to expound further. And her question was not out of panic now, but more like a student who wanted to have some idea of what to look for in a chemical experiment.

He almost said no. Because he felt that way honestly, and he didn't feel he could go on deceiving her. But then that was not right either—he had lived all his life as a minister with a shaky, unproven faith. He had no right in this hopeless situation to convey to even one helpless soul that God was not here, that a miracle was not possible.

"You said you believed in God back there, Miss Randolph," he answered, standing upright now to look down at her tired, empty eyes, wanting this leverage of position to add strength to his words. "There is no reason to disbelieve Him now . . . in fact, maybe it's time to start believing as you never have. . . ."

He walked away from her when she didn't answer, because he didn't want to go on with the conversation that might show up his own ingredient of doubt. He had chased down those blind corridors of his faith long enough, trying every door, feeling for even a small ray of light. He did not want to be confronted now with the apparent hopelessness of that chase. All he wanted was to keep moving, as if there were honor and vindication in staying on his feet to the last.

But her voice caught him before he had gone ten feet from her.

"Would you say a prayer with me, Mr. Sebastian?"

He stopped, his back to her, and Barbara Churchill looked up suddenly from her work over the child as the commanding tone cut into the silence of the morning. Ida Randolph had decided to make the test of him, to prove

225

the strength of his own belief, and he knew she would not get up and walk unless he did pray with her. For she had nothing left now—Mabel Stockton's betrayal had nailed the last of her will to the winds, and it had long gone. She had to have some indication of a living God in an empty, hopeless world—or else there was no point in attempting what lay ahead.

He went back and got down on one knee. "Pray for a miracle, Mr. Sebastian," she said, her eyes big and intense on him now.

And then that laugh cut in rudely, and he looked up to where Brelsford lay, propped up on one elbow not more than thirty feet away. "That's right, Sebastian," he called with a mocking wave of his hand. "Go ahead and pray with the lady . . . look, not a cloud in the sky, not even a thread of vapor anywhere. It's a good time for the miracle—pray, Sebastian, for rain! Remember the prophet who prayed and shut up the heavens for three years? You ought to be able to get rain for four people—or has God changed since then? Hey?"

He hesitated while Ida Randolph waited. Could he muster up enough of his own shattered faith to pray like that? Could he dare convey to this ghost of a woman that he was not certain himself that God was going to do anything but bring them to their appointed graves this day? He thought that perhaps he ought to take the time to prepare her rather for her future beyond death—that would be more in keeping with the circumstances. But he knew she would not accept that—she had to know his faith, to be sure of him, before he could communicate anything else. For God was only as big as a miracle, even to Brelsford now, and for all of them.

"Lord, as You gave water to Thy servants of old on this parched and empty ground," he began, lifting his voice for Brelsford too. "Have mercy on us who count for little in the earth and Thy kingdom, but are Thine neverthe- less. . . ." He paused, feeling for words that would not be so irrelevant, for he was so new to this, to praying in such hopelessness. "And give us courage to keep going on, courage to believe that You do all things well. . . ."

"A—A—A—men!" Brelsford shouted.

He looked up at Ida Randolph, and she still had her eyes closed, drawing on his words like they were some kind of magical smoke to inhale as some kind of cure-all.

He got up from his knees, not wanting to say more, and he looked just once at her dull, tired eyes as she opened them, and he caught just a trace of new hope. How many times had he looked into the same eyes of dying people who knew they were dying, but who dared to believe that a single prayer could alter the inevitable plunge? It was there in her eyes too—desperate hope, fighting to get astride the mountain of impossibility, timid in its demands, finally to be slowly inundated by the swamping facts of the circumstances.

He went on to Brelsford, and the man was sitting up in his blankets now, a weird, twisted smile on his ulcerated lips. He waved a hand of acquiescence to Sebastian as he approached and croaked, "You don't have to pep talk me, preacher! I wouldn't miss the rest of this for anything. This old, dying body will follow you straight to the valley of dry bones. . . . I got an interest in you, Sebastian, like I had with my Daddy way back in Oklahoma. But smell the humidity?" And he sniffed loudly, giving a mocking display of ecstacy with his hands, like he was smelling a fragrant garden. "It's here, Sebastian—maybe a few hundred feet down—but all you got to do is ask God to sink a shaft and bring it all up to us. . . ."

He walked away from Brelsford because there was no point in exchanging with him now. And Brelsford began to laugh, and it rose to a long peal of hysteria, uncontrolled, rocking with the lyrical half sobs that went with borderline madness. Once Sebastian made a move to go back to Brelsford to help him snap out of it, but Miss Churchill said, "Leave him alone . . . it's got to come out sooner or later. . . ."

So they waited. Dennison looked around in confusion

now as the high-pitched sounds broke through his veil of other worlds. Ida Randolph merely rolled up her blue blanket and stood up unsteadily, hardly paying any heed at all to Brelsford's long cackle, accepting it as a normal part of this world.

Then it ended. And Brelsford fell back into his blankets limply, his hands over his face as if to cover the shame of this performance. Then he moved slowly upright, leaving the blanket there, for to him it was but excess baggage. To him there would not be another night to worry about—he had figured his chances on that slide rule of his, and the very act of his abandonment reached out to Sebastian to add another nail to the mounting futility of the moment.

Sebastian turned then and without a look at Miss Churchill, he started out. Once he turned to look back, and the sight of them squeezed hard on his drained emotions—a staggering, bedraggled, debilitated specter of humanity, hanging on to the thin thread of life that was snapped taut and straining by the lack of will within and the building elements without. He was actually all that moved them now—Ida Randolph followed to see the miracle, Brelsford followed in his stumbling, drunken gait, only to mock the lack of miracle, and Dennison was but a mechanical unit, conscious only that he was to imitate the movement in front of him. And as for Barbara Churchill, it was duty—for her she had no place to go, for Bir Milhan only meant confrontation with defeat. But she would play her role to the end, not necessarily for him, but because it was what her training dictated. And as for himself—he did not know truly why he kept moving his legs out in each painful, weary, torturing step, except perhaps that if he did not there would be no one else. It wasn't because of his clerical role here, divine instinct, or duty—if anything, he did what he had to do now because he really didn't want to face God taking up the rear. It had become a slowly building conviction, that if he had to die here, he wanted to be out front, where the church ought to be anyway.

He followed the wheel tracks left by the Land Rover Mabel Stockton had fled in earlier. It left a clear trail in the white sand, and he noticed that she must have been going at a fast clip, for the ruts showed long, digging, clawing marks as if she had skidded or had fed gas to the engine in the heavier sand spots.

There was no way to explain the heat. He had been in a steam bath once and fought the jarring heat that threatened to cut off his breath—but here every breath was a sucking up of fire. There was no sweat left at all now. They were human gears running hot against the cams and rock metal of the Negev, the smoke rising from their bodies, and it was almost as if he could smell the burning flesh as they went through the torturing slow bake.

In the first hour he had to stop repeatedly to help Brelsford, who kept falling in the heavy sand. Each time he would prod the scientist by saying, "Come on, O man of science, prove thy tensil now . . . you going to let the church walk in without you?" And each time Brelsford would respond by dragging himself back to his feet and staggering on blindly, groping like a child with his hands in a dark room.

Or else it was Dennison who kept wandering off in other directions, pursuing the sound of bugles from the past, calling out to former heroes, charging strange enemy entrenchments that crowded up into his warped mind. Each time Sebastian led him back, talking him gently back to some semblance of reality.

And once he fell into the sand himself, and he was conscious immediately of the others stopping and waiting, wanting to lie down too, and hoping that he would stay down so they could do the same.

"Don't you think we ought to stop to rest?" Miss Churchill said after he had fought back to his feet and started walking again.

"You know better than that," he said, breathing hard. "If we stop now, we stop for good. . . ." He paused to squint against the shimmering furnace in front of him and asked, "I seem to have lost the Land Rover track—you figure we're off target?"

She didn't answer for a long moment. "You'll just have to trust we hit friendly nomads soon. . . ."

"How's the traffic in nomads about now?"

Again she paused. "In summer like this, they aren't as frequent, but. . . ."

He waved his hand to her to let her know she didn't have to try to inject any further hope. "Save it," he said, and turned back to the concentration of keeping one foot ahead of the other.

The sun was everywhere now. It poured out of the sky, that same ruptured ball of magnesium spilling itself over the inverted saucer of the sky. It was hard for Sebastian to keep in a straight line—he was sure he was going in circles. He could only go on, there was nothing else to be done. And as he walked, he kept staring at something ahead which seemed to come swimming toward him on the heat waves. Mirage. He had come to that too. Again and again it kept coming into his vision. Finally he called to Miss Churchill who angled slowly to his side, clutching the child to her.

"I keep seeing something moving ahead of us," he said. "Can you pick it out—or is it just me?"

He waited. After awhile she said, "Yes, camels. Three of them."

"You sure?"

"Quite sure."

He didn't say anything, not allowing the rising stab of hope to get very far.

"How far ahead?"

"About a mile. . . ."

Again a pause. "What are they doing wandering around here?"

"Probably got loose from their Bedouin drivers. . . ."

"Could we . . . can we catch up to them?"

"Maybe . . . but it's very hard to mount a camel that isn't yours. . . ."

230

"You're sure they're not mounted already . . . you're sure they're not friendly nomads maybe?"

Another pause while she looked, her one hand lifted to shade her own smarting eyes. "I'm sure," she said finally then. "They're not mounted, and I don't think they would be wandering around here if their drivers were anywhere near. . . ."

Nothing more was said. He kept glancing up now and then to see if they were gaining at all on the camels. Slowly he sensed that the animals were getting clearer in his vision. They were walking all right, but not very fast, sometimes pausing to nudge each other as if having repeated discussion as to where to go.

"And when she had given him drink," Sebastian said, remembering the Scripture in Genesis, "she said, 'I will draw water for thy camels also, until they have done drinking.'"

He paused, feeling her eyes on him for a brief moment, not comprehending what relevance that had. Then he said, "I thought camels never got thirsty?"

She didn't answer. They walked on. Now the camels were not more than fifty yards ahead. As yet none of the others had even indicated they had seen them. Sebastian waited, not wanting to start a panic among the animals, for if there was one last thread of hope for them, it was in those four-legged beasts.

He had gotten within twenty yards, enough to actually smell them, when Brelsford spotted them. He began running at the same time, half stumbling, sliding, gripping his side as he did, moving out in front of Sebastian before he could be stopped. The animals were spooked by the suddenly slashing yells of Brelsford, but they milled around bumping into each other, all trying to go in different directions. Brelsford in that time managed to grab the saddle stirrup of one, but the beast was not about to be taken in by this wild enemy out of nowhere. The camel whirled its head around and nipped sharply at Brelsford's shoulder—Brelsford went down into the sand with a cry of pain. The camel trotted off after his companions.

Sebastian was running after Brelsford all this time, yelling to him to let the animals alone. When he got up to Brelsford lying in the sand, it was certain the man had given all his strength to the one last effort. He just lay in the sand giving off long gasping breaths that rode a small whimpering sob.

"Get up, Brelsford," Sebastian urged, sensing the others wanting to fall down and rest. There was no movement from Brelsford. He lay there out flat, and a small blue-greenish fly was circling around his open mouth, the first official ambassador of death. Sebastian brushed it away.

"Leave him," he heard Barbara Churchill say from a long way off. Then she was crouched down facing him across the unconscious Brelsford. "You're all we've got now!" and her voice rose to try to batter down his flimsy but stubborn defenses. "If you die carrying him, then we've lost our fix! Can't you see that? Leave him here, we'll send someone back if we get out—if we don't, it won't make any difference to him!"

He looked at her, genuinely confused. Her argument was logical. Her insistence was convincing. His aching body lent strength to it. He didn't even know if he could get Brelsford up.

"I said . . . I said we'd go out together or die together," he mumbled. "If I die, you . . . you take over . . . anyway, what difference does it make who . . . leads or follows at this point. . . ."

They managed after much tugging, pulling and exhausting effort. When he got him up, he fell down, Brelsford tumbling over him.

"How much more do you have to do to prove whatever you're trying to prove?" she shouted at him again, and her hand gripped his shirt front and shook it weakly in an attempt to get him to see the folly of this.

"He's going!" he snapped back at her. "He's going—especially him! I came all this way . . . and I want him in

232

on the finish! Live or die, Brelsford is going to be there—and so is everyone else!"

She knew it was hopeless and dropped her hand from the front of his shirt. They went about getting Brelsford back up on his own shoulders. This time he managed to stay on his feet—and they started out again.

"Look for those camels!" he called to her. "They may lead us out of here. . . ."

But they couldn't see the camels at all for awhile. It was Ida Randolph who saw them and called out her discovery. But by then it was almost impossible to go on. The pains in his chest and lungs made him cough fitfully, and now he was spitting blood. But he couldn't stop. Ahead of them the camels were moving in their awkward gait not more than a half mile—now and then they were lost in the dips in the sandy plain. Then they appeared again—hanging there before them, mocking them in their movements, always just far enough ahead. But keeping them in sight kept the rest of them moving—at any moment they expected to see Bir Milhan or other friendly nomads. As long as those camels were there, they would put that extra effort in, push a little harder, dismiss the relentless pressure of death drowning them now. . . .

He knew then that it had to stop here. He had been keeping burning eyes fixed on a jutting piece of something sticking out of the desert ahead. He hadn't the strength to tell Barbara Churchill to keep her eye on it—so he did it himself, while the bouncing body of Brelsford on his shoulders cracked new pain down through his own. His eyes weren't focusing very well now—the world around him was on that fast merry-go-round again. Voices called to him from a long hollow corridor, incriminating, mocking, laughingly accusing: "He saved others, himself he cannot save . . . I'll tell you how you'll get water here, Reverend . . . the same way the people in the past did it, using their minds and conquering their environment . . . not waving some magic wand around . . . like the Middle Bronze people

. . . or the Nabataeans, whose genius perpetuated water storage . . . it's man genius, Reverend. . . . you see, its science and man's ability to conquer his environment. . . ."

Then he stopped. The world stopped spinning. He was facing the giant rock that he'd been following for a few miles. It was greenish looking, as if it were made of copper . . . Dennison would know what that metal was. He peered around the same world of sand and heat . . . and he saw the camels standing there only a few feet ahead . . . their snoots were down to that same hot sand . . . why should they stop? By now his own breath was coming out of him in gasping sobs . . . he fell with Brelsford on top of him . . . but somehow he kept his mind open, fighting unconsciousness . . . he rolled over and looked back. . . . they were all down now . . . even Miss Churchill, sprawled out in a misshapen bundle of khaki, the child lying ahead of her a few feet where she had apparently rolled out of her arms . . . Ida Randolph was flat out on her stomach, her arms reaching out, fingers digging in the sand. . . . Dennison was down on all fours, animallike sounds coming from him, his moves feeble. . . .

"Get—get up!" he tried shouting, but all that came out was a long, hoarse grating sound, his words burned out by the fire in his throat. Breathing heavily now, he forced himself up on his feet again . . . turned toward the camels who lifted their heads to watch him wearily . . . he moved woodenly forward, his hands out to try to quiet them. . . .

"Please," he heard himself saying like a child beseeching a parent, "please . . . stay right there . . . for them You can help . . . please . . . God!"

He made a lunge for the halter of one. The head snapped upward and he fell forward, missing the rope. He smelled the dust as they trotted away . . . and all he had was sand in his fists.

"Is this what You want?" he tried to yell now, looking up at the open furnace door of the sky. "Must they die with Your name sticking in their throats? Don't reward them for my sins, God! Take me if You must—this miserable blob of humanity . . . take me . . . but don't let them plunge into hell because of me! Are You there, God? Or is it true You don't belong here after all? God of Moses! You who gave water to the Israelites in this wilderness. . . ." And now he stood up again and raised his arms to the sky, stumbling forward again, "Is it too hard for You to do the same thing? Is it asking too much?"

He fell again, and the sand was hot under him. He groaned in the agony of his soul . . . and in that anguish he dug his hands deep into the fiery sand, clawing at this earth, this volcanic ash that mocked his desperate cry to God . . . and he cried, and the sand gritted between his teeth . . . and all the torture of a soul that had been bitterly disappointed by the silence of heaven welled up in him . . . so that his arms went deep, following the clawing fingers as if seeking there some tangible touch with God. . . . And then as his will gradually melted to the tormenting world around him . . . as tired nerves and muscle succumbed to the terrible agony of burned and broken things within him . . . suddenly the voice shot through his clouded mind, cut deep into his numbed senses:

". . . any fool can go out there and die. That's an easy way out and a kind of cheap demonstration of involvement. . . . I don't intend to follow you out there to witness your voluntary crucifixion so that you can make up for your shoddy past. If you want to prove anything to this group, you'll have to go there and come out alive!"

He lifted his head out of the sand, turning to see if she were calling to him. But she was still lying there, not moving. He pushed at the sand, trying to find leverage to boost himself up. The pains shot through him with serious intent, as if death was not about to let go its hold now. He fought it off, the groan coming to a scream in his throat.

He got to his feet, stumbled back to Miss Churchill. "Get up!" he yelled, rolling her over and pulling her up by her shoulder. She looked up at him quickly, and the glaze of death was in her eyes already, but she reacted now like a sleeper who had suddenly realized she had slept through the alarm.

He moved on, shouting, "Get up! All of you! Get up! Dennison! Miss Randolph! Brelsford!"

But they did not respond. Ida Randolph made slow, feeble movements with her arms after awhile. Dennison tried humming his "Waltzing Matilda" like a soldier trying to put back the fallen flag. But Brelsford didn't move at all.

He fell down next to the scientist, feeling that if he could get the man up on his back, the rest might follow him out. He tugged at the dead weight, flogging him with threats. "Get up, Brelsford! You want to go down in history a victim of circumstances you couldn't tame? No victory in science in that . . . they'll laugh at you, Brelsford. . . ." But there wasn't much coherency or depth to his argument now. He tugged at the body, got the shoulders off the sand with great effort, but then had to let it slump back as his own dissipated energies failed. He paused, on all fours there in the sand, mindful now of the loud whistle of his breathing.

"Don't do it!" he heard Miss Churchill say next to him then. He turned his head, and he caught her face dancing in front of his tortured vision, and he saw there the emotion laid bare, the tears that made clean, white marks in the dust on her face like the first rivulets of rain on a dirty windowpane; he saw the unguarded, unpretended venting of feeling from the rock of expressionless personality that she was.

"You're crying!" he said, and it sounded like a strange peal of triumph coming from him.

"Don't do it! she repeated, and her hands touched his shoulder. "If you have strength . . . then go! Go and get help—let us remain, leave us . . . don't try carrying us all out . . . you've proven enough!"

"Ha!" he fought back, wondering why he did, since it

made no sense, and it cost him so much to even breathe. "We go out . . . we go out together . . . or . . . or we die together. . . . that will . . . that will make a wonderful slogan . . . someday . . . on somebody's church steeple. . . . Anyway . . . thank you . . . as last I've seen you are . . . you are a woman . . . a person. . . you can cry . . . feel . . . my God, thank you. . . . I think I can die even with that much. . . ."

He coughed hard, and he gagged on something big and spongy in his throat. He tried to get up, one hand reaching for Brelsford . . . and then the agony of a thousand hot spears ran through his chest . . . he saw the shadow of night cross his vision . . . and from somewhere a cool wind was coming in. . . . There was a long sliding feeling, a gentle coasting through a soft vapor of multicolored substances . . . it came to him like cotton candy . . . and he sank into it. . . .

"Now into Thy hands, Lord, I commend my spirit . . . have mercy on these I must leave . . . remember them when they come into Thy kingdom . . . bless this sweet girl whom I have come to love. . . ."

* 14 *

He felt the silk of the sand under him. But it wasn't like before. He could not feel the graininess of it, the heat of it. It was firm, flexible. He lay there a long time with darkness over him, not wanting to wake up again to that hell. . . . Lord, let me die now, let me come to You!

He opened his eyes. Just cracks. He saw green first the green rock? No, It was solid green, light green, pale green . . . the green that went with cool things . . . green that went with life and water . . . WATER?

His eyes came open wider . . . he saw that it was all green. And it stayed that way, and he followed it with his eyeballs gently rolling to the left, then back to the right. Until he stopped at white and blue and grass—and sun. But not the same sun . . . no, it was a kind of sun that touched the gentle delicate fingers of plants, that designed shafts of innocence on a brown wooden casing . . . this was not the devil of the Negev. . . .

"Ah, I'm glad to see you are awake, old man!" the voice came to him sounding as if it were at the end of a long pipe, as if someone were yelling through a culvert, the sound echoing and spiraling down to him.

He waited. He closed his eyes again. Now he felt the tight, constricting armor that bound him. His hand explored and felt the hardness, and it mystified him, but his mind would not work or form logical conclusions.

"That's all right, take your time, old boy!" that voice sang out to him again, and he wanted that voice turned off, because it seemed loud and jarred deep into his brain demanding of him that he acknowledge.

Now he opened his eyes again, slowly. This time he saw the brown khaki, the pointed chin with the blue line of freshly shaven face . . . the mouth was a jagged line of tissue like a snowman's melted in the sun . . . but the teeth were good and strong . . . the nose was a bit pointed and the eyes were dark and friendly like a dog's . . . but who was this?

"You've had a bit of a go," the voice went on, and that mouth moved so that the jagged lines fell into place. "But you're all right now . . . I'm Duncan Alexander. You're at the British Archaeological Laboratory in Elath, my friend . . . you've been unconscious about a day now since we picked you up. . . ."

Alexander? Sorry, nobody in my party by that name. But then as his eyes focused clearly on the man, and the message penetrated, the cottony sense of surroundings began to settle.

He opened his mouth but nothing came out. He felt his lips with his tongue . . . the ulcers were still there, but they didn't smart as bad. His tongue, too, didn't seem as swollen, and he could swallow without pain.

"That's all right," the man said, lifting his hand to restrain him from trying to talk. "Let me just fill you in while you get your bearings. . . . It's a bloody miracle we ever found you, you know that?" The man paused and then said, "Sorry, that's hardly the language to throw at a man of the church, leastwise one who can't talk back. . . ." He decided he liked this man Alexander's smile. It was like having Sparks there again.

"Well," he went on, his voice rather lyrical in its tone, "I was sent over here to fill you in when you came to so you wouldn't aggravate yourself in worry over all the details. . . . You don't have to talk now," he added

239

quickly as Sebastian opened his mouth to try. "Just let me fill you in as best I can. . . ." He paused, waiting to be sure apparently that Sebastian was staying awake. Sebastian could only stare up at the circular ceiling fan as it revolved its blades, fascinated by its quiet, easy motion and the peaceful touch of air that it blew across his face. He had no desire to talk—it was good just to lie there and let the man tell him, feeling as though it were something that happened to someone else.

"Anyway," Alexander went on, then, "it's those camels that did it . . . how you had sense enough to follow those stupid beasts is beyond me . . . anyway, we would never have gone out looking for you if it wasn't for the fact that a tribe of nomads found a Land Rover at the bottom of a crevass about six miles out of Bir Milhan. . . ." Sebastian dropped his eyes from the fan and looked back at the man, who, sensing his interest, said, "I'm sorry . . . the machine was burned to a pile of liquid metal, with whoever was inside . . . anyway, those nomads came in here carrying some navigational charts that must have been thrown clear . . . they had the name of the airline on it and since by then everybody was hunting you in Egypt where you were supposed to be and hadn't even begun in the Negev yet—well, we figured you had to be out there somewhere, nobody just comes charging across the South Negev alone in a Land Rover, you see. . . .

"So we followed the Land Rover tracks back, but we would have missed you even then . . . you were off that trail by at least a mile . . . just happened one of our chaps was doing a bit of a scan with the binocs and saw those camels hanging around that rock . . . camels will do that because they've got the idea that they can find water around any rock that sticks out of the desert . . . well, we got curious and happened on you just like that . . . a bit of a fantastic miracle you're alive, old man . . . nobody lives in the Negev very long without food and water . . . that's why even the nomads don't travel much in summer, there isn't much of a chance if you get cut off. . . ."

He paused again. Sebastian let it get through, the wonder of it half perplexing him. He wanted to ask more, but it seemed too much of an effort.

As if sensing his desire, Alexander went on, spinning off the account like yarn off a spindle. "Strange thing about that Land Rover . . . nobody goes riding into the South Negev at night, or even at dawn, unless they know the country like the back of their tatoos, you know? And even if they know they don't . . . too risky. But the charts are what get me . . . the navigator of your plane had a straight ruled line to the point of the crash and then drew in another one in different color pen showing the exact way into Bir Milhan from a point about fourteen miles south of the wreck . . . he even put in that particular dog-leg jog around the Valley of the Skull . . . but I can't understand why your man didn't heed to it as clearly as it was on that map."

He waited again, and now Sebastian, fighting off the seeds of curiosity himself, found that he had to get it out even though it sounded weak and strange. "How . . . how about the others?"

Alexander's jagged lips curved into a smile of apology. "Sorry . . . that's where I should have started, I guess . . . you all came out all right. Except the man named Dennison. He'll have a bit of a go for six months with the psycho boys, he's just one step from being out of his mind . . . but that's the Negev sun for you, it'll suck your brains out and let you walk around empty-headed, you know . . . but give him time and he'll be back at it. . . ."

"Brel—Brelsford?"

"The archaeology chap? Well, yes, he'll have a stitch in his side a long time, and he's had a nasty crack on the head in a couple of places . . . but he'll mend . . . he's got an archaeological first, too, to help him. . . . the way we figured it he stumbled on the Well of Sheba . . . we've been hunting those wells where we figured the Queen of Sheba watered her animals when she came to visit Solomon . . . you know? Could never find it—been at it for

241

half a century of digging now perhaps . . . actually it's an underground spring we figured, comes up once or twice a year maybe then just disappears like that . . . well, Brelsford stumbled on it back at Iqfi and that's part of the reason I'm here, to get you to verify that he actually did. . . ." Sebastian thought of Brelsford and that water hole where he almost died. "He found it, just as he says," he said simply.

Alexander let out a sigh. "Anybody else we'd have to have more proof . . . but we figure a clergyman's word ought to do it. . . ."

"What about—Miss Churchill?"

"Ah, yes. Well, we haven't had much to do with her. . . . She's been behind closed doors with a few Jewish chaps down from Jerusalem . . . can't figure out what an airline stewardess would have so much to say to two Jewish generals . . . but she's in pretty good health . . . in fact, if you don't mind my saying so, Reverend, she's in very attractive health. . . ."

He managed a smile to put the man at ease, for he looked embarrassed. "She knows about the Land Rover—in the—the Skull?"

"She rightly does, I'll say . . . I had to drive her out there this morning after those two Jewish generals came in . . . they poked around that heap most of an hour, and that girl isn't even out of the worst of her ordeal even yet . . . messy business that was."

He paused again, wanting to be sure he met Sebastian on his own strength and level. Then, satisfied, he went on, "As for the child, well it was touch and go . . . she was in tough shape when we brought her in . . . the docs aren't sure she's out of it yet, but today the little cutie took solid food for the first time since she came in so there's every hope now . . . and that schoolteacher, Miss Randolph, she's mending nicely too . . . you must have prayed with a fury, Reverend . . . you can't explain how any of you are alive without it. Just goes to show you, I guess, if you expect to get shipwrecked anywhere, make sure God is along . . . hey?"

Sebastian felt the warm folds of sleep touch him gently. "By the way," he heard Alexander say from that hollow pipe again, "you were walking around out there with a cracked rib that was poking a sliver of bone into your lung, did you know that? You could have had it any time out there . . . good thing we found out when we did, you were beginning to bleed pretty bad. . . ."

The voice went on in that peculiar British sing-song, but for Sebastian the cloud was gone, the weight had shifted some. The pieces of the puzzle that didn't fit in yet could wait. Now he let the sweet feel of sleep take him, and nothing was ever so beautiful to him as that first, gradual peaceful slip into unconsciousness.

He was up two days later. On the afternoon of the fourth day after rescue he received word by Duncan Alexander that he would be flown out to Jerusalem the following day and then on Pan American to New York. Alexander also brought a set of uniform khakis cut strictly along the British military lines. After Sebastian dressed, Alexander looked him over.

"You're a bit of a lanky Yank for that, but it's pretty close anyway," he said with a smile. "You might even pass General Monty's inspection at that. . . ."

Sebastian grinned and then asked, "Anybody been around to see me while I slept it off?"

"Only the charming Miss Churchill and two very important looking Jewish generals," Alexander returned. "But you were babbling in fever then and none of it made sense. . . ."

Sebastian felt some inward relief in the knowledge that she had after all been concerned enough to do that.

"Incidentally the big man himself, Sir James Richardson, Director of this Center, has invited you to dinner this evening," Alexander added, "I gather that Miss Churchill will also be there."

Sebastian turned to look at him, wanting to be sure the bantering Englishman wasn't pulling his leg. At the same time he felt a twinge of regret that he should have to share his last evening with her with someone else. He had been searching for a way to get her alone, because it was so important now that he could talk with her on neutral ground.

"What time?" Sebastian said.

"Around eightish. . . ."

"Then I've got time yet to see Brelsford . . . can you tell me where he is?"

"Across the compound where the archaeology chaps hang out," Alexander replied. "Room E 113 I think it is . . . he's bunking with a man named Jessup." Sebastian made a move to the door, and Alexander called to him, "Don't start laughing or pounding each other on the back—we don't want you popping your ribs against the cage of plaster we got on you."

Sebastian nodded, made a mock British salute as he went out, and caught the quick grin from the likable Englishman who seemed to take particular trouble to watch over him.

The fact that Brelsford hadn't come to see him at all was indication enough that the man was quite content not to have anything more to do with him. But for Sebastian it was necessary to at least have one last encounter in the hope that perhaps something might have happened to the man that might show a crack in the hard crust of disbelief. If Brelsford were hiding away, afraid to admit whatever work of grace might have occurred in his life through the ordeal, then he wanted to bring it out in the open. For he had not found any point of vindication of divine personality yet—all he had to show for it all was a few superficial wounds, a peeling sunburned nose, and the haunting specter of two grave markers representing men who had slipped through to a Christless eternity.

He found E 113, knocked, and a muffled voice told him to enter. The room was small with two beds and a large window looking north toward the desert. It was neat, polished to a luster, and had everything in its proper place. Brelsford was standing at the window smoking a long-stemmed pipe, dressed in a faded purple bathrobe that fit too tightly on his bulky frame. He did not have his yellow turban around his head now. Only a small white patch on his right forehead testfied to the wound he had suffered in the crash. His crew-cut salt-and-pepper hair had grown out some, so that it was more like a bushy crop of mesquite, poking up uncertainly trying to find proper direction. It brought out his years with striking reality, and it also gave him a rather scattered, out of sorts look as though he'd just come out of a long sleep and was trying to find the handle on life again.

"Well," he said, his voice neither pleasant surprise nor testy aloofness, "I was just wondering what they'd done with you. . . ."

Sebastian stood by the door, not sure if he should push into the room or not, for he wasn't sure yet that Brelsford was in the mood to accept him.

"I'm off to New York tomorrow," he said, trying to form a proper excuse for his visit. "I thought I'd at least come and say good-bye."

"Hmmm," Brelsford said in acknowledgment, as if this were only right, drawing on his pipe and hiding his face behind a column of blue smoke. "Have a seat," he added, and kicked a wicker chair by his bed.

Sebastian sat down, and Brelsford sat on the edge of the bed a few feet away, not giving himself completely to it as though he wanted to spring up at any time. He blew more smoke ceilingward, and the bowl of his pipe seemed to get as active as a volcano. Then, as if making up his mind, he looked up and pointed a stubby finger at Sebastian and said, "There was no miracle out there, Mr. Sebastian. Everything that happened is traced to natural causes. Those camels were riderless because their drivers were shot off in a tif with those pursuing Egyptians—you can't say God shot them off just to lead you to that rock where Duncan and his party could find us. . . ."

Sebastian smiled in spite of Brelsford's high-pitched

recital-like voice that he had come to inwardly despise.
"It appears that you've been thinking about it anyway,"
he said pleasantly, surprised himself that he could face
such an archenemy without any desire to even the score.
"But if we wanted to argue about it, those camels didn't
have to cross our path at that particular time, Mr.
Brelsford . . . that desert was big enough for them to go
elsewhere. . . ."

Brelsford grunted as if to say he expected that kind of
answer that didn't come up to his idea of adequacy at all.
"It wasn't what I was looking for," he returned flatly. "You
were supposed to get a fountain of water in the desert,
manna from heaven . . . in that sense you failed misera-
bly."

"I don't claim to be a rainmaker or one who pulls rabbits
out of hats. . . . Whatever your opinion of success or
failure in religion, I make no claims for miracles. I made
no big claims out there in the desert either. . . ."

"How else can you prove God then?"

Sebastian hadn't especially wanted to talk this way with
Brelsford, for he wasn't sure enough himself yet what God
had taught him in the experience. "If I had to have
miracles to keep my faith alive, then I would have hung
up long ago."

"Then you're reduced to the common substance of all of
us," Brelsford jibed, a note of triumph in his voice now.
"The uniqueness you claim is shattered—for without a
miracle man has no reason to believe God exists. You've
got no more than we of science—you grope after a vapor,
but at least we seek answers on the solid facts of history."

"You have more of some things perhaps—very little of
others."

"Like what?"

"Mr. Brelsford," Sebastian said, then with a sigh,
knowing talk was not going to accomplish much at all, "I
will never win an argument with you. You've got the feel
of polemic that far outclasses me. So I think I'll let that
go by the board. But—you're alive, sir, by an act of God

and only an act of God. Even the best of minds would admit that our survival can only be explained as supernatural. . . ."

"Rubbish!" Brelsford snapped. "Coincidence, purely coincidence. . . . God doesn't fit into it in any way as I see it."

Sebastian knew it was no use to press on with that. "What I also came over here for was to congratulate you on your discovery of the Well of Sheba. I see now why you were so insistent on dying that day at the water hole."

"Do you?" and his voice seemed to be more subdued suddenly as he stared at the smoking bowl of his pipe. "Well, actually I wasn't sure it was Sheba then—I wanted that water, because I didn't want to die of thirst. And it wasn't that I was afraid to die—I just didn't want to go that way that's all. I would have rather died by those Bedouin bullets."

He paused, then, and it looked as though he was a bit embarrassed at having admitted a weakness. His demeanor had taken on the appearance of a man groping through his words, sorting them out, not wanting to use what came up. "I appreciate you supporting that find out there," he went on, and he busied himself with packing down the burned tobacco in the pipe bowl with the forefinger of his right hand as if he didn't want to look up when he talked now. "That discovery meant a lot to me. . . ." He waited, and Sebastian didn't answer because he wanted to let him get it all out in the immediate context. "That's what I don't quite understand—why you supported my discovery to the authorities here after all I've done to discredit you out there in the desert. Mind you, what I said was true—but in spite of it, you endorsed my discovery, and you must have known that they probably wouldn't have accepted it without a reliable witness. . . ." He didn't look up yet, finding the pipe of intense interest suddenly.

"You found it. I was there," Sebastian said simply, feeling a little sorry for the man in his obvious discomfort

247

of having to admit a kindness in another, especially a man of the cloth.

"But you didn't even see it," Brelsford insisted, frowning at the floor. "You didn't see the water like I did—how did you know it was even there?"

"You wouldn't have been willing to die for anything else is the way I figured it, Mr. Brelsford. Sometimes the greatest demonstration of something existing is in the action of people who claim the discovery. . . ."

There was a long pause during which Brelsford remained quiet, speculative, thinking to himself or else not knowing how to proceed from there. Sebastian, sensing it would be far better to leave him with that, arose to go.

"Wait," Brelsford said before Sebastian could get to the door. He got up, pulled open a desk drawer and took out a worn copy of a Bible. It stunned Sebastian for a moment, for it looked as out of place in his hands as a bouquet of flowers in the hands of a general.

"This was my father's Bible," he said, but he sounded as if he were referring to a useless souvenir. "He gave it to me when he died—I was seventeen then. Don't think I've kept it for inspiration—not on your life. The day he gave it to me I vowed then that I'd use it to take me to Bible lands and prove that all this divine presence in Jewish history was nothing but a myth. I was going to make archaeology prove that—and I made a few scores in my time, Sebastian." He paused then to let that sink in, staring at the black-covered Bible that had frayed edges as if he was making the point to his dead father too. Then he turned the cover and stared long and hard at the inside. "My father put a Scripture verse in front especially for me, he said. It was his way of wanting me to get his kind of religion I suppose—but anyway it says here in front, 'For a good man one would dare to die; but even while we were yet sinners Christ died for us!' Now I don't accept that last part, naturally, but the fact that for a good man one would dare to die . . . I have pondered that for some hours now, Sebastian, in the philosophical sense. . . ."

Now he paused and looked up at Sebastian. His eyes were unreadable, except perhaps for the trace of uncertainty there that didn't do much to dilute the hard concentration of his scholarly mind and view.

"You know I won't and can't apologize for what I said or did to you out there," he said then.

"No, and it isn't really necessary. . . ."

"There ought to be an apology . . . you saved my life, I know that. But what gets me is why. For a good man another would dare to die for him—but to you I wasn't good, I was evil . . . yet you packed me around . . . this I will wonder about. I am a scientist, Sebastian. I pursue answers to mysteries in the universe—there has to be an answer, and I will find it."

"When you find it, I wish you'd write to me or come see me," Sebastian said, wanting to press home the need for acknowledging that the mystery here was in God, not in the physical.

"I will," Brelsford said, his voice still a little dreamy with preoccupation with the thought. Then, a bit hesitantly, he stepped forward and put out his hand. Sebastian felt a bit surprised at the gesture, but he took the thick palm in his own, looked back into the eyes that said nothing more than "this much is costing me a lot." "I intend to go on in my archaeology to prove my old man a liar, you know that," he added.

"I know. . . ."

"And to make you a liar, you know that?"

"Of course. . . ."

Then squeezing the hand more firmly in his own he added, "You're a lousy driver, and you couldn't follow a straight course across the desert if you followed a plumb line—but you aren't afraid to sweat and get your shoes full of sand. I like to shake hands with an opponent I respect. Good-bye, Mr. Sebastian."

"Good-bye, Mr. Brelsford."

When he got to the white stucco house, he was ushered into a large, well-furnished room of teakwood and oak, with a huge sailing ship on the mantelpiece, various paintings of ships on the walls, and many repainted relics of archaeological diggings that went back undoubtedly thousands of years. It was a room that resembled a museum in one sense, but the furniture and props were so arranged that it gave the impression of history suddenly becoming contemporary. He stood a moment in the room that had softness to it, feeling dwarfed by the high ceilings, the symbols of science that breathed an awesome fragrance of intelligence and mastery. He felt suddenly a bit shabby in his borrowed uniform that rose high above his ankles. He picked out the soft theme music in the background as being Moussorgsky's "Pictures from an Exhibition." It was good to listen to that, to feel the continuity of things, of life, of beauty, of significance.

He noted the shiny dark mahogany table carefully set for three, then walked through the carpeted room toward the terrace that faced the desert. He expected Sir James at any time—or better yet Miss Churchill. But for now he merely stood and looked back across the sand that was turning bluish-purple as the sun sank for other worlds. It was strange viewing an enemy like that from the sanctuary here—it was hard to imagine that he had been in its grip once, so recently, and how soon he was forgetting, like a woman forgets her pains of childbirth so soon afterward. He tried to remember the agony of it, the heat, the merciless mockery of it—but all he saw now really was sad, lifeless, innocent, inanimate.

He was studying it and reflecting when he sensed she was there. How quickly his nerve endings responded to her! Yet, perhaps they were even more sensitive now—even more than before. He caught the faint scent of jasmine before he turned, and it made him heady and almost afraid—as if the smell of a beautiful woman posed challenges he was not sure he was able to meet. Then he turned—and he saw the sharp contrast of the blue dinner dress against the flash of golden hair. The image was breath-taking, like the daring splendor of a bluebird in the sun after a rain. His heart beat a heavy pulse in his throat, and he swallowed quickly.

She approached him with a gliding, effortless movement, and her eyes now were reflecting the relaxed mood she was in, not studious, detached, but soft in response to a world of natural things. Her mouth, lightly touched with orange lipstick, had just a trace of pleasant smile so that it curved into a tormenting line of solicitation, even though probably not intended by her. Her hair had been redone, and it gave her entire body an aristocratic beauty as though she were a piece of sculpture that had suddenly come alive.

He reached out his hand to her, not even sure he knew what to do, and she took it, placing it lightly in his as she mounted the four steps to the terrace. The only intimate touch he had had with her all this time was in that moment, and he wanted suddenly to hang on to that cool flesh that filled him with a sense of sureness and desire.

"You even look like Abraham Lincoln," she said as she paused only a few feet from him, her eyes looking into his with the soft lights of the strangely and beautifully mysterious evening flickering there.

"I didn't know it was that obvious," he said, holding on to her hand, keeping in check his own fluttering emotions.

"I wouldn't have really thought about it, perhaps, except you were babbling the Gettysburg Address when I visited you in the hospital." Her quick smile was a flash of white, a shooting star in the night.

He smiled, and dropped her hand as it went loose in his. "I was Abe Lincoln every year in Nashville, giving that famous speech before the Lincoln memorial. The kids loved it." He paused a moment as she moved by him to stand by the terrace rail, looking out across the desert. "Did I say anything else?" he asked to make conversation.

She hesitated a moment and then said, "Yes—Psalm 139, I think it is. 'Whither shall I go from thy spirit? or whither shall I flee from thy presence? If I ascend up into heaven, thou art there: if I make my bed in hell, behold, thou art there.' . . ."

She kept her eyes on the desert, as if not wanting to look at him.

"I'm sorry your two Jewish generals had to sit through that," he said.

With that, she picked up the small blue bag she had with her and removed a long white envelope from it. "On the contrary . . . they know that biblical truth as well as you." She turned then and handed the envelope to him. He took it. "Those two generals run the Israeli Secret Police . . . they wanted me to extend their own apologies that they had to leave for Jerusalem before you were well enough to receive them. They wanted you to know how much they appreciate what you did to keep the film out of enemy hands. That letter there is a rare piece—it is sealed with the official seal of the Prime Minister. Only a few people I know of outside of Israel ever got that kind of honor. The letter is a statement of thanks for your part in the Christopher affair. It's not the kind of honorary ceremony we would have liked—but since they want to keep the newspapers out of this, they are doing it this way. . . ."

Sebastian felt a bit stunned. "I really didn't have that much to do with this Christopher thing," he contradicted.

"When I told them what you did, they thought otherwise," she replied, her voice was light, slow and carried the warmth he never thought she had.

He put the envelope in the side pocket of his tunic, feeling that she knew what was in the letter anyway. He fished around then for the right approach to take to other matters.

"I—I saw Brelsford," he tried, "but didn't get to see the others yet . . . Brelsford is riding high on his new discovery, I suppose you know that."

"He needed that," she replied, turning away from him again to the desert. "You may not have known it, but he was about through as an official archaeologist with

252

Princeton. The Well of Sheba will reestablish him for awhile."

He didn't know where to go from there, so he moved over next to her, feeling the same wonder at her moods that were shifting constantly from polite pleasantry to tones of introspectiveness and some hesitation.

"I wish I could have found as suitable a wardrobe as you did," he said then. "That dress is absolutely stunning." He noted the creamy tan of her bare shoulders, the long sweep of her neck—where was there ever such perfection?

"Thank you," she said and turned her head to look at his khaki uniform. A slight smile tugged at the corners of her mouth, and he saw the childlike trace of genuine amusement there. "I see Alex has succeeded in reshaping you into General Montgomery. . . ."

"He did mention that I could pass General Monty's inspection. . . ."

"Well, Alex served with Monty in North Africa, so whenever he gets the chance to reincarnate his idol in someone else he does it. You come pretty close at that. . . ."

He felt a bit self-conscious now and somewhat out of sorts because the conversation even yet was not loose enough. They were both groping around for that natural gateway that would bring the warmth they both needed.

"I'm both sad and glad about Miss Stockton," he said, "which is the constant ambivalent attitude of most preachers to death as you know. I'm glad for you, though, that it didn't turn out the other way." She didn't answer, so he added, "Alexander in his running account mentioned the charts—I take it you drew that line in from the wreck down to Bir Milhan?"

"It was a long shot," she said, saying it to the desert, as if explaining it to that unseen but so very real spectre of the Negev hanging around out there. "I figured whoever Christopher was he'd look for those charts—so when Brelsford slept that night after the encounter with the

253

Bedouins I put in the course, deliberately giving the right way in."

"You've been this way before then?"

"Once a few years back I was here and drove out twenty miles with Alex. . . ."

"But why draw in that course the right way? It would seem more logical to give the wrong approach and drive him to the skull that way. . . ?"

"I figured Christopher would suspect my chart line to be a work of the counterspy in the group . . . he'd figure I had deliberately altered the course by the dog-leg to send him into trouble, so he'd go straight instead. It was a hundred to one chance, but in this case she did exactly that. . . ."

"But you were never sure it would go like that?"

"No. I was more sure she'd follow the line as I put it in. . . ."

He let it die there on that. He didn't want to talk any more about the past. There were still some dangling strings he wanted to pull up and tuck into the ball of yarn, but he wanted more pleasanter things to happen now.

As he sought new areas of coversation, the servant who had let him in earlier appeared at the bottom of the terrace steps. He said something to her in a language Sebastian couldn't understand. She answered. When the conversation finished, and the servant had gone, she appeared almost resolute, as if bad news had come and she were bracing herself as if it were inevitable.

"Sir James sent word that he can't make it—he's called to some other emergency meeting. He asks us to take dinner together and make ourselves at home as his guests. He'll join us later. . . ."

She didn't look at him when she said it. She appeared hesitant, not sure if she wanted it this way.

"What a stroke of fortune!" he said, genuinely glad for this new circumstance he had dared to hope and even secretly prayed for. "I told God out there in the desert that I wanted to live for a number of things—but one thing mostly was that I'd get to see you over a dinner table with candles and soft music. . . ."

She gave that half smile again that was only half acquiescence, and he took her by the elbow and guided her back to the dining area. The steward had rearranged the places so that they sat opposite each other in the middle, the candles between them. He seated her, then walked around to the other side. He sat down, giving her a quick smile. The sparkle of her earrings, the flashing of the diamond brooch on her dress that pinned the single shaft of blue over her shoulder—all of it mesmerized him. She sensed his fixation, his continual watchfulness, and it was beginning to make her feel a bit self-conscious.

"Back to Nashville tomorrow then?" she said politely, trying a bit of her soup.

He didn't want to go that way. There was finality in it, and it brought panic to him to think of leaving—without her.

"Yes, I suppose so," he admitted. The steward came in, and poured her wine and then moved to him. Sebastian shook his head, and she said something to the steward. The steward backed away politely.

"Alcohol one of your vices?"

"In a sense—that and grenades."

She gave just a trace of a smile in acknowledgment. "Wine is good for the stomach here in the Middle East— that's why Paul told Timothy to take a little now and then. Water here will kill you in the end."

"I don't condemn it in others," he said, "so there's no need to rationalize your own habits."

"There is no attempt to rationalize," she shot back. "I'm only trying to help you drop the barrier for your own health's sake."

He smiled. "There we go again, Miss Churchill, we're back on the old trail—check, counter-check. Forgive me for provoking you."

She hesitated, peering at her wine, then smiled, and that was a picture he wanted to keep forever, for it was genuine, because it showed in her eyes too, and all the warmth and beauty of her character was there.

After a pause, she said, "Back to the pulpit again? You'll have many illustrations to support your propositions now, won't you?"

"I don't know," he said, wondering if this was only polite talk for the meal. "I must confess I don't have much to go home with—I lost two men whom I haven't any assurance of their being in the right place in eternity . . . I could come up with no miracle to prove God lives in the Negev as well as in Nashville . . . it will be a little difficult telling this to my hopeful and critical congregation. . . ."

She waited while the steward served the main course. When he had gone, she said, "But if you consider Heinrich Zimmerman, what he was, and what he did out there, I think that alone should make up for some of the problem you think you have. No man who was an SS trooper like Zimmerman would have thrown himself under a half-track with a live grenade to save anyone else. You have to know the hard core of the Nazi mind to appreciate that. Something happened to Zimmerman in that desert—I don't know what or the exact experience, but I'm positive it was the fact that you suddenly emerged the way you did, a man who represented the weakest element in society suddenly rising to the forefront in a daring attempt to do the impossible. You shocked Zimmerman more than any of the others I'm sure—and there was no more confused man than he when you rode that Land Rover out—and at the end there was no more convinced man than Zimmerman as to who was, actually, fundamentally the strongest of any of us . . . including himself. Zimmerman's military mind saw the situation—and perhaps for the first time in his life he saw something worth dying for . . . whatever he said to God before he died, if anything, is not for me or you to judge . . . but the fact remains that the hard-core Nazi was willing to give his life for the least common denominator in the world, the church . . . that should tell you something. . . ."

He hadn't touched his food. Neither had she. Suddenly the night was building up to new dimensions. She was leading him now deliberately into new areas of thought that had to have some definite application to both of their futures.

"Thank you for that," he said. "It really helps." He hesitated a moment and then said, "And what about you?"

She lifted her head to stare at him a long moment. She had not touched her wine. Her soup was growing cold in front of her as was his. "Do we have to eat—now?"

"No, I'm not hungry yet," he replied.

"Then let's get out where there's air."

They stood on the terrace. Behind him the sound of Listz's "Hungarian Rhapsody" lent a peculiar kind of drama to the setting. She stood facing the desert again, as if it were easier to talk with the past experiences before her.

"I think you knew why I didn't want you to tackle that Egyptian camp," she began, then going at it carefully.

"I figured it had something to do with how you felt about your father," he offered, glad she was willing to touch that dangling string now.

"Yes, it had to do with him . . . my whole concept of the church and ministers was a bitter one. I grew up with the Jewish cause in Palestine. My father's only concern was for the souls of the Jews, not their political aspirations. I didn't think you could separate the two. I still don't. You have to understand the demands made on Jewish people. No one can claim immunity from the struggles of a people to be free by using the church or God. Jewish history does not support such a position. I knew my father's position was New Testament and the Sermon on the Mount. But it did not fit Israel—so the issue came finally. He refused to take in a wounded member of the Haganah—that's the Jewish underground fighters—he refused to lend his car to the Haganah when they needed a way of escape. All he wanted was to be detached from it to save Jewish souls— right as that was—but not to touch their blood, or bind

257

their wounds . . . so I judged him for it . . . and I turned from the church; it hurt him what I did. . . .

"Then . . . then you came along . . . and you fit the role exactly . . . back at the wreck telling me you didn't want to get involved . . . so I made you the test case . . . I wanted to prove that all clergymen were the same as my father . . . I wanted to be sure . . . so I shoved you up front, manipulated you into leadership, controlling the events all the time, but keeping the fire on you . . . I wanted to see you fold up in the pressure . . . I knew that you could and would only go so far and then no more. . . .

"But then you threw that plan to invade that Egyptian camp . . . and that frightened me . . . that was more than I expected . . . and suddenly you were not like my father at all . . . and it confused me . . . if you went into that enemy camp and pulled it off, then I had the awful condemnation on me for having judged the church, my father, even God as weak instruments in the universe . . . so I had to fight you on that . . . only I knew it had to be done . . . and I had to go along to prove you one way or the other . . . either you were weak and would run for your life when the shooting started . . . or else you'd actually rise to this thing and prove me a liar . . . you did just that. . . ."

She paused, and he waited, a few steps behind her, not pressing, letting her get it out.

"So . . . now my father is dead, and I can't beg him for forgiveness . . . he had his right to minister as he felt led . . . I had no right to judge him for that and certainly not to conclude the church weak because he didn't. . . ."

Now she turned to him suddenly in a quick move that startled him. He saw the tears in her eyes, the patches of color showing up on her cheeks. "You say you have seen no miracle in that desert to prove God? Well, understand me well now . . . the greatest miracle out there is what happened to you, Sebastian . . . you came into that desert weak, all mush, whining about the need to be detached from the bruised, confused people who had survived . . .

remember? I hated you, I despised you that night for that weakness . . . well the end of the journey was different . . . you were in a sense invincible . . . not miraculous . . . but you were a man risen to the commission to lift the helpless, to daringly, in instances, effect deliverance when you even didn't know how . . . to me, that is my concept of God in the universe . . . and you brought Him to me in all His glory. . . ."

He wanted to hold her, for the sweeping, gripping sense of his love for her was suddenly overwhelming. She lifted her hands though as he made a step towards her, restraining him, wanting to be heard completely out. Her body was building up that high amperage again, charged with feeling, intensity.

"Hear me out," she pleaded, flicking quickly at her moist eye with her right hand. "I closed the Christopher file today . . . it is our custom to always put the name of the Israeli agent across the front, the one who has solved the case or directly affected it . . . normally mine would go on there . . . but I put yours . . . code name Sebastian. . . ."

She waited to let that get to him. He didn't get it. He said, "I don't understand. . . ."

She sniffed and went on, "Well, you're not The Reverend Raymond Sebastian to me anymore . . . you are indeed code name Sebastian . . . I want that name to go with you . . . for it symbolizes a man who must not be content with standing in a safe, comfortable pulpit away from the bleeding, broken mass of humanity . . . it symbolizes a name that means a man is ready to go into the hundreds of Negev situations around the world, giving himself to lift people from the slavery they are in . . . this is what God has done for you, my dear Sebastian, and for the world in all of this. . . ."

He didn't like the vaporous fog coming between them. He saw her slipping away, and his soul cried out in protest. "All I know is that I love you!" he said to her, his hands on her shoulders and feeling the warmness of her smooth skin. "I don't want any other name . . . I want you, I want to start with you . . . go to Israel, work with you. . . ."

She shook her head, and the tears were fresh on her cheeks again, and her lips trembled for a moment. "Listen . . . we can never do it . . . I have my life in Israel as an agent, poor as I may be . . . you . . . you have your life for God ahead of you . . . we will always be too concerned for each other to let either of our commissions be fulfilled . . . you I expect and am sure will go on from here to other worlds . . . you must! And I must go back to mine. . . ."

"Do you deny you love me?" he insisted. "Just tell me if that's what all this is all about . . . are you trying to put me off this way so you won't have to tell me you love me?"

Again she shook her head, and her eyes closed, and the tears were there again. Then, with a sigh, she got hold of herself and said, evenly, "Do you think I could have come through all this with you . . . to be knit to you all the way . . . to fight with you . . . to lay myself open to you as I did out there . . . do you think I could reveal myself to you and not—not love you?"

"Then, in the name of Heaven, let's stop playing with this code name Sebastian business," he argued. "You make me sound like I'm an international Robin Hood all of a sudden . . . I'm not superman . . . I can get scared, I tremble . . . I don't know anything about helping people in their fight to be free of anything except sin . . . what I did out there was because I had no choice . . . in any other case, I certainly wouldn't go looking for trouble. . . ."

"But you will," she said stubbornly. "Because that's what God did for you here . . . and you will never be content again until you are out there where the agony of man is . . . even as I finally identified with Israel in its suffering, so will you with the world . . . in that light I don't think about love for you . . . I avoid it . . . I refuse to accept it . . . and so must you!"

Her voice rang with finality. He knew then that he would never be able to cross over to her—ever. It left him with a deep sense of tragedy. He dropped his hands from her shoulders and turned to lean against the terrace rail, to look out at the Negev.

"Somehow I knew that desert would have the last laugh," he said gloomily.

He felt her step up behind him and her arms go around his middle pressing against the tape and her head rest against his back. "No, dear Sebastian, you know what the Scriptures say: 'He that sitteth in the heavens shall laugh'? God has had the last laugh here . . . the desert has lost, that bone that stuck in God's throat has been dislodged . . . the desert sought to destroy you, instead it has made you into something useable. . . ."

He turned slowly then, and her face was only inches from his, and he saw all the longing and love there that she was permitting for only this moment. And he kissed her gently on that soft, tender mouth—and for only those brief seconds she responded, and all that she felt was there. And it was sweet, overpowering, so right.

And then she removed herself from him, and they stood looking at each other, seeing all that could have been, two people who by all the laws of physical chemistry should be amalgamated as one for life. But instead the magnetic power was being canceled by the sheer act of will—mostly by her. He wanted to reach back and recapture that moment, to shatter all the silly nonsense about code name Sebastian, for it was the wildest, most ludicrous statement about himself. But from her nothing was ever wild or ludicrous—this is what sobered him and kept him standing there unsure, bewildered and fighting to get some sense of balance in it all.

"Hello, there!" came the voice from the inside, and it jerked both of them back to time and place. "I say, didn't you people have dinner?"

Suddenly a tall, heavy-set man in white dinner jacket was standing below them looking up at them. "Sir James," she said, and she was conscious that she had been crying, and it was an embarrassment to be caught that way for her. So Sebastian stepped forward, went down the stairs, and introduced himself.

"We got carried away with other matters," he said to the perplexed host.

"Well . . . I see, but you sure you won't eat now?"

"We'd be glad to join you!" she called from the terrace where she was touching up her face.

"Good show!" Sir James said, and he gave Sebastian a knowing wink as if he sensed that they were in an embrace all this time, and that he understood.

When Sir James disappeared into another room to call the steward, he turned as she paused on the stairs to come down. He looked at her long and hard, a prize he would never win, a part of him he could never keep. And she looked back with that same sense of awareness as the gulf widened between them—and it was finished.

He waited at the airport gate for most of thirty minutes but she did not come. Perhaps it was better this way. Why provoke new feelings over it? He knew it would be harder again to say good-by here—for good. But he wished for just one last word, anything, something he could take now for the journey home.

With only five minutes to boarding time, then, she was there. She was dressed in a casual white blouse and khaki skirt, her beautiful bare legs in loafers—and it was the person he had known in the Negev, totally different from the one he had kissed and said good-by to last night. She was different too. He saw the studious look in her eyes again, that all business demeanor that went with an agent of the Israeli Secret Police. With her was Duncan Alexander.

"I had to come to give you greetings from Ida Randolph," she said simply. "She's applied for a position to teach in a kibbutz on the Negev frontier around Beersheba."

"Miss Randolph?" he said in disbelief, and he tried to see that self-pitying, selfish, crying cowardly woman in a kibbutz. He looked back at Miss Churchill, and he saw there something of what she had been trying to tell him the night before—that somehow through it all, people had been reshaped, transformed. For some the Negev would take credit—but for her, it was him and what he had done to make God real in the common sweat of a struggle to live. He wasn't sure of that even yet, but her sureness about it had during the night penetrated his foggy senses—somehow it had credence coming from her.

"I say, when we went out to that Land Rover the other day I brought in some of the things that had landed clear," Duncan cut in then. "I brought this aluminum shaft back—and when the chap Brelsford saw it, he wanted it. Acted as if it were some kind of magical wand or something. Anyway, he gave it to me just before I left to come here and said this really belongs to you . . . so here it is. . . ."

Sebastian took the familiar stick, fondled it, then looked back at the girl. There was a trace of a smile on her lips again. He thought of Brelsford, awed by the fact that the man would remember so little a thing as this. Perhaps it was intended to be an example of his own sarcasm again—or maybe he was actually saying that this "Moses rod" actually did belong to Sebastian. He would never know.

"Well, you've got a decent suit of clothes on," Duncan chirped. "It doesn't do as much for you, but as least they'll accept you in New York now."

"Thank you, Alex," Sebastian said. He turned then to her and took her hand, looked into her eyes, saw now only the steady gaze of a woman who belonged to Israel. "May the God of Abraham, Isaac, and Jacob watch over you, Miss Churchill . . . and may the Lord Christ light your way through every experience in life. . . ."

"*Shalom*, Mr. Sebastian," she said, and he gave her hand a final squeeze.

"Don't let that welcome committee punch you around that rib cage," Duncan reminded him with a grin.

That was all then. The attendant urged him out to the tarmac. He walked out into the Negev sun. It seemed a long walk. But he walked straight—maybe the taped rib cage made him stand taller. When he got to the top of the ramp of the plane, he turned and looked back. They were there still watching, Miss Churchill out in front of Duncan a few feet. He lifted the aluminum shaft to the sun in one hand, the last salute to her, the last touch on her of the things that they had known together. She gave one simple wave of her hand. Alex Duncan gave a quick British salute—and that was it.

He didn't look out of the plane again until they were airborne and skimming over the Negev. He looked down at the miles of sand and rock, the emptiness, the waste, the deplorable death of it. And then he leaned his head back on the seat, the aluminum shaft between his legs.

"AND GOD SAW EVERYTHING THAT HE HAD MADE, AND, BEHOLD, IT WAS VERY GOOD."

Epilogue

He stood alone in the church office. He heard the slowly fading murmur of the crowd outside as they dissolved in the balmy September Sunday, and to the sun that would dilute their wonder and temper their perplexed minds.

He was leaning against the file cabinet when Les came in. He stood there a moment, a big man carrying a well-packed frame on a six-foot carriage, dressed impeccably as always, for Les Bennington believed that Christianity was as much vindicated by careful dress as by careful speech and deportment.

He took off his glasses now and held them up to the light as if he had been seeing things peculiarly all morning and was tracing the trouble to his spectacles. There was a small smile on his mouth, that perpetual token of the vastness of the gentility that was in him.

"The rest of the board held a caucus and decided I ought to be the one to talk to you," he began. He paused to hold one lens of his glasses up to his mouth, clouded it with his breath, and reached in his pocket to pull out a neatly folded handkerchief. "That was your shortest sermon in nine years," he said, carefully polishing the lens.

"And I hope the best and most welcome," Sebastian replied.

"It shook them up quite a bit. I don't think they expected your resignation—they came to hear what the newspapers didn't say about you."

"The newspapers said it all—no miracles, no dramatic conversions . . . it was pretty common and ordinary. . . ."

"But God did something surely. . . ."

"Of course. He did something inside me . . . that's what I said this morning. But it wasn't anything greatly dramatic."

Les let that go and said, "You don't have to resign."

Sebastian smiled. "You mean I've got enough publicity now so that people will accept me on that if nothing else?"

"No, not exactly. I think something happened to you all right. The letter you sent me from Jerusalem was the same tone of the man I've known for nine years—uncertain, groping, a man running down blind alleys and pounding on doors. But the man I heard this morning, though appearing the same, had a different quality about him. I think the people sensed it too. You had command of yourself for the first time—and I think you could lead the church on that alone."

"You're kind as usual, Les, thanks. But that isn't enough to hold them, it'll wear off—and what happened to me is too deep to hold me. I don't even know what it is fully myself—but I know I'll have to go on following what glimmer I've got."

"You quoted Bonhoeffer this morning . . . how did that go again?"

"Bonhoeffer said, 'The church must get out of the cloister and into the world . . . man is challenged to participate in the sufferings of God at the hands of a godless world. He must therefore plunge himself into the life of a godless world without attempting to gloss over its ungodliness with a veneer of religion or trying to transfigure it. He must live a worldly life and so participate in the suffering of God. To be a Christian does not mean to be religious in a particular way, to cultivate some form of asceticism . . . but to be a man.' I've read Bonhoeffer

266

before, but I never got the significance of that until yesterday when I reviewed all that happened to me in that desert."

There was a pause for a moment, and then Les said, his high forehead creased with perplexity. "Have you never been that—before?"

"Do you think so, Les?" And when Les didn't answer, Sebastian went on, "I think you knew that was my problem all along. You've kept the board from asking for my resignation all these years in hopes that I'd make connections with a spiritual experience that would put iron in my blood. And I think it was mostly your money too that sent me on the Holy Land quest. Well, I think it has finally come—but with it the urge to extend it elsewhere. . . ."

"And where might that be?"

"I don't know . . . it won't be another pulpit, that I'm sure of. Even you know I'm not a pulpit man."

"And money? Livelihood?"

"I know you'll want to give me a check," Sebastian said with a smile. "Bless you for that, Les. But I'm letting God take care of that. I've enough to get by for a while."

"We really ought to have a formal farewell," Les tried again. "Just walking out like this seems so abrupt. . . ."

"I don't think the young preacher, Randal, my substitute all this time, can use any extra epitaphs that may come out of that . . . he's a good man by the way. You ought to call him officially. He's got what I prayed for but never did get."

There was a pause again, and both of them were trying to find the most natural way to cut nine years of close friendship.

"You'll keep in touch with me?" Les asked then.

"Of course."

"You must promise to get in touch with me if you need anything at any time."

"I will."

They stood looking at one another, each waiting for the other to move. "May I take you to dinner?" Les asked.

"No," Sebastian replied, "It would only make it harder. Anyway, I'm catching a plane at 1:30 for Philadelphia— I want to see my father and share with him this strange thing God has done."

"You think he'll understand?"

"Not in the slightest. But he should know it from me."

They walked to the door. By now the people had dispersed, except for a few who were hanging around in that pose of uncertainty that followed some kind of calamity.

"Where can I contact you?" Les asked as they stood in the open doorway facing the street.

Sebastian hesitated a moment and then reached into his pocket, pulled out his wallet, removed a card and handed it to Les. Les looked at it, his eyebrows lifting in wonder. "Code Name Sebastian?" he read. "Number One Jubilee Drive, Chicago?"

"The building belongs to my father," Sebastian explained. "I simply cleared out the top suite and moved in. I'll make that the base of my movements—whatever they are."

Les still didn't appear to have grasped it. "You had these made up?"

"No—a lovely girl named Churchill had them printed up in Jerusalem and sent them to me through an Israeli government office in Chicago."

"This—code name . . . it sounds a bit odd to say the least."

"It's just a clue to where I go from here," Sebastian said and smiled.

Les peered at Sebastian closely again just to make sure he could not see signs of deliberate humor in his face. Then carefully he put the card into his inside shirt pocket like he was putting a carnation in his coat lapel.

Les took his hand then and said, "Then go to it, Sebastian. Take your cause to the gates of hell itself. And may God go with you!"

He took the firm hand in his own, and then walked down the steps and up the familiar walk lined with elms.

When he got to his car the church chimes began to toll noon. It was a fitting farewell. He paused only a moment to look up at a passing jet that thundered its derision of earthlings. He watched it until it disappeared, for planes now had associations for him and warm memories.